The Weirdness

THE
WEIRDNESS

a novel

JEREMY P.
BUSHNELL

MELVILLE HOUSE
BROOKLYN · LONDON

THE WEIRDNESS

Copyright © 2014 by Jeremy P. Bushnell
First Melville House printing: March 2014

Melville House Publishing   8 Blackstock Mews
  145 Plymouth Street   and   Islington
    Brooklyn, NY 11201   London N4 2BT

mhpbooks.com   facebook.com/mhpbooks   @melvillehouse

Library of Congress
Cataloging-in-Publication Data

Bushnell, Jeremy P.
  The weirdness : a novel / Jeremy P. Bushnell. — First Edition.
    pages cm.
    ISBN 978-1-61219-315-1 (pbk.)
    ISBN 978-1-61219-316-8 (ebk.)
    I. Title.

PS3602.U8435W45 2014
813'.6—dc23

                                          2013041263

Design by Christopher King

Printed in the United States of America
1 3 5 7 9 10 8 6 4 2

To Atwood's Redraft, for everything

CHAPTER ONE

THE FUNDAMENTAL WEIRDNESS

BANANAS AND CIGARETTES • 80,000 YEARS OF COMMERCE •
PEOPLE HAVE PETS • WHAT ELECTRONIC MUSIC CONFERENCES
MIGHT BE LIKE • PLACES NOT TO HAVE SEX • NICE EVENINGS •
FUCK THE PAST TENSE • THE WORLD IS A RIDE • REALLY GOOD
COFFEE • THE LIGHTBRINGER

Billy Ridgeway walks into a bar with a banana in his hand.

It's November, and gloom has settled over Brooklyn, but this bar generates its own warmth, running forced heat over a narrow room crammed full of humans. A clientele mashed into intimate proximity by shared need, if not exactly by fellow feeling. They drink together. Someone picks out old L.A. hardcore songs on the jukebox to correct for the sins of the person who picked out a block of Texas swing. Someone else picks out masterpieces of East Coast hip-hop to correct for the sins of the person who picked out the block of hardcore songs. They generate friction, these off-duty waitresses and delivery guys and dog walkers. They rub elbows and bellies and backs, and together they hold winter and its wolves at bay.

Billy finds Anil Mallick at the end of the bar, where he is managing to defend two stools against the throng through some combination of fast talk and physical maneuverings. Anil is a chubby guy who wears half-moon spectacles and favors tweedy blazers; his round head is topped with a sumptuous mass of lanky curls; he works in the kitchen at a sandwich shop, but anyone here, in this bar, could mistake him for a kinda hot young academic. Anil is Billy's coworker and oldest friend, and Anil, tonight, is testy.

"I thought you were just going to get cash," says Anil. "You've been gone for"—he checks his watch—"twenty-two minutes."

"Yeah, sorry," Billy says.

Anil regards this apology. "There's a *bank* literally two doors down from here," he says.

"Yeah, I just—got distracted." Billy puts the banana on the gouged bar, between them. "Take a look at this."

"A banana," Anil says.

"Right, but, where did it *come* from?"

Anil blinks.

"I mean, yes," Billy says. "It's a banana. We *get* bananas from, what, from the bodega."

"Sure," Anil says, patiently. He sips his Scotch. "Like a lottery ticket. Or cigarettes."

"Well, sure," Billy says. "Except a banana isn't like a lottery ticket or cigarettes. I mean—it has to *grow*."

"Cigarettes grow," Anil says.

"Yeah, but—hear me out."

"I am hearing you out."

"We live in *Brooklyn*," Billy tries. "It's the middle of *November*. And yet we can go into any corner store and buy a *banana*. Where do they come from? Who grew them? I mean, I go into the store to hit the ATM, and I see these bananas sitting there, and I just stand there for a second, in the store, looking at them, and I'm thinking about, like, Costa Rica or Ecuador or some shit and it's just—I'm sorry, but it's just blowing my mind a little."

"This took twenty minutes?" Anil says.

"I thought that you, of all people, would appreciate the fundamental weirdness of the whole thing."

"You left me here for twenty-two minutes," Anil says. "Are you asking me to believe that you spent a significant portion of those twenty-two minutes staring at a *banana* in some kind of trance? Forcing the better-adjusted members of our fair city to steer around you to complete their own humble transactions?"

Billy frowns. "Admit that it's weird," he says.

"It's not weird! It's normal. Humanity has at least eighty thousand years of commerce under its collective belt; the details of that should no longer seem *opaque* to you. You want to talk weird? Open a newspaper. Last week? You see that thing about the Starbucks in Midtown that disappeared? They think the employees went on the run together, stole everything out of it to sell on the black market or something. *That's* weird. The shit that happens to you is not weird."

"Commerce is weird," Billy says. "I mean, think about it. People *buy* things."

"And *I*," Anil says, "am buying *you* a drink. Put that goddamn banana away."

Here's the thing about Billy. Bananas are not the only things that get him going. It can be anything. Just a week ago he was on the subway, sitting across from a woman with a tiny dog in her purse, and as he watched her tickle the little goatish beard under its chin he made the mistake of beginning to think about the very existence of dogs in general. People have pets. He repeated it. *People have pets*. It began to become odd; the very concept of *pet* began to slide out of his grasp. How did it get to the point, he wondered, where we began to keep *animals* as, like, accessories? He spent the rest of the ride staring at the dog, thinking basically: *Holy shit, human beings, the shit they come up with*. When he got back to his apartment he looked up *dog* in Wikipedia and from there started opening tabs and lost the rest of the day. By midnight, he had drifted to looking at videos of fighting Madagascar cockroaches, actually developing opinions on the cockroach-fight-video *genre*. He was cold. He was alone. He was uncertain as to what exactly had happened.

It had long been like this.

Blame his father: Keith Ridgeway, a pipe-smoking antiquarian bookseller, who had filled the entire first floor of the family's gabled three-story Victorian house with books. Billy had spent his formative years wandering among heaped codices, studies and catalogs and compendia, brochures and pamphlets, extended inquiries into every conceivable topic. From the very existence of these books he learned one primary truth: that everything in the world was enveloped in great skeins of mystery into which one could bravely probe but which one could never fully untangle.

Blame his mother: Brigid Ridgeway, a professor of medieval studies at the local university, who tied her red hair in a long braid and kept a collection of a dozen swords in a restored barn at the rear of the property. Billy remembers her standing in the sun-drenched open space of the barn, on Sunday mornings, practicing thrusts and parries, grunting and sweating, her heavy feet thudding on hard wood. Afterward she would spend hours at a workbench making chain mail. For fun. When Billy thinks back on her, he remembers her looking him in the face and telling him that she loved him, that he was special. Special and unique. From this, he learned a lesson that she may not have intended: that his differences were his merits. She loved him, he believes, because he *wasn't* normal, he wasn't a boy who was rambunctious and active and courageous, but rather a boy who was dreamy and inquisitive and delicate.

But now he is thirty, and his mother is dead and his father has drawn back into some sort of isolating crankdom that Billy doesn't quite understand. And when Billy checks in with his peers, when he looks at pictures of their kids on the computer, he notes that they've all begun to amass some share of money or power or career advantage or relationship stability. Then he looks at himself. He's barely managed to amass a goatee. He's unmarried. He's skinny. His mess of strawberry-blond hair is not quite receding, but it is thinning enough that it generates some small anxiety when he checks on it in the mirror. He makes $12.50 an hour at a sandwich shop run by an angry Greek. He's still writing, yes, but what does he have to show for an entire adult life pursuing his quote-unquote craft? Half a novel, plus some short stories (gathered into an unsellable collection that in a fit of self-abnegation he decided to entitle *Juvenilia*). These moments of accounting lead him to understand that somehow he is exactly the same as he's ever been: curious, confused, poking out an existence from which can be derived no clear utility. And in these moments Billy wonders if maybe he wasn't wrong about believing that his differences constituted his merits. On certain days he wonders if he, in fact, has any merits whatsoever.

"So," Anil shouts, over the growing roar of the bar. "Denver."

Billy winces, turns his empty shot glass around in a circle.

"You said you wanted to talk about her," Anil says.

"I know," Billy says. "It's just—things with Denver and I are really, uh, *challenging* right now."

"You might as well tell the story."

"It's hard to know where to start. I mean, I guess it started when Jørgen disappeared."

"Wait. Jørgen *disappeared*?"

"Oh, man. I didn't *tell* you this part?"

Anil removes his glasses with one hand so that he can press his other hand slowly into his face.

"I mean," Billy says, "he hasn't *disappeared* disappeared. Like, I don't need to call Missing Persons or anything. He's just—not around."

"Jørgen's a tough guy to lose," Anil says.

True. Jørgen, Billy's roommate, is six foot four, with shoulders that give you the impression that there are certain doors that he can only get through by turning sideways. A big, broad, hairy dude. Basically a Wookiee who has maybe shaved a bit around the facial area. But nonetheless, he is, indeed, somewhat lost.

He had sat down with Billy one morning, two weeks ago, over breakfast—eating half a box of Cap'n Crunch's Peanut Butter Crunch out of his mixing bowl, while Billy picked at two pieces of toast—and he'd explained to Billy that he was going to be attending some kind of electronic music producers' conference, so he'd be away for a little while.

"Cool," Billy had said, breaking off the corner of a piece of toast, blasting crumbs into his pajamas and the recesses of the couch. In retrospect, Billy probably should have gotten more information, but he assumed he'd hear more details before Jørgen left. But Billy hasn't seen him since that morning. Two weeks now.

Maybe producers of electronic music have these epic conferences that Billy doesn't know about? That go on for, like, a month? He tries to picture what a hotel might look like after two weeks of being inhabited by dudes like Jørgen and all he can picture is the scorched landscape of some heavy metal album cover, littered with chunks of rubble that look like fragments of a blasted monolith.

Two weeks with no sign of Jørgen: maybe Billy should have been more worried. But he'd been enjoying having the tiny apartment to himself for a while. It had given him an opportunity to finally attempt to have a private sex life with Denver.

Denver, a filmmaker, lives in Queens. She shares her co-op house with eleven other people. She sleeps in a hammock in the attic; somebody else sleeps in a hammock at the other end of the attic. Her place is not a viable site for sexual activity. Not that Billy's place is any better. He sleeps in a loft above the apartment kitchen, and the loft doesn't have a door. In fact, it only has three walls. Basically if you're standing in the living room you can see directly into the loft. Especially if you're six foot four, like Jørgen.

To make matters worse, Jørgen stays up late, sitting in the living room till one or two a.m., smoking weed and listening to drone metal albums on his (admittedly awesome) Bang & Olufsen unit. Thank God he uses (admittedly awesome) wireless headphones; this at least gives Billy and Denver a chance. But adults shouldn't have to fuck like that, trying desperately to finish before some third party decides to turn around. And the whole experience of rushing it? The clenched teeth, the film of flop sweat emerging on his forehead, the near-total uncertainty as to whether Denver is deriving any joy or pleasure or comic relief from the experience? It all cancels out whatever pleasure he gets from the grudging orgasm his body eventually spits out.

He'd return to having sex in the backseats of cars except neither he nor Denver owns a car. He has considered, on more than one occasion, signing up for a Zipcar account just to have a place to furtively fuck, but he never gets far enough in this plan to actually propose it out loud. Something about imagining that hundreds of other people around the city had also come up with this idea, and that he might end up fucking Denver in some car that somebody else had just used as their own roving fuckatorium . . . he envisions clenching buttocks, or a woman's greasy footprint stamped on the window, and queasily dumps the whole idea.

So he was excited when he knew that Jørgen would be away. He'd used money that he didn't really have to buy a nice bottle of wine, the start of a plan for a good evening. He'd told Denver that they'd be able to have some time alone. She'd been excited and pleased. Which was good. They were approaching the six-month mark in their relationship. A tricky point in a relationship, that six-month mark. Half a year in. Assessments get made when you're half a year in. Half a year in is a good moment to instill excitement and pleasure, Billy thought. He thought it would maybe be the right time to say *I love you*, a task he had not yet accomplished.

Except then somehow he'd blown it. He'd gotten nervous about the exact scheduling of what he had come to think of as "The Event." He'd been surprised that Jørgen had left as soon as he had after the conversation, and then had gotten confused about not knowing when exactly Jørgen was destined to return. So he began to hedge on inviting Denver over. Part of him thought that he should just call her over as soon as possible—immediately—but for the first couple of days he wasn't entirely sure that Jørgen had, in fact, actually left. And then after that it seemed probable that he could return at any moment.

Billy sent a series of texts. He sent two e-mails of inquiry to the address that he thought was current for Jørgen. He even sent an e-mail to the address that he was pretty sure Jørgen wasn't using anymore (*Hotmail? That can't be right*, he thought, even as he was sending it). None of these efforts yielded any response. And a couple of days ago, with Jørgen already gone for twice as long as had ever seemed probable, he had to face up to the fact that he'd blown it. There would be no Nice Evening, no Event.

When he explained this over the phone, Denver had pointed out that if the Nice Evening had been truly important to him he would have been more careful to get a more detailed explanation of Jørgen's plans.

"It *is* important to me," he'd said. "I mean, it *was* important to me, I guess. I'm just—I've just never been good with details. That's just part of the way I am."

"So," she'd said, after a pause. "What you're saying is that you're a fuck-up."

"Not—not a *chronic* fuck-up."

She'd pointed out that she could come over *right now* and they could still have a Nice Evening. The odds that Jørgen would choose this specific night to return—didn't it seem unlikely? And it *did* seem unlikely. But Billy had gotten it into his head that the Evening was now impossible, and somehow he was unable to disabuse himself of this notion.

"Why don't you just call him?" Denver had said. "Instead of sending e-mails and texts?"

Billy had responded with a kind of *tsk*ing sound. "That wouldn't do any good. Jørgen's one of those guys who never actually uses his phone to, like, *receive a phone call*. If you can't reach him by text you might as well just hang it up."

"You could try," Denver said, an uncharacteristic pleading note entering her voice.

"I don't know how to put this without it sounding bad?" Billy said. "But that idea has just basically no value."

The conversation began to go downhill from there.

"Look," Anil says, after Billy has explained enough of this. "Just cut to the chase."

"The chase," Billy says. He knocks back the new shot that the bartender has set up for him. He wipes his chin with the back of his hand. "*The chase* is that at the end of it she said she just wanted me to say one thing. She just wanted me to tell her that everything was going to be okay and that things were going to get easier from here on out."

"Okay, yeah," says Anil. "And you responded by saying—?"

"I responded by saying that it would be ethically unsound for me to make a claim, for the purposes of comfort, that I couldn't be certain was true under the present circumstances."

Anil opens his mouth and then shuts it again. Finally he offers this: "No offense, man, but you're a fucking idiot."

"I'm aware."

"Fucking," Anil says, ticking it off on his thumb. "Idiot," he concludes, ticking this one off on his pointer finger.

"Thank you, Anil, I heard you the first time. And Denver and I will sort it out. I just—I just want to give her a couple of days to cool off."

"Right, right. 'Cause that's what everyone loves when they're upset. To be left *alone*."

"I haven't exactly been leaving her *alone*. I've called her, like, six times. If I *left her alone* any *less* I'd be stalking her. And no one wants that."

"No one wants that," Anil agrees. He holds his shot up to one of the exposed halogen bulbs above the bar, contemplates the play of light in the alcohol for a moment, then throws it back. "It's too bad," he says, once it's gone. "I liked Denver."

"Don't say it in the past tense like that," Billy says.

Anil shrugs.

"I liked Denver, too," Billy says. He did. Or he does. Fuck the past tense. He thinks back to June, the night they met, on the rooftop of some art space in the Bronx, a program of experimental video screenings. One of the videos was hers, a work in progress called *Varieties of Water.* Twenty-five minutes of river foam, swirling drains, trash floating in city gutters, lake surfaces. Backyard pools thrust into abstraction by the activity of children's play.

Watching it, Billy had been mesmerized. By the end of it he felt like he had learned things about pattern and light, about perception, about nature, about humans, about himself. She'd been sitting in a metal folding chair just past the edge of the screen and every once in a while he'd look away from the film and his attention would settle on her. She reminded him a little bit of the ballet students he'd sometimes see hanging around Lincoln Center: tiny, wiry arms jutting oddly out of her loose sweatshirt, her face a little severe. During the entire duration of the video she'd kept her eyes shut.

Once the screenings had wound up and the crowd began to separate into clusters of conversation he made his way over to the very outer rim of her orbit. She thanked a few people quietly and then popped some kind of multi-tool out of a pouch on her belt and went to disassemble the stand for the projection screen, efficiently breaking it down into components that fit into a single black nylon bag. He edged up to her and looked at all the shit clipped to her belt. Some kind of folding blade, a stubby flashlight, a green iPod Nano, a few photography-oriented gizmos, a ring of keys larger than he'd ever seen on someone who wasn't a janitor. *She's like—a female Batman*, Billy thought. *Batwoman?* He had no idea whether there was such a character or not. Whether there was such a character was not the point. The point was that Billy was fast figuring out that she was talented, pragmatic, and competent: pretty much exactly the kind of woman who he typically felt terrified about approaching. But the video had filled him with a sense of spirited determination, and so he took his best shot.

"I liked your video," he mumbled.

"Thanks," she replied automatically, without really pausing in the process of packing things into the bag.

Billy, determined to nurture the exchange until it became a conversation, went on: "It was like—it was like being on a very benign drug."

She did not treat him as though he'd said something stupid.

What happened instead: she stood, wiped her hands on her jeans, and asked him, somewhat tersely, to imagine a film that operated like a malignant drug and describe it to her, which is exactly the kind of left-field question that Billy is actually kind of good at imagining answers to.

Conversation went to David Cronenberg's *Videodrome* (Billy had seen it; Denver hadn't) and then to D. W. Griffith's *Birth of a Nation* (Denver had seen it; Billy hadn't) and then to Leni Riefenstahl's *Triumph of the Will* (which they'd both seen). Billy started talking about the recommendations that Netflix had started giving him after he'd watched the Riefenstahl, and he'd gotten Denver laughing, and in the first moment that she laughed he felt insanely grateful that she'd taken the stupid shit that he was saying and made it into a decent conversation. Made something wonderful out of the common flow of gutter water.

"All right," Anil says, fishing a bill out of his wallet. "We gotta work tomorrow."

"True," Billy says, depositing his own bill on the bar. "You headed home?"

"Yes," says Anil. "But first I am going to go out back and get high."

"That sounds excellent," Billy says, either forgetting or deliberately refusing to recall the knowledge that getting high on top of getting drunk almost always gives him a horrible case of the veering spins. By the time he and Anil part ways he literally can't walk in a straight line. Instead he has to lurch from lamppost to lamppost like the world is some kind of fantastically disorienting carnival attraction. Like the world is a ride. Complete with swallowing back the need to vomit.

He gets back to the apartment, lets himself in: no Jørgen, still. That fucker. Billy drops the bruised banana into the fruit bowl, then opens the nice bottle of wine which he and Denver will now never drink and uses it to fill a Boddingtons pint glass. He collapses onto the sofa, hauls his laptop up to his chest and navigates clumsily to the website for *Argentium Astrum*, this online-only supernatural police procedural he's been watching. There's a new episode available but he can't get it to stream properly: the opening credits load all right but then the images devolve into glitches and optical noise, as if the video compression algorithm has grown overzealous, opting to cheerfully crush the visual data into unparsable blocks. He watches fields of color shift for a minute and then slaps the laptop shut, drains the pint glass in three great gulps, and stumbles into the bathroom, where he stares at the toilet, trying determinedly to make it stop drifting around in his field of vision. He never quite manages it, but he doesn't throw up either. He calls this a partial win and stumbles up to bed.

He wakes to the smell of coffee and the sound of his phone buzzing away. *It's Denver*, he thinks, and he experiences a brief feeling of hope, which is promptly demolished by the realization of exactly how hungover he is. He feels like a corpse being reanimated by means of savage jolts, one fresh burst of current direct into his rotten nervous system each time the phone vibrates. His limbs jerk uncoordinatedly. He flings an arm onto the bedside table, where it crashes onto the edge of a saucer covered in coins, flipping it into the air. Pennies rain down onto him. He groans and curses and pulls his head to the level of the bedside table, forces himself to open his eyes, winces. The phone's not there. It's on the floor. Each time it rings it scurries further away from the bed. *Fuck it*, he thinks. He pulls his pillow over his head. At long last the phone goes silent.

He plants a hand on the floor and anchors his stomach to the mattress, stretching his torso into space, sending his other hand way out, all the way out to the phone. Gets it, reels it back into the bed. When he checks the screen he sees that it's not Denver who called him at all. It's his dad.

He pulls the pillow back down over his face for a long minute. What could his dad want? Nearly every conversation they've had since Billy dropped out of school involves Dad urging Billy to read this or that esoteric book or article: something *Maleficarium*, something *Lycanthropia*, something *Carcieri Infernus*, whatever, whatever, whatever. Billy always says that he will do it, even though they both know by now that he won't do it. Well-meaning, Billy supposes, and in his more charitable moments Billy is even a little touched by the continuity of his father's faith in him, but that is not the kind of conversation he wants to have right now, or today, or maybe not this month at all, so Dad is going to have to wait. It is decided.

His head pounds. His stomach clenches.

Okay, he thinks. *Okay. We can survive this.*

He checks the time on the clock. It's just past nine. He needs to be at work at eleven thirty. That maybe gives him a little time to look over some of his writing; he's been invited to perform tomorrow night at a reading put together by this new lit mag, *The Ingot*, which is allegedly going to publish some of his stuff. But most of the stuff he's been writing lately isn't exactly what he would call *well-adapted to the reading format*, so he'd intended to spend the morning digging up something older, taking an hour or two to give it a little polish. He has an hour, maybe, but he can barely open his eyes against the oppressive daylight; looking at words on a computer screen might just finish him.

No, he thinks. *You can do this.* He sniffs the air. *At least there's coffee.*

Wait. Why is there coffee?

He sits up. He looks over the railing, down into the living room. There's a guy sitting on the couch, looking up at him. It's not Jørgen. It's not anybody Billy recognizes.

"Uhhh," says Billy. He pinches the bridge of his nose, blinks hard. Maybe the guy will disappear. But no. There's definitely a guy down there. He's wearing a suit, a pretty nice-looking olive suit.

He's got a shaved head, looks a bit like he might have once been a bike messenger. "Hi?" Billy tries. He gets out of bed, feeling a bit exposed, just standing there in his boxers. He hurries to get his legs into a pair of jeans.

"Take your time," says the man.

"Uhhh," Billy says again. "You must be . . . a friend of Jørgen's? He's away."

"No," says the man, while Billy's head is stuck inside a T-shirt. "It is you, William Harrison Ridgeway, with whom I intend to speak."

It is you with whom I intend to speak? Billy thinks. *Who the fuck talks like that?*

"Call me Billy," Billy says reflexively, heading down the stairs, wondering, not entirely idly, whether he should be looking for something that might constitute a weapon. "So—okay? Hi? Are you—with the landlord?"

"I am not," says the man. He hasn't moved from the couch, and he continues to watch Billy with evident interest, which freaks Billy out a little bit, but on another level he feels surprisingly relaxed about the whole thing. The guy doesn't match Billy's image of a psychotic murderer. He's clean. He's got probably a day's worth of stubble but it's clearly part of the overall look. Billy doesn't like the steady gaze, that's freaky, but it's also a calm gaze, the dude isn't wild-eyed or anything. He's not sitting there twitching. He's just, like, hanging out. His suit has clearly been tailored, which suggests money. So the guy probably isn't here to rob him either. It must just be a misunderstanding, something that can be resolved with ease.

"There's coffee," says the man.

"Thanks," says Billy, heading into the kitchen, while still trying to maintain a kind of half-cautious watch over his shoulder. He's prepared to be miffed that the guy broke into his coffee reserves without permission but he looks at the counter and sees that the guy actually brought his own beans. A bag of something called Fazenda Santa Terezinha, which smells pretty goddamn good. He fixes himself a cup.

"Okay," Billy says, holding the cup in both hands, up close to his face. "So you said you wanted to talk to me?"

"Have a seat," says the guy, gesturing at the armchair across from the couch.

"Um, yeah, no," says Billy. "I'm doing fine over here." *You're being ridiculous*, he tells himself. But, fuck it, so what? There's a steel counter between him and the guy and he's got bunch of knives within arm's reach. From that perspective he's got the best space in the house.

"As you wish," says the guy.

Billy sips the coffee. It's really good.

"This is really good," he says. It's really fucking good.

"I am glad," says the guy, "that you are enjoying it. But now. Let us get properly introduced."

"You already know my name," says Billy. "So why don't you tell me yours?"

"I shall," says the guy. He produces a business card, seemingly from nowhere, and places it carefully on the coffee table, among the messy piles of CDs, drug paraphernalia, and magazines. Billy makes no effort to approach to retrieve it, staying exactly where he is, in the kitchen, near the knives, drinking this really fucking good coffee.

"My name is Lucifer Morningstar," says the guy.

Billy sighs with annoyance because it turns out this motherfucker is crazy after all. He'd really hoped he was going to make it through the day without having to stab a dude.

CHAPTER TWO

TOUCHED IN THE HEAD

THE SAFETY MANAGER • CULTURAL NORMS AND WHEN TO
IGNORE THEM • IMAGINARY COPS • THE CONCEPT OF A LIGHT
SWITCH • INTIMACY AND CONSENT • LUCIFER'S PREFERRED
MEDIUM • NOVELS VS. SHORT STORIES • EARNING IT •
A LEAK AND TWO ASPIRIN

But he doesn't reach for the knives, not actually just quite yet
thanks, even though his optimism about the situation has just sustained a major hit. There's still got to be a route to resolution here.
A plausible reason why this guy is in this room, saying these things.

"Lucifer Morningstar?" Billy asks. "What is that, your *World
of Warcraft* name?"

"William," Lucifer says, and then he gives up a small, patient
smile, the kind of patient smile that primarily communicates just
how tolerant its bearer is being.

"Just Billy," Billy says. "Please."

"Billy, then. No, Billy, Lucifer Morningstar is my true and
given name."

"That's rough," Billy says. "Hippie parents?"

"Not exactly."

Billy picks up his cup of coffee and begins to step around the counter, heading closer to the guy. *What are you doing?* says the cautious part of his brain, the part Billy thinks of as the Safety Manager. *Don't get closer to this guy. He's a nutjob.*

Let's just see, says some other part of him, the part that Billy sometimes, in retrospect, calls the Well-Meaning Idiot. *It's stupid,* this part says, *to maintain, like, a twenty-foot distance between you and someone you're talking to.*

That's a cultural norm! says the Safety Manager. *You get to ignore cultural norms when some stranger shows up in your apartment! They're already violated!*

But by then it's too late. He's sitting in the armchair across from Lucifer. He reaches out to the coffee table, uses the back of his hand to push some garbage aside, making a space for his mug. He still feels pretty certain that he's not in real physical danger.

"Sorry about the mess," Billy says, holding both his palms up, beseechingly. "I've been busy."

"That makes perfect sense," says Lucifer. Billy feels a little flattered by this. Lucifer nods at the business card he placed on the table earlier, wedged between a heap of bills and a tangle of charging cords. The gilded edge catches Billy's eye, and he picks it up. Sure enough, it says "Lucifer Morningstar" on it, in a nice serif font. Underneath that it says "Comprehensive Consulting." There's no number or anything. Billy thinks about pocketing it before remembering that there's no good reason why he needs to be polite to this guy. Maybe playing it tough is the way to go. He flips the card back onto the table, leans back in the chair, crosses his arms, and puts on a face that's intended to say something like *You ain't shit to me.* Lucifer regards it placidly.

"Billy," he begins. "I wish to communicate something to

you directly. Our time is limited, so it is important for me to be frank here at the outset. I am a supernatural force. I have existed since time immemorial. I am what you would colloquially call the Devil."

This gives Billy a significant dose of pause. He lifts the coffee and gulps down a strong bolt of it, as if that will help.

"So—wait," Billy says. "What you're saying is . . ." He frowns. He's not really sure what else Lucifer Morningstar might be saying.

"What I'm saying," Lucifer says, "is exactly what I have said. There is no misunderstanding."

Billy, suffering a jolt of alarm, looks this guy straight in the face. Lucifer meets his stare and holds it, which does nothing to help him relax, so he looks away, electing to stare, instead, at the rim of his coffee mug.

"Yeahhhh," he says eventually. "But . . . you get that that's not a normal thing to say, right? I mean—I'm not a, what would you call it, a *religious man*. I don't believe in the Devil. So, what I'm saying is that you're kinda freaking me out here. I mean, if we're being frank, I'm, like, half a second away from picking up the phone and calling 911, reporting this as a home invasion, and getting on with my day."

Lucifer nods in a way that confers a certain sad understanding. "You are welcome to do that," he says, "but I guarantee it will not advance this conversation in a fruitful way."

For a minute, Billy thinks about doing it. But then he imagines having to deal with the NYPD. His past run-ins with them have never exactly elicited a high level of what you might call *customer satisfaction*. He imagines having to go through the process of hiding all the drug paraphernalia on the coffee table, imagines the long statement he'd have to give to some asshole force veteran.

And he imagines the whole process making him late for his shift at the sandwich shop, and late is the one thing that he cannot be. Giorgos, his boss, already wrote him up once and at that juncture it was made very clear to him that Giorgos was not in the business of writing up people twice. Billy's struck with an urge to check the time, but there's no clock in this room and he thinks it'd be rude to pull out his phone. The point is, he's really got to be moving this whole experience toward a wrap-up as quickly as possible.

Lucifer speaks again. "Billy," he says. "We have a limited amount of time."

"You're telling me."

"In order for you to understand what I have to say, it is imperative that you believe that I am who I say I am," Lucifer says.

"Fine," Billy says. "But you gotta give me something here, 'cause right now? I'm just not feeling it. You want me to believe that you're the Devil? Show me something. Show me something you can do that an ordinary guy can't do. Make it fucking rain blood or something."

"That would cause more problems than it would solve," Lucifer says.

"Then—I don't know," Billy says. He slaps his hands down on his thighs. "But you better come up with something, 'cause otherwise, it may be time for you to go."

"There is one technique which might meet your needs," Lucifer says. "I can simply make you believe me."

"You can *make* me," Billy says. "Tell me how that's going to work?"

"It's simple. Imagine a light switch in your brain. A light switch has two positions, on and off."

"I'm familiar with the concept."

"Little beliefs in your brain work the same way. Like a vast set of little switches. You prefer chicken. You prefer pork. You like eggplant. You don't like eggplant."

"I do like eggplant," Billy says.

"Wonderful," Lucifer says, giving Billy a full-on smile which lasts exactly a second, then vanishes. "However, if I reached into your brain and flipped that switch, your liking of eggplant would cease. Whether you treat any individual utterance as true or false is a simple binary belief, a switch. And I can change those."

"So if you can go into my head and change shit around, why haven't you done that already? If you can just *make me* believe you, why didn't we just *start* there?" Billy says, annoyed with himself that he's even dignifying the argument this way.

"It is intimate. People typically do not wish to have an intimate procedure performed on them without permission. The procedure does not strictly require consent, but consent facilitates the experience."

"You sound like an R-rated hypnotist," Billy says. "You're supposed to be the goddamn *Devil*, and you care about whether you have permission to change people's *minds?*"

Lucifer produces no evident reaction.

"Fine," Billy says, out of patience. "You have my consent. Go on ahead in there. Touch my brain. Make me believe you."

"I shall," Lucifer says.

Great, thinks the Safety Manager. *Here we go.*

Billy hears something. A tiny pop, like somebody had been shuffling their feet on carpet and then poked him in the back of his head. And something happens in his skull. Something shifts, grinds, as though his brain is a pile of rocks and one, deep in toward the center, has just disappeared. And suddenly something is different. He doesn't see the guy across from him as just a guy anymore, or even as a potentially-dangerous crazy guy. He sees him as the physical embodiment of a grand architecture of evil. The Devil. The Prince of Darkness.

The first thought Billy's new brain has is: *Holy fucking shit.*

The second thought is: *Call 911 now.*

Billy rears upward in the armchair.

"One moment," Lucifer says.

Billy's busy patting down his pockets in search of his phone and he doesn't quite hear that. He finally wrangles the phone out of his jeans, but his motor control has gone completely wack: instead of opening the phone's flip-top he manages to flibber the gadget right out of his hands. It caroms off the wall and vanishes entirely from Billy's perceptual awareness.

Billy turns to Plan B.

Plan B is to get the hell out of here. He considers making a run straight for the window; smashing through it, barefoot; and plummeting two stories to the street below. *We can survive it*, insists the Safety Manager, who has pretty much gone crazy from overwork at this point. *C'mon! Let's go!*

"One moment," Lucifer says again, rising from the couch and extending his palm toward Billy. "This requires adjustment." And Billy hears a lot more of those static-electricity pops, less like someone shocking the back of his head and more like someone peeling a synthetic shirt off of a blanket when they've both just come out of the dryer. The rock pile in his head grinds some more.

"Ugh," says Billy. He drops into a huddle. "What are you doing?"

"Cleanup," Lucifer says. "Tidying."

"No," Billy says, although the shower of spark sounds is already beginning to subside.

"Do not panic," Lucifer says. He is speaking a little absently and he has a look of partial concentration on his face, like somebody working a Rubik's Cube. "I'm just reducing some of the secondary effects: The anxiety. The adrenal residue in your limbic system. I'm grooming your neural pathways."

"I withdraw my consent," Billy says, miserably. "Get the fuck out of my head."

"This is the easy part," Lucifer says. And sure enough, if Billy were really to be honest, he'd have to admit that this part feels comparatively gentle, maybe even kind of good, like the feeling you get when you smell a cinnamon bun somewhere nearby.

Slowly he gets back to his feet, dusts himself off.

He looks at Lucifer, tries to see him again as he saw him a moment ago—magnificent, fearsome—and he can't quite muster it. Whatever Lucifer just did in the cleanup, it made him go back to just looking like a sort of ordinary dude. An ordinary dude who Billy believes to be the Devil. Intellectually, Billy understands that he should still be spasming in the grip of vast cosmic terror but the part of him that was able to do that seems to have burned out. But still. There's no possible way he can be safe right now.

"Um," Billy says, patting himself down again for his phone, only half remembering that he dropped it. "I still kind of feel like I should call 911?"

"Certainly that is your prerogative," Lucifer says, although he sounds a little bored by the prospect. He bends down, picks Billy's phone up out of the corner, and hands it over.

Keeping one eye on Lucifer, Billy flips open the phone and punches a nine into it. He pauses there, taking a moment to rehearse exactly what it is he is going to say. *The Devil's in my apartment?*

What would the cops do if they even showed up? Mow Lucifer down in a hail of bullets? Billy guesses that if it was that easy to get rid of the Devil, someone in the long history of humanity would already have done it by now. And when he actually tries to play out how it would go in his mind, all he can foresee is *himself* getting shot in the kind of inevitable mix-up that always seems to befall him. He ponders for a long moment and finally claps the phone shut again.

"Come," Lucifer says, returning to his seat on the couch. "Sit. Let us talk."

Billy cautiously settles back down in the armchair. He picks up the coffee and takes another sip. It's cold.

"Okay," Billy says. He crumples a little, recognizing defeat. "You want to talk? Let's talk."

"Fantastic," says Lucifer. He leans over the side of the couch and hauls a messenger bag up into his lap. He pulls open the bag's flap, a tremendous roar of rending Velcro powerfully reminding Billy that his hangover has not gone away. What the fuck. The Devil can groom his goddamn *neural pathways* but doesn't bother to clean up his hangover while he's in there?

Lucifer produces a beat-up ThinkPad from his bag. Billy notices that part of the casing is patched with electrical tape. He tries to imagine the Devil using tape.

"I've prepared a PowerPoint presentation that will cover the basics of what I wish to discuss with you," Lucifer begins, opening up the ThinkPad.

"Stop," Billy says. "PowerPoint?"

"It's my preferred medium," says Lucifer.

"No," Billy says. "Just no. You want to talk? We can talk. But I'm hungover, I'm annoyed, I'm still kind of losing my shit, I'm not watching a freaking *PowerPoint presentation.*"

"PowerPoint is actually quite unfairly maligned," Lucifer says. "In the right hands, it can produce presentations that convey a lot of information and border on the beautiful."

"Look," says Billy. "I don't know why you're here, and I don't know what you want, and—I mean, if we're just two dudes hanging out, talking, then I can maybe deal with hearing what you have to say. But otherwise—"

"Yes, fine," Lucifer says, a touch of irritation creeping in. He shoves the laptop back into the messenger bag. For a second he looks really pissed and then his features clear, his expression reverts back to neutral.

"Billy Ridgeway," he says, in the affectless tone that seems to be his default. "I have a proposition for you."

"I gotta be frank," Billy says. "I sort of feel like the choice move here is just to say no right out of the gate." Another sip of the cold coffee. He wants a refill but feels like now is not the time to get up and go back into the kitchen.

"I wish for you to do something for me," Lucifer says. "It is a simple task which will require a minimal amount of your time. In exchange, I will do something for you."

Billy's prepared to reiterate his *choice move* line, but then he allows himself to grow intrigued. "You'll do something for me? So, okay, wait. Exactly what?"

"I can see to it that your book gets published," Lucifer says.

A tiny burst of excitement spikes within Billy, which is almost immediately swallowed by a yawning chasm of skepticism.

"Which book?" Billy says, cautiously.

"The novel," Lucifer says. "There are people I can get to publish the novel. Short stories, though—that's a tough sell."

"A major publisher?" Billy asks.

"I am prepared to promise you a major publisher and a five-figure advance."

A five-figure advance! Billy thinks, even though a quick mental process in which he tacks zeros onto a one helps him to remember that the figure he's envisioning might only be $10K. *So*, he thinks, suddenly canny, *let's deal.* And then he realizes what he's doing.

"Wait a second," he says. "This is some kind of make-a-deal-with-the-Devil-type shit."

"Technically," Lucifer says, "yes."

"This is one of those things where I end up saying *Oh, tell me more* and the next thing I know I'm signing away my soul." He doesn't actually believe in the soul, but he does know that if the Devil shows up and asks you to sign yours away, you should probably say no.

"Billy," Lucifer says. He offers the patronizing, patient smile again. "It doesn't work that way. I'm not interested in your soul."

"You're the Archduke of Lies," Billy says. "How can I possibly believe you?"

"Souls are like ideas," Lucifer says. "Everybody has one that they think is worth something."

"Yeah, no," Billy says.

"But—"

"Just no. I don't feel safe around you and I sure as hell don't trust you. And although your offer is very intriguing—and I *would* love to see my work in print—so if you know anybody and feel like putting in a good *word* for me . . ." Noting that he's beginning to backslide, he makes the decision to just shut up.

"Let me tell you what you'd have to do," Lucifer says, smiling with the radiant false force of a salesperson.

"I don't *care* what I'd have to do," Billy says. "It could be the simplest thing imaginable. Something I was going to do anyway. *Go to the bathroom, take a leak and two aspirin. Then, bam, you're a famous writer.* I'd still say no." As he says this, he feels a pang deep in his chest, like a piece of gravel hitting a bell, and he realizes that it may not, in fact, be true.

He thinks for a minute about how his life would change if his book got published. He contemplates the feeling of validation he'd enjoy. The ability, at least for a little while, to say *You were right to do this.* To give up time every day, precious time, the resource that other people seem able to turn into *billable hours* or *functional relationships*, to working on putting words together, to making declarations about people who don't exist, to saying that they did things they didn't do. To spend money on books instead of clothes or a haircut. To fail out of school because he spent a semester trying to teach himself Polish in order to read a Stanisław Lem collection he'd bought at a bookseller's kiosk in Greenpoint (and, not incidentally, because he used Krakowianka, a Polish blackberry vodka, as his primary study aid). If he were holding his book in his hand he'd be able, for once in his life, to look at all his choices and say *You were right.* What would that feel like? Billy doesn't know. He would like to know.

But he does know one thing. He knows that if he says yes, in this way, under these circumstances, and he gets what he wants, he won't exactly be able to say that he earned it. And he wants to earn it.

And so Billy decides. He says, "This discussion is over." He rises. "Thanks for the coffee." He heads for the kitchen to get that refill he's been wanting, leaving Lucifer sitting, blank-faced, there on the couch.

After a minute, Lucifer rises, straps the messenger bag across his chest, dons a pair of aviator sunglasses, and fishes the business card out of the junk on the coffee table. He meets Billy in the kitchen on the way out.

"I'm disappointed," he says.

"And if you were my dad, that might matter to me," says Billy. *Call your dad back*, says Billy's brain.

"I'll respect your wishes," Lucifer says, ignoring the retort, "and be on my way. Do keep my card, though. In the event that you change your mind."

"I very much doubt that I'll be changing my mind," Billy says. But he pockets the card.

"Good day to you, Billy Ridgeway," Lucifer says. Billy half expects him to disappear in a great cloud of violet smoke, but he heads out the front door like a normal person.

Billy gets a great flash of jubilation as soon as the door latches. *I was tempted by the Devil*, he thinks, *and I walked away.* He suddenly realizes that Denver was wrong—he's not a chronic fuck-up! This is proof—ironclad, dishwasher-safe proof. He has the moral high ground and he intends to hold it. He notes a few little shoots of regret and doubt fringing the edges of the high ground, but, hey, who cares, that's normal.

Another sip of the really good coffee. He notices that Lucifer left the beans. This day is going to keep getting better.

He takes a leak and two aspirin. And in the blessed dark of the bathroom, for which his hangover is grateful, he decides to keep going on his winning streak. He's going to get Denver on the phone. If he can look the Devil in the eye and emerge unscathed then surely he can work things out in his personal life. He feels good. He feels confident. He flips his phone open and eyeballs the time.

"Son of a bitch," he says.

CHAPTER THREE

PROFOUNDLY SUCKING

IDEAL DESKS • BLACK SHIRT AND KHAKIS • THAI FOOD AND
BOURBON • NOT CHARLIE OR CHUCK • DRUNK SENIOR
EDITORS • A FUCK-TON OF HINDUS • JESUS, TAXES, PEDOPHILE •
POSSIBILITIES OF AN UNCERTAIN WORLD • BAD PUBLICITY

I wish that I was the kind of person who owned an appointment book, Billy thinks, as he frantically grubs around in the bottom of his closet, looking for the button-down shirt that completes his work uniform. He's never owned an appointment book but he pictures it as this serious leather-bound thing, sitting on his desk. In this fantasy, his desk is nothing like the desks he's ever actually owned— desks which quickly go invisible under unmanageable mountains of unopened mail and tech cables—it is instead one huge square slab of monochromatic wood, with nothing on it except this imaginary appointment book, his laptop, and maybe some interesting artifact. A piece of river stone. And, in this fantasy, when people approach him with some kind of demand on his time, he simply says *I'm not sure if I can see you right now. Let me check my appointment book.* And he can flip it open and examine the day dispassionately and say *Ah, yes, today is no good. Today I shall be selecting pieces of fiction for tomorrow night's reading and then I must depart for my shift at the sandwich shop. Perhaps next Wednesday?* And then he wouldn't have days like today, where somebody shows up and devours his available time, and then the next thing he knows he's on his knees, in the closet, pulling shirts out of a heap, hoping he can make it to work before Giorgos decides to fire him.

He finally finds the black button-down he was looking for. It hasn't been washed anytime recently but fuck it, the dictum says *black shirt and khakis*, he's never heard Giorgos say *The black shirt shall smell fresh* or *The khakis shall not bear mayonnaise stains that could be mistaken for semen.*

Bang, he's out the door, down the stairs, through the vestibule, and out into the cold, clear Brooklyn morning. Running for his life, or at least the version of it where he has this job and lives in this apartment.

If Billy loses this job he won't make rent. In fact, even with the job it's often a struggle. That $12.50 an hour adds up pretty slowly. He's had months, plural, where he's had to turn to Jørgen for a little financial help. Billy thinks on this for a moment as he angles through a cluster of kvetching grandmothers and it occurs to him that if Jørgen doesn't return before the end of the month then he's going to have to cover the entire rent himself. This is not actually a possibility. *Just call him*, Billy thinks, as he barrels past discount electronics shops and the bagel place that he likes. *Denver was right. You should just call him.*

Denver. He imagines the thought of her name stopping him dead in his tracks. (In actuality he is already stopped by two elderly Romanians who have chosen to use the sidewalk to angrily negotiate the sale of a pair of ancient Nintendo Entertainment System consoles.)

The point is: he misses Denver. And as he gets around the Romanian guys and heads into a final sprint toward the subway stop, he thinks about her, he reflects back on the normal times, the downtime, the evenings that he'd spent with Denver just flumped out in his bed, eating Thai takeout, drinking some incredible bourbon that she'd brought over, watching stupid YouTube videos on her MacBook, listening to her plot out a piece of conceptual video art that she wanted to make out of uploaded footage of cats, seeing her smile at his jokes. Pressing his face into her shoulder as the hour grew late. Not having sex kinda 'cause of Jørgen and kinda just 'cause they were both too sleepy. The memory is a lamentation. Right now he feels like he would do anything even to be *not* having sex with Denver.

Too bad she figured out that he was a fuck-up.

But no, he tells himself. *You're not a fuck-up. You met the Devil and you walked away. That proves something. She'll see when you tell her.*

But how can he tell her?

And then, right as he reaches the subway stop: inspiration.

He has it.

He knows how he can explain his feelings toward her, reassert his competence, and convince her to accept the major epistemological shift he's experienced today. It all holds together. In his mind it's an intricate crystal made of pure motherfucking eloquence. He just has to get her on the phone, now, before it all dissolves into slush.

He judders to a halt on the stairs, halfway through his descent into the station. The last possible point where he'll have a phone signal. A person directly behind him stumbles into his back and emits a few terse syllables of what may be Korean invective.

"Sorry," Billy mutters, but he isn't, not really. He struggles his cell phone out of his pocket, angles it up the stairs at a chunk of sky, and punches the single numeral that autodials Denver.

And of course it goes straight to voice mail.

"Fuck," Billy says. He's never done well with voice mail.

It's okay, he thinks, *you can do this.*

And he speaks: "Uhhh, yeah, hi, Denver, I just, I was just thinking, I know we're—I know things are—I've just had a really strange day today, and it got me to thinking about us, about you, and I just would really like to talk to you again, sometime, when you can, I know you probably don't really want to because, I don't know, I think you're still mad at me or something, but I kinda hope that you'll look past that and call me back and maybe I can explain a couple of things. Okay? Uh, that's it I guess. Call me!"

He hangs up. *Fuck,* he thinks, *that was horrible. Do yourself a goddamn favor and never speak again.*

The taste of failure still rank in his mouth, he hurries down the stairs, swipes his card at the turnstile, and bolts to the platform just in time to see his train close its doors and pull away.

When he finally gets to work he's ten minutes later than the five minutes late he thinks of as permissible. Fifteen minutes is late enough that he's inarguably late but still close enough to on time that maybe nobody noticed. Giorgos's idea of management is to stay in the upstairs office for most of the day, on the computer, possibly looking at whatever kind of porn tiny, angry Greek men indulge in, so he's not always up-to-date on the precise status of any given employee.

The only person in the kitchen is Anil, who looks up from

his station at Billy, looks at the clock, and looks back at Billy, all without pausing in his sandwich assembly. Guy is kind of a machine.

"Late again," Anil says. "You run into a bunch of bananas that you couldn't resist?"

"Very funny," Billy says. "Does Giorgos know?"

"I think you're safe," Anil says. "But, come on, man, this job sucks enough even when we're working *together*; could you please make a little more effort to not get shitcanned? In the name of some motherfucking *solidarity*?"

"Yeah," Billy says, getting his latex food-prep gloves on. "But it wasn't my fault."

"Right, it's never your fault," Anil says. "That's some bullshit, though."

"True," Billy says, taking his spot at his station and reviewing the three sandwich orders in the queue. "But I gotta tell you, it's been a weird-ass day today."

"Ah, yes, Billy and the ten thousand weirdnesses," Anil says. "Spare me no detail."

Billy contemplates the prospect. Tell him. Find a way. Anil already knows that shit sometimes goes down in Billy's life. It was Anil who showed up at Billy's apartment when Billy failed out of school, made him open his blinds, change his clothes, shave his face, pour the last of the Krakowianka down the drain. And when Billy confessed, in that dark time, to having been too drunk and disordered to have gotten it together to go back home for his own mother's funeral, it was Anil who volunteered to drive Billy to Ohio—eight hours—so that Billy could look his father, Keith, in the face, and apologize. Anil had slept on a couch that no one had ever found comfortable and then driven Billy back the next day. Ate the cost of the gas and the tolls and the cigarettes without complaint. Billy remembers that trip, the two of them out of their minds on rest stop coffee, listening to Anil's Minutemen cassette over and over and over again, the only cassette Anil's crappy stereo hadn't long ago devoured. After the tenth time they listened through it Billy had memorized the album's entire collection of gnomic pronouncements; by the time they rolled back into Brooklyn he was bellowing them out the window. Each line seemed like a slogan for the new and better life that he believed Anil had bought for him. Surely you could talk to someone like that about the Devil?

Except you can't, not really.

"Forget it," Billy says, finally, not without a little sadness. "You would just—you would think I was a real nutjob."

"Instead of just a fuck-up?" Anil says.

"I'm not a fuck-up."

"Whatever you gotta tell yourself, man."

Fuck-up or not, Billy fulfills his duties well as the day wends along: he reduces heads of lettuce to ribbons with some deft knife-work, he folds sliced turkey artfully atop ciabatta bread, he musters a passable level of cheer when Giorgos passes through. All the while, though, he's thinking of how he could tell Anil about what happened this morning. Telling Anil would be a good trial run for telling Denver, and if he can tell Denver, he feels like his life will fall back into some kind of recognizable order.

"Hey," says Anil, at one point when they have a breather. "After work I'm meeting the Ghoul down at that vegetarian place he likes. Gonna talk some shop for a little while. You want to join us?"

The Ghoul: his real name is Charles but to them he's always been the Ghoul. What else can you call someone with that particular waxy complexion, that long, bony face, those deep-set eyes set loosely in crumpled bags of empurpled flesh? No other nickname seems available: nobody is going to mistake this guy for a Charlie or a Chuck or a Chazz. Put a pair of fingerless gloves on him and he could be somebody who died of consumption in a garret somewhere near the end of the nineteenth century.

It doesn't help that he's a poet. Anil and Billy are both fiction writers and they view poets with definite suspicion: they treat them the way you'd treat someone who claimed to have descended from elves. Poets seem to have collectively learned a particular type of intonation to deploy at readings: Anil calls it "Poet Voice." It's a cousin of what he calls "NPR Voice." On more than one occasion Anil has cracked Billy up by reading random things around the kitchen in Poet Voice: recipes, auto circulars, credit card offers, personal ads. He once stood on a stool and made Billy nearly herniate himself with laughter by using Poet Voice to recite a crass rhyme that Billy remembered from childhood ("Milk / milk / lemonade / round the corner / fudge is made").

But in spite of themselves they like the Ghoul. For all his anachronistic look-and-feel, he's actually the most twenty-first century guy they know. He has this phone that he never seems to put away. It's all tricked out in some ultra-complicated fashion that involves RSS feeds or Google Alerts or some shit. Billy doesn't claim to have a grip on the particulars but he knows that the Ghoul's phone is like a gleaming portal opening onto the entire New York literary scene. Every five minutes it trembles or coos and the Ghoul fusses with it and then, miraculously, he is in possession of some detail that seems, suddenly, crucial to what they think of as their *careers*: "Three senior editors from HarperCollins are getting drunk on Dark and Stormys two blocks from here." And they're off on some adventure.

Furthermore, he's on Twitter, *active* on Twitter, like dozens-of-tweets-a-day active, and what's more, he's *funny* on Twitter. If he ever wanted to give up poetry he could make a decent go at stand-up. He could get up there, looking exactly like he does, and read tweets nonstop for twenty minutes. Anil and Billy still kinda struggle just to get their minds around why Twitter even exists.

So, yeah, Billy likes the Ghoul. And even though he should be taking the evening to select pieces for tomorrow night's reading, he agrees to go out, not just because he wants to see the Ghoul but because he won't quite give up on the idea of talking to Anil about the Devil.

So then it's after work and he and Anil are standing in the alleyway among the Dumpsters and hot pizza exhaust from the parlor next door, and Anil's having one cigarette before they head to the vegetarian place, and Billy decides to just plunge in.

"Hey Anil. Remember when I said I'd had a weird-ass day?"

Anil gives a perfunctory nod. His face is pressed into his cupped hands, where he's shielding his lighter from the wind. Once he gets his cigarette going he returns to full height—five seven or thereabouts—drags, exhales, and says, "Bet it seems less weird now that you've made sandwiches for eight hours straight."

"Yeah, but shut up a second," says Billy. "This is actually important."

Anil draws and exhales again. "Okay," he says. "Tell me."

"It's hard to know how to start," Billy says. "Things are a little mixed up in my head—that's part of it, actually—so I'm not a hundred percent sure how it'll sound to somebody who hasn't had the same experience I've had."

"This is why I don't write memoir," Anil says. "There's an inherent intransmissibility to experience that memoir purports to be able to breach? You know, thus grounding itself, as a very genre, in a lie?"

"Yeah, no," Billy says. "Not like that. Well, maybe like that."

"Why don't you just tell me?" Anil says.

"I met the Devil today," Billy says.

Anil contemplates this, drags on his cigarette again.

"The Devil," he repeats.

"Yeah, the Devil."

"Which one?" Anil says.

This throws Billy for a second. "Which *one*? You know, Anil, *the Devil.*"

"My family is Hindu, man. We don't have just *one* devil."

"Oh, shit," Billy says. "I didn't think of that."

"So, I don't know, if you're really telling me that you met the Devil—and I'm still kind of hoping that you mean 'the Devil' as some kind of metaphor, like maybe you faced your own personal demon, or you smoked heroin or something—but if you're really telling me that you met the Judeo-Christian Devil, with the embedded implication there being that Judeo-Christianity is somehow ontologically more *real* than the Hindu beliefs of my own tradition—I mean, shit, Billy, I'm not the best example of a devout practicing Hindu, but don't take that to mean that there aren't a fuck-ton of them out there. And I'm not saying that a billion Hindus can't all be wrong—I'm pretty sure they all *are*, in fact—but if they're all wrong, I guarantee you that the motherfucking *Christians* aren't *right.*"

"I don't mean to be offensive," Billy says, cringing. "Is this offensive?"

"Yes," Anil says. "You're basically a racist."

"I'm sorry," Billy blurts.

"No, man, would you relax?" Anil says. "We've been friends for like ten years and you still don't know when I'm fucking with you?"

"He did something to my brain," Billy says, morosely. "He did something to my brain and nothing makes sense any more."

Anil gives him a long look.

"Okay, see, now you sound like a crazy person," Anil says. "This seems like an actual step down from when you were just going on about the Devil. Maybe you'd better start over."

"I woke up this morning," Billy says, "and there was this *guy* in the apartment." That seems like a workable way in. He continues from there. Anil finishes his cigarette and starts a second one and doesn't interrupt. When Billy finishes he closes his eyes, waiting for judgment.

"So what about God?" Anil says, finally.

Billy opens his eyes. "I don't know."

"If you believe in the Devil now, you should believe in God," Anil says. He points upward, by way of illustration.

"Yeah," Billy says. "That would make sense. But remember the part where I said things don't make sense any more?"

"I'm going to say a word and I want you to tell me if you have any special feeling about it, okay?"

"Okay."

"Ready?"

"Ready."

"The word is: Jesus."

Billy throws out his hands, exasperated. "Really, dude? Really?"

"What?"

"*Jesus? Jesus* isn't exactly an *emotionally neutral* word for *anybody raised in the goddamn Western world.* It's maybe one of the top ten words that we have *special feelings* about? 'Jesus,' 'taxes,' 'pedophile,' and I'm sure there are seven others? But if you're asking me if I have any special feeling about that word that I didn't have yesterday, then the answer is no."

"Okay," Anil says. "That's weird."

"Yeah, asshole, I know. That's where we came in, remember? Give me a cigarette."

"I thought you quit."

"I reserve the right to be un-quit in a *mental health emergency* such as the one we clearly have before us today."

"Fair enough." They huddle together to get Billy lit, and then they separate, standing there for a minute, eyeing one another somewhat suspiciously.

"I dunno, man, you seem normal to me," Anil says, finally.

"I *feel* normal," Billy says. "Except there's like this one *belief* in my head that I just can't make fit."

"You know what I think?" Anil says. "I think you got pranked."

Billy, dragging on his cigarette, shakes his head with a vigorous no, but Anil carries on: "I think Jørgen and some buddy of his got the best of you. You said he was out of town, right?"

"I guess," Billy admits. "At the electronic music dude convention."

"He probably had some buddy who was coming into the city and needed a place to crash. He probably got in touch—*Hey, buddy, can I stay with you?*—and Jørgen was like *Perfect, I'm not even there, you can crash in my bed. I'll send you the key. I got this roommate though* ... One thing led to another and they got into their heads that it'd be a good idea to freak you out. I mean, did he know *anything* about you that Jørgen doesn't know?"

Billy considers this. "No."

"This whole *devil* thing sounds like something one of his friends would come up with. You remember he spent like all of last year palling around with those death metal dudes? Guys with a kinda Jotunheim look about them? Dudes in druid robes who maybe had a White Power background?"

"Yeah, but this guy didn't look like *that*," Billy says. "He just looked kind of normal."

"I don't know," Anil says. "Maybe somebody who grew out of that stage?"

Billy considers Lucifer's shaved head and stubble. "Could be," he concludes. "But what about the part where, you know, where he reached in and like *touched* my *brain*?"

"Tricky," Anil says. "But someone who has maybe some stage magic experience? Somebody who had done some hypnotism?"

"Yes! He sounded like an R-rated hypnotist!"

"Coupled perhaps with an unusually receptive, naïve subject ... it's not ironclad, but it makes loads more sense than the alternative. I'll bet they got the whole thing on video. It's probably up on YouTube right now. You'd better hope you comported yourself with your usual dignity throughout the experience."

Billy remembers cowering in the corner, and he winces. "Is that legal?" he asks. "To put me on YouTube without my permission? With an ... intention to humiliate?"

"Dude," Anil says. "You're not going to *sue your roommate* just because he punk'd you."

"Don't say *punk'd*," Billy says. "That is not a word."

"Don't worry, buddy. If they did something like that, it's cool, they'll take it down as soon as they know you figured it out. Look, we're going to go see the Ghoul, right? We should have left ten minutes ago, I'm just saying. If you're online somewhere, looking like an idiot, the Ghoul will be able to find it. Fuck, he's probably already seen it. So you call Jørgen, you admit that he punk'd you, you guys'll have a laugh, he'll take it down. That'll be it. You'll go home tonight, the quote-unquote Devil will be there, you'll get to meet him a second time and you'll see that everything's cool, tomorrow you'll be all like *He actually turned out to be a really funny guy.*"

Put that way it doesn't sound so bad. Billy's been meaning to call Jørgen anyway. And as they head out, he can almost make Anil's version of events seem plausible. There is only one problem with it. The switch in Billy's head, the one that tells him that this guy was actually the Devil? It's still stuck, determinedly, in the ON position.

"Gentlemen," says the Ghoul, his heavy-lidded eyes rising from his phone to regard them as they tramp in and shake off the chilly November as best they can.

"Hey, G.," says Anil. "How's the poetry biz?"

"Predictable," says the Ghoul. He's already gotten started on his meal, having worked halfway through his usual, an enormous platter of vegetarian chili nachos. The waitress proffers menus before Anil and Billy are fully settled in; they wave them off, putting in orders for their own respective usuals.

"So," Anil begins. "It's been an interesting day."

"Uncovering new horizons in sandwich-making?" says the Ghoul.

"As ever. But no. The interesting part involves our buddy Billy here." He claps Billy on the shoulder. "Billy had, I don't know, you might call it an unusual epistemological occurrence? Maybe a brush with the divine?"

The Ghoul slowly arches an eyebrow.

Anil turns to Billy. "Do you want to tell it?" he asks.

"Why don't you tell it," says Billy. He wants to hear whether it sounds crazy coming out of someone else's mouth.

"Let me lead with a question," Anil says to the Ghoul. "Did you see anything online today that might have embarrassed Billy?"

The Ghoul's face contorts into a grimace of sympathy, revealing an answer. Billy crumples a little, mortified, but there's some relief in it: he understands that he can maybe begin to relax into knowing that the whole thing was just a joke.

"I wasn't sure that I was going to bring that up," says the Ghoul, not unkindly. "I didn't want to cast a pall over the evening unnecessarily. But you've seen it?"

"I haven't seen it," Billy says. "But Anil guessed that it was probably out there."

"He guessed?" the Ghoul says.

"I'm just an unusually perceptive motherfucker," Anil says. He leans back, seemingly satisfied that his role in this drama is complete.

"Interesting," says the Ghoul.

"I want to see it," says Billy. "Can you get it up on your phone?"

"I can. You're not going to love it, though."

"I can take it," says Billy.

"A brave mind is an impregnable thing," says the Ghoul, using his long fingers to complete a design on the glossy surface of his phone. Moments later, Billy is peering into its depths. It's not YouTube he's looking at. But he recognizes it, the pink of its banner is an instant giveaway. It's Bladed Hyacinth.

Why is he looking at Bladed Hyacinth?

Bladed Hyacinth is a blog. It's a literary gossip blog that they all read, a blog that they all are influenced by, even though none of them, no one they know, in fact, ever really wants to admit to being influenced by it, because then you would have to admit to being the kind of person who is influenced by Bladed Hyacinth, which none of them want to be. But the bottom line is that once Bladed Hyacinth says you're cool then everyone kind of tacitly admits that you're cool, and if Bladed Hyacinth says you're over, then you're over.

"Why are you showing me this?" Billy asks. It isn't really a question. The Ghoul has directed him to a Bladed Hyacinth posting entitled "Tomorrow's *Ingot* Reading a Nonevent."

"Oh no," Billy says. Horrified, he looks at the byline. His heart sinks to see the name of Anton Cirrus, the founder and editor in chief of Bladed Hyacinth, the most notoriously mordant member of the loose gang that runs the site. They all want to believe that Anton Cirrus is a guy who feels vengeful toward all writers because he can't write, but word is that he has the talent to back up his acerbic nature. The latest gossip reports that he's just signed a six-figure deal with Knopf, for a memoir. Nobody seems to know anything about Cirrus's early life but somehow the memoir is already rumored to be "explosive." No one knows what exactly stands to be exploded, or why, but the book already has an aura around it, whispers about how it's going to change everything. "Asshole Writes

Incredibly Good Book, Dismaying Observers" is not exactly stop-the-presses-type news for anybody sitting at this table. But seeing said asshole mention the *Ingot* reading gets Billy on full alert. He reads:

Recently at the offices we received notice of an approaching reading at Barometer, last year's literary-tavern-of-the-moment, tied to the upcoming release of the debut issue of *The Ingot*. The invite promised an evening of "the best innovative new writing," and we confess to having felt a momentary stirring of hope, despite the fact that we have come to believe that promises of this sort—having been offered so many times, by so many similar comers—border now on the unfulfillable. But we did not recognize the names prominently featured on the invite—poet Elisa Mastic and fiction writer Billy Ridgeway—and we here at the Hyacinth aspire, always, to retain an open mind. Perhaps, we thought, perhaps these two truly do represent the best innovative new writing. Certainly the possibility is there, in an uncertain world. We concluded that more research was in order. We were able to track down Ms. Mastic's first book—*Sanguinities* (2010)—and a smattering of short fiction that Mr. Ridgeway has published in a set of small magazines that do not merit recounting here. We sat down, braced for amazement. Sadly, our optimism was unfounded. Our research revealed that Mastic and Ridgeway do not, in fact, represent a new guard of innovative writing, but are merely the latest pair to stumble, wide-eyed, into the ravaged storehouse of tired forms and stale devices. These creators have yet to realize that they are offering us not wonderment but familiarity, familiarity of the most familiar form, and that by so doing what they have brought upon themselves, editorially speaking, is our contempt. Thanks for the invite, *Ingot*, but we find ourselves in a position where we must decline.

And, with that, Billy thinks *Anton Cirrus thinks I suck.*

"What does it say?" says Anil, craning in to get a look. Billy lets the phone go out of his slack, defeated hands.

"The ravaged storehouse of tired forms and stale devices?" Billy says, from memory. He seems to have memorized the entire thing with only a single read, as though it has been branded into his mind. "It basically says that I suck. Am I wrong here?"

"You're not wrong," Anil says, staring numbly into the screen.

"Anton Cirrus," Billy says, "just said that I suck."

And he's right, Billy thinks. *All that time, all those hours spent in front of the computer, practicing, doing the work, and in the end all it will ever mean is that I just suck more and more profoundly.*

"This could be one of those things," the Ghoul says.

"What things?" Billy says, hollowly.

"Any publicity is good publicity?"

"No," Billy says. "This isn't good publicity. This is bad publicity."

"As long as they spell your name right . . ." Anil says.

"Are you kidding?" Billy says. "Anton Cirrus just told, what, twenty thousand of the most influential readers in the country that I suck. Is this—is this the first thing that comes up when you Google my name now?"

"I don't know," Anil says, fumbling with the phone.

"Google it," Billy demands.

"Don't Google it," says the Ghoul. "Just leave it alone."

"Give me the phone," Billy says.

A brief scuffle ensues, ending with the Ghoul's phone firmly in the Ghoul's bony grip.

"Just let it go," says the Ghoul.

"I don't believe it," Billy says, although he clearly does. "I suck."

No one seems to be in the mood to correct him. They all stare awkwardly off in different directions for a minute and then the food hits the table. Billy gazes dispiritedly at his eggplant Parmesan sandwich. He doesn't want it.

"You should eat," says Anil, after a minute.

"I don't want to," Billy says.

"Eating is a small, good thing in a time like this," Anil hazards.

"Fuck you," Billy says, but he takes the point. He lifts the sandwich to his mouth, and bites in. Something is wrong, though. It tastes disgusting.

"Eccch," he says, around the bolus of food in his mouth. "This is wrong."

"The sandwich is wrong?" says the Ghoul.

"It's disgusting," Billy says. He thrusts it toward Anil. "Taste this."

"I don't know why you persist in thinking of me as the kind of person who would taste something prefaced with *It's disgusting*," Anil says.

"It's just—I dunno," Billy says. "It just tastes *off*. Will you just try it? I'm having the kind of day where I need a second opinion to make sure I'm not going crazy."

Anil shrugs, leans over and gives it a bite. Chews, swallows, makes a thoughtful face. "I don't know," he says. "It tastes normal to me. What's *off* about it?"

"I don't know," Billy says. "The eggplant just tastes disgusting somehow." And then he realizes what has happened.

"That fucker," he says, rearing to his feet. "That soulless, black-hearted motherfucker."

They assume he's still talking about Anton Cirrus, and they try to calm him, but by this point Billy is inconsolable. He throws some money down on the table and storms out, leaving his sandwich uneaten, making a beeline for the subway. He wants to go home. He wants to go home, throw himself down onto his bed, and cry. Or at the very least smoke some of Jørgen's weed and watch some online video, disappear into *Argentium Astrum* if he can get it to stream right.

On the platform he checks one final time to see if Denver has tried to reach him. He holds the phone in his hand for a good long time, willing it to do something. He resists the urge to dash it to pieces on the track. And then finally he shoves it back down into his pocket, and while his hand is in there he digs around through the trash he's accumulated over the course of the day, and he pulls out Lucifer's business card.

Lucifer Morningstar, Comprehensive Consulting. No number or anything. How the fuck was this even supposed to work? Not that he would call even if there was a number there. It's been a bad day, everything important to him ruined and tattered, but even so, that doesn't mean that he should just become Satan's lackey.

You should have at least heard him out, he tells himself, *just found out what he wanted you to do. Maybe it wouldn't have been so bad.*

Maybe, maybe. But maybes do him no good now: his chance, whatever it was, has passed. Billy puts the card back in his pocket and gets on the subway and rides for three stops: miserable, racked with regrets, but at least feeling certain that there's nothing to be done now. He feels resolved, nearly calm. And perhaps it's something about this near-calmness that causes him to be not exactly one hundred percent surprised when he climbs the stairs to his apartment and keys in to find the Devil sitting there, on the sofa, as though he had never left.

CHAPTER FOUR

WAVING GOODBYE FOREVER

DIETARY CONCERNS • TWO REASONABLE GUYS • FOCUS • WHAT
AQUINAS SAID • DORM ROOM WITCHES • SCARY ARCHITECTURE
• BECKONING, TECHNICALLY • INFINITE FIRE IS BAD • THE ME
GETTING KILLED PART • OH YEAH DON'T FORGET ABOUT GOD

―――――――

"I want eggplant back, you bastard," Billy says.

"I understand," Lucifer says, holding his palms out. "Please be assured that my primary intention was not to cause you undue distress."

"You didn't *intend to*— You *vandalized* my *brain* and you didn't think it would cause me *undue distress?*"

Lucifer shrugs. "Causing you distress was not my primary intention," he reiterates. "Let's call it a by-product."

"What the hell was your *primary intention?*" Billy asks.

"I sought to provide something that would serve as a reminder of my visit," says Lucifer. "I thought it would perhaps stimulate some curiosity in you, a desire to meet again."

"A *reminder?*" Billy says. "You're the fucking Devil; it's not like I'm going to *forget* that we met."

Billy slumps into the chair, across from Lucifer, back in the positions they were in this morning. The setup is taking on a feeling of familiarity. Billy isn't exactly thrilled about that. He does not want Lucifer as a roommate. He does not want his life to become some kind of theological buddy comedy.

"You gave me permission to adjust your beliefs," Lucifer says. "I remained within the bounds granted me by that permission. Regardless, you will be pleased to learn that the effect is temporary. It was designed to last for only one exposure to the substance in question."

Billy considers this. Sure enough, eggplant is beginning to seem good again. He thinks of his sandwich, back there on the table, going to waste, and he feels a vague sadness. His stomach growls.

"But," Lucifer says. "You didn't summon me here to talk about your dietary concerns."

"Summon you?" Billy says. "I didn't *summon* you."

"Actually," Lucifer says, "you did. You held my card in your hand and you experienced palpable regret that you didn't hear me out. It's a delectable emotion, regret. It reads very clearly. There is no mistaking it."

Billy contemplates protesting this, but he knows that it's essentially accurate and the idea of constructing a big front of fake outrage just seems too exhausting right now.

"Before this conversation continues," Billy says, glumly, "I would like to get high."

"That's reasonable," says Lucifer.

"Is it?" Billy says, as fishes a baggie of weed out of the accretion of junk on the table. "Reasonable? Really?"

"Reason is the servant of the passions," Lucifer says.

"Uhhh, sure," Billy says. "Why the fuck not."

He finds his pipe, gets it loaded and takes a long draw.

"You want a pull on this?" he says, proffering the bowl to Lucifer.

"Normally I wouldn't," Lucifer says, "being here, as I am, on business. But—how did you put it? Why the fuck not? I admire this as a basis for decision-making. You have inspired me to follow your lead."

"Mr. Reasonable," Billy says, watching as Lucifer takes his own draw.

"*C'est moi,*" says Lucifer, after a long exhale.

"You and me," Billy says. "Two reasonable guys."

"Indeed," says Lucifer.

"Having a reasonable discussion."

"Precisely."

That hangs in the air for a minute. Billy takes another draw. Lucifer stares off into space, his face eerily impassive, like something carved out of rock ten thousand years ago, before emotions were invented. It's creepy. It kind of makes everything that Billy has done or seen or made or thought suddenly feel like piffle. He wonders how he's managed, so far, to even *talk* to Lucifer, to just sit here, twice now, carrying on a conversation, like they really were two reasonable guys. Or two guys, at least.

A minute passes. The silence is really creeping him out now. *Say something,* Billy insists to himself. But now that he's freaked himself out about even having a conversation he's not sure what to say or where to begin. He feels like a fruit fly attempting to address a volcano.

Say anything, Billy tells himself. *Talk to him like you'd talk to anybody else. You're just two dudes, getting high. Maybe it* can *be like a buddy comedy.*

"So," Billy ventures. "I got a question."

"Shoot," Lucifer says, without the expression on his face really changing.

"You brought really good coffee with you this morning."

Lucifer says nothing for a long time. "That's not a question," he says, finally.

"Uhhh, sorry," Billy says. "Question! My question was: I bet you can also get really good pot."

Another lag. Billy waits, apprehensively.

"That is also not a question," Lucifer says. And then another really long lag. And then, like an ancient machine starting up: "However, your assumption is correct. I rely upon a grower in Mendocino, when the situation calls for it."

"Okay," Billy says, relieved. "You have to get me some of that. I definitely want to try that."

"I'll consider it," says Lucifer.

"I mean," Billy says, anxious that maybe he's overstepped his bounds. "Just to try it."

"You would like it," says Lucifer, peacefully.

"Good," says Billy. "I like shit that I like." He feels a little better. He takes a long blink. Geometric brocades shiver and furl behind his eyelids.

"Although I should point out that this," Lucifer says, "is not bad." Billy can hear him taking another pull.

"Yeah, my roommate has some connection," Billy says. And he begins thinking about Jørgen. He frowns concertedly. He opens his eyes. He remembers Anil's theory, the idea that Lucifer was actually just some out-of-town friend with Jørgen's key, pulling an elaborate prank. It still doesn't *feel* true, not even a little, but for Billy, marijuana has a way of making things that aren't true seem suddenly probable. So he offers some bait: "You know him?" Billy says. "My roommate? Jørgen?"

Having set this trap, he feels pretty sly, but Lucifer does not give any sign of recognition at the name. Something does happen, though. What happens is Lucifer's face loses the dreamy vacancy it had mere moments ago; his eyes turn alert and fix acutely on Billy's own. He abruptly appears to be no longer high: a little bit alarming given that Billy is still drifting in some entheogenic dreamtime halfway between Brooklyn and Shangri-la. Billy feels a little stab of panic, remembering exactly what is happening here: Lucifer is not his buddy, not a volcano, not an impassive stone face. He is some kind of straight-up other intelligence, thoroughly alien, like a great white shark or an evil clown.

"Billy, it is time," Lucifer says, "to return to our agenda."

"Um," Billy says, his mind reeling at the thought of discussing anything resembling *business*. "Wait, right now?"

"There will not be a better time," Lucifer says. He pulls his messenger bag into his lap and rips its Velcroed flap open.

Okay, shit. Billy has to concoct a response to this. But at the same time he remembers that he had a question on the table, something about Jørgen, that he never got an answer to. He could ask it again, it's at least possible, and he knows he could follow the path of that possibility right into the future, the future where he is asking the question. He's stoned, so he can see it, as an image. But then he sees the other possible avenue the conversation could take, hearing what Lucifer has to say, another path, and each path sends off finer path-shoots, branching into a plentitude of futures . . .

Jesus Christ, man, focus, Billy thinks, while Lucifer begins to set up the computer. He rubs his face vigorously to clear his mind of the image of infinite fernlike branchings. *Focus.* The very word itself makes his mind spin off down another avenue. He's suddenly getting contemplative and abstract, asking himself *What is focus, anyway?*

Focus, he remembers from somewhere—a *Times* Style piece? a fortune cookie?—*is having the inner resolve to ask the most important question.*

So what's the most important question, when you're making a deal with the Devil? He thinks about this for a second, and realizes that the most important question he can ask is not about Jørgen. It is not even *Can you vindicate all the choices I've made in my entire life by the time I give my reading tomorrow?* The most important question you can ask the Devil is *How is this going to screw me?*

Lucifer has completed booting up his ThinkPad and he appears to be launching PowerPoint.

"I have a question," Billy says.

"Watch the presentation," says Lucifer, through a veneer of patience that seems to be beginning to crack and peel. Billy imagines a black nebula of unearthly malice swirling behind it. "The presentation will answer many of your questions. It will also raise some new ones. I'll be happy to address all your remaining unanswered questions at the conclusion."

"But," Billy says, gathering resolve. "No. I have a question."

Lucifer sighs loudly, but he stops poking at the ThinkPad's little pointing stick and trains his attention on Billy.

Billy does not ask *How is this going to screw me?* What he asks, instead, is "Is there a Hell?"

"Billy," says Lucifer. He folds his hands in his lap. "I'm going to be frank with you. Just one hundred percent up-front. There *is* a Hell."

"Oh," Billy says. He presses his face into his hands and tries not to envision horrible shit like being on fire. He's seen a guy on fire before: an accident, at the first kitchen he ever worked in, and it left an impression on him, the impression mostly being: it's not cool to be on fire.

"But Billy," Lucifer says. "It's not like people say. It's not Hieronymus Bosch creatures and torture chambers. There aren't saints looking down on you from above, enjoying the perfection of their beatitude by jerking off to the punishment of the damned."

Billy raises his head out of his hands. "People say that?" he asks.

"Aquinas said that," Lucifer says. A hitherto unnoticed bass note in his voice seems to subtly double, and his face contorts into an expression of what appears to be genuine anger. "That fat fuck."

"Aquinas said *jerking off*?" Billy asks, a little spooked. This is the first time Billy's seen an expression on Lucifer's face that doesn't look like it was learned from some kind of demonic field guide to human emotions, and he finds himself hoping that it'll go away quickly.

"He didn't say *jerking off*," Lucifer concedes. "But he *implied* it." His expression goes blank again.

Billy's face goes back down into his hands. "So, what?" Billy says. "Is this the part where you tell me how awesome Hell is? That it's, I don't know, like I'm going to be getting hot oil massaged by virgins the entire time I'm there?"

"Billy," says Lucifer. "You still appear to believe that I'm attempting to defraud you. That I am after something ineffable, that I want to lock you into some horrible cosmic payback. It will not be like that. This is simpler. Much simpler. I have a thing that I need to have done, and I can't do it myself. If you do it for me, I shall ensure that your novel gets published. And then our obligations to one another will be mutually concluded. I don't get your soul. You don't burn in eternal torment. You get to be happy, and I get to be happy. That is the extent of the transaction."

You get to be happy. "Well," Billy says, considering this. "Okay. What's the thing you need done?"

"Watch the presentation," Lucifer says, curtly. He points at the laptop, and Billy looks.

"This," Lucifer says, "is Timothy Ollard."

First slide. Billy peers at it through his stoned daze. It depicts a tall, thin man, sitting on an overstuffed ottoman, his knees higher than his hips. Youngish-looking, maybe in his early thirties. Smiling into the camera, a variety of self-confidence around the eyes, a smugness, like he's quite certain that he's the brightest person in the room. He's wearing a very twee suit, and an ascot. It might just be because Billy is high, but he takes an instant dislike to the fellow.

"I don't like him," Billy says.

"That's good," Lucifer says.

Lucifer clicks again and a name appears over the image in, like, 48-point font:

TIMOTHY OLLARD

"So what's his deal?" Billy says.

"Timothy Ollard is a warlock," Lucifer says. "In my estimation he is the *key* warlock on the eastern seaboard."

"A warlock?" Billy says. "Like, a wizard?"

"A warlock isn't a wizard," Lucifer says. "A warlock is a male witch."

"Okay . . . ?" Billy says. He frowns. "So, this guy is a witch?"

"A warlock," says Lucifer.

"This is a real thing?" says Billy. "People go around calling themselves warlocks?"

"You never met anyone who called themselves a witch?" Lucifer says.

Billy thinks. "Well, sure," he concedes, "but they were mostly chubby girls who liked herbal tea and burning incense in their dorm rooms. I thought it was kind of a thing that most people would give up by senior year. I didn't think it was exactly a *career path*."

"You're more correct than you know," Lucifer says. "Most American witches don't get very far. And most American warlocks get even less far—there are fewer of them to begin with. There are, however, a few witches and warlocks who excel, who remain active for a longer period than most, and at some point they begin to become a problem."

"So how long has this guy—Ollard—how long has he been, what would you call it, *warlocking*?"

"I cannot say precisely when he began. But I have known Timothy Ollard to be practicing high-level black arts in New York City for the last eighty years."

"Eighty *years*?" Billy says.

"Take a look," Lucifer says. New slide. An old photo. People at some sort of Jazz Age party: a crowd reveling among streamers and glittering curtains. Lucifer clicks for the caption: 1924. He clicks again and a red circle pops up around the face of a guy standing way off to the edge of the photo, a dour face among the partygoers.

"Is that supposed to be the same guy?" Billy says. He can't tell for certain: there are shadows on the guy's face and the hair is differently styled. It could be the guy's grandfather or even just a random guy with a similar facial structure. The ascot is the same.

"It is him," Lucifer says. "As near as I can tell, the last time he aged was a single afternoon in 1945, during which he went from age thirty-three to thirty-six."

"Good trick," Billy says.

"His current base of operations is here," Lucifer says.

Slide. A stone tower. Dank, rotting, covered in creepy crenellations and greeble. It's got these scary bits hanging off it that look like they might be made out of long chains of human ribcages, like something you might dream up after a tour of Cambodian genocide sites. Every available surface has shit spanged onto it: wires or pipes or crumbling gargoyles drooling black autumnal slime.

"Yeesh," Billy says.

"Don't be too impressed," Lucifer says. "The edifice you see is mostly illusory."

"What even . . . ," Billy says. "What part of the *planet* is this on?"

"It's here," Lucifer says. "It's in Manhattan."

Slide. A Google Maps screenshot with one of those little red bulbs pointing at a corner that looks like it's somewhere in Chelsea.

"Huh," Billy says. "You'd think I'd have heard about some freaky-ass black tower being in the middle of Manhattan."

"People can't see it," Lucifer says. "Ollard has cloaked it. Wrapped it in a perceptual blind spot."

"So, what, eight million people walk past this building and nobody notices it?"

"No cloak is perfect," Lucifer says. "So it is likely that people *notice* it all the time. Hence Ollard's choice to make what lies behind the cloak appear fearsome. When people get a glimpse of something that troubles them, that disturbs, their minds *turn off* toward it. They *unnotice* it. Their defensive human psychologies effectively partner with the cloak. In the end, people see what they want to see: a Manhattan without a—how did you put it—a *freaky-ass black tower* in it."

Lucifer clicks through to the next slide. It's a picture of one of those cat statues that Billy has seen in every sushi bar he's ever been in.

"This is the Neko of Infinite Equilibrium," Lucifer says.

"That's a lucky cat statue," Billy says.

"Neko means cat," Lucifer says. "And don't be confused. This particular lucky cat statue is unique."

"What does it do?"

"It waves."

"Well," Billy says, "sure."

"Technically the gesture is supposed to represent a form of beckoning."

"Huh," Billy says.

"Ideally, it does not do anything else. Ideally, the Neko sits on a shelf in Hell, doing nothing. Beckoning. This was the state of affairs until two weeks ago, when Ollard saw fit to divest me of it."

"He . . . divested you of it?"

"He stole it. He stole the Neko and placed it in his tower. It is crucial that it be retrieved. Part of my function is to retain possession of certain items that would have unfortunate effects if they were used by human beings."

"Uh. Define *unfortunate effects*."

"The Neko beckons," Lucifer says. "It beckons endlessly. It does not require a source of energy. This makes it"—he pauses to contemplate—"abhorrent to this world's thermodynamic laws. Once fully in this world the Neko's surplus energy will be given off as heat. Since the Neko has, effectively, an infinite amount of surplus energy, it has the potential to produce an infinite amount of heat."

"Infinite heat is bad?" Billy asks.

"Infinite heat means that you are starting a fire which can be neither extinguished nor contained."

"That sounds bad."

"Nothing could stop such a fire," Lucifer says. "It will burn until it has consumed the entire atmosphere. It will burn until it has consumed the combustible matter that constitutes this planet and the life on it."

"Oh," Billy says.

He takes a moment and tries to let this sink in. He momentarily reviews all the things in the world that qualify as combustible matter, tries to think about them vanishing into fire. Vietnamese spring rolls. The Black Flag T-shirt he bought fifteen years ago, which is now the most comfortable item of clothing he owns. Anil's Xbox. Anil himself. Denver. Everyone. And at that point his capacity to imagine the annihilation of all earthly endeavor fails.

"Why would somebody want to do that?" he asks, quietly. "Torch the world?"

"I do not know what he hopes to gain," Lucifer says. "It could be some sort of necromantic rite, a bid to attain godlike supremacy. The thanatotic power released by murdering a world would be substantial; Ollard may be able to put it to some use. But his ultimate aim is obscure to me."

"So, wait, why aren't we dead right now? Like—is Chelsea on fire right this second, or will it take a while to really get going?" Billy asks, hoping that maybe he can add *supernatural fire* to the list of things that might kill him at some point in the future but that are out of the range of his direct control, like global warming, or the world's collective failure to develop a superpowered laser to blow up giant earth-threatening asteroids.

"The Neko has a set of protective defenses. When taken out of Hell, a set of six seals sprang into place around it. Until those seals are dispelled the Neko technically has not entered this world; it exists effectively in a sort of limbo. Over the last two weeks Ollard has dispelled four of these six seals."

"Four?" Billy says. His stoned brain tries to calculate a percentage. "That's a lot," is what he ends up with.

"The remaining two are—challenging," Lucifer says. "They may thwart him. They will, at the very least, slow him down."

"Slow him down?" Billy says. "Can't you—stop him?" A pleading note that he isn't entirely fond of has entered his voice.

"I intend to stop him."

Billy feels a surge of hope. "You're going to save the world," he says.

"There are challenges involved. Ollard knows that I seek the return of the Neko, and he has prepared accordingly. He has thrice-warded the tower against me. I can't enter it. I can't get within five hundred feet of it."

"So—" Billy says. And then he stops. He does not plan to be the one who completes this thought.

"So that's where I need you," says Lucifer. He clicks again and a picture of Billy comes up. It's from earlier that night: Billy standing on the subway platform, with Lucifer's business card in his hand. Billy jumps a little in his chair, seeing this.

"William Harrison Ridgeway," Lucifer intones. "I task you

with this objective. Enter Timothy Ollard's tower, retrieve the Neko, and return it to me. At the completion of this objective you will be rewarded. The challenges involved will be minimal."

"Minimal?" Billy says. "The most powerful warlock in the eastern United States, and the challenges will be *minimal*? He's powerful enough to make an ugly tower invisible to eight million New Yorkers? Powerful enough to steal some dealie from out of Hell and do the thrice-ward thing you were talking about? If he can fuck with *you* then what's going to stop him from hitting me with a lightning bolt or—you know," he churns the air with his hands, "killing me in some other wizardly way?"

"Well, he's not a wizard," Lucifer says. "He's a warlock."

"Yeah," Billy says, "but the important part is the Me Getting Killed part."

"He won't kill you. Ollard has warding powers, but I have ones of my own. I can ward you against him."

"That would work?"

"It will work," Lucifer says.

This is crazy, Billy thinks. He does not think about what it would be like to get his book published. He does not think about reconciling with Denver. He thinks *This is a good way to die*.

"Billy," Lucifer says. "I care about this world. I do not wish to see it come to harm. I need your help."

"Man," Billy says. "Aren't you supposed to be *evil*? Why aren't you asking me to do some evil shit that I could say no to? Why do you care about the world anyway?"

Lucifer looks at Billy for a long second.

"You know what I do?" he says, finally. "I *tempt* people. I've done it for a long time. I *like* it. I'm *good* at it. And if the world goes away there will be no people left to tempt. There will be cinders and there will be ash. And looking at cinders and ash for the rest of eternity strikes me, frankly, as no fun at all."

"I have to think about it," Billy says.

Lucifer looks at his watch. "How long do you think you'll need?"

"I don't know. I don't know. How long do we have?"

"Maybe a week," Lucifer says, after taking a moment to pause for some kind of calculation.

"Okay, then," Billy says. "I had a long day. I'm tired and I'm high and even if I *weren't* it'd *still* be a good idea to sleep on it."

Lucifer watches Billy's face, reading something in it, then says, "As you wish."

"Let me do the reading, get that over with, and then *after* the reading I'll have a decision for you."

"After the reading," Lucifer says.

"Yeah," Billy says. "But I don't necessarily mean the *second I step down off the stage.* I mean, like, a *while* after."

"I am reasonable," says Lucifer. "I agree to these terms." He closes the laptop and stuffs it back in his messenger bag, swaps it for a manila folder. "I'll leave you with these for your review."

Billy takes the folder. Inside is a printout of all the PowerPoint slides. "Uh, thanks," says Billy.

"Until after the reading," Lucifer says. As he turns to go, something nags at Billy, some question that Anil raised.

"Hey, wait a second," Billy says, remembering.

Lucifer, half out the door, pauses.

"What about God?" Billy says.

Lucifer frowns.

"I mean, if I believe in you—the Devil—then it reasonably follows that I should believe in God. But I don't know if I believe in God, not really. So—I don't know—I just thought I'd ask you, like, *is there a God?*"

Lucifer looks at Billy.

"Don't talk to me about God," he says, and then he's gone.

Billy stands there, at the doorway, for a long time. He latches the chain. He tries to get back to having the feeling he had this morning, the victorious feeling he had at having turned the Devil away the first time. But it's not working. He no longer feels like turning the Devil down is proof that he's not a fuck-up. This time, with the fate of the goddamn world hanging in the balance, he only feels like a coward.

Why me? he wonders. *Why put this on me? There are people out there who infiltrate places for a fucking living. Navy SEALs. CIA spooks. Fuck, send a UPS guy; he could at least get Ollard to open the door.*

It's because you're desperate, he thinks. *The only person desperate enough to say yes.*

But that can't be it. There are plenty of desperate people. He lives in New York; he sees buttloads of human desperation every time he goes out to get a coffee. So why him?

Eventually, Billy convinces himself that it doesn't have to be him at all. *I might be desperate, but I'm not a dumbass,* he tells himself. *Lucifer will ask someone else, someone braver. Someone stupider. Someone more morally corrupt.*

Or maybe more morally prepared? Billy tries to picture saint-like people, risking their lives in the scary tower for the good of all humanity. He envisions Martin Luther King Jr., back from the dead, kicking open the door. An Uzi in his hands, spitting out fire.

Okay, he thinks, jarred out of his reverie by this image. *Let's think about something else.* And he does. He checks the phone again to make sure Denver hasn't called. He ravages the cupboards for a dinner, ends up eating two bags of Mixed Berry Fruity Snacks and a half-dozen fistfuls of oyster crackers. He washes each fistful down with a slug of Jørgen's Scotch.

He gets online. The tab for *dog* is still open in Wikipedia. For a minute, he stares glassily at this sentence: "The domestic dog (*Canis lupus familiaris*) is a subspecies of the gray wolf (*Canis lupus*), a member of the Canidae family of the mammalian order Carnivora." Eventually, against his better judgment, he clicks over to Bladed Hyacinth and rereads the pan of his work. His stomach sinks in the exact same way it did when he read it the first time. *I've wasted my life*, he thinks. *The world is going to end and all I'm going to be is a guy who sucks.*

Not necessarily, he thinks. *Just walk into the horrible tower and get the stupid cat and give it to Satan and everything could be different. You could get your book published. You could save the world.*

To this, he thinks both *Yeah right* and *No way* so closely together that he can't discern which one comes first.

So be it. He envisions the Neko, its little paw oscillating. Not beckoning, but waving goodbye. Waving goodbye forever. To him, to the world and all its combustible matter, to everything and everyone.

Something else, he tells himself. *Think about something else.*

Back to the computer. He Googles Elisa Mastic, tomorrow night's poet, reads one of her poems online. It might be good, but it's poetry, so he can't really tell. He kind of likes the line about the "deleted world," but that gets him thinking once again about fire destroying everything.

He looks at some porn. He must be depressed, because tits don't seem sexy. He considers for a moment the horrible prospect that whether he likes tits is contingent upon some light switch in his head that could be flipped off.

Okay, if not porn, then narrative. Maybe he can catch up on *Argentium Astrum*, although he's not entirely sure he's going to enjoy its particular brand of supernatural mystery now that there's so much goddamn supernatural mystery jammed into his everyday life.

He loads the page; there are three episodes he hasn't seen. He clicks one and the opening sequence begins to stream as normal—the familiar sheriff's badge rises, gleaming, from inky, mistshrouded depths—but then the stream glitches again. First there are a bunch of jittering bars, then a quick flash of what looks like a block of random numerals, then the bars again, and then the little video window just crashes into a block of solid blue. Then it changes to red. Then blue again. Then green. Then a black field with six white dots in it. Then back to blue. The effect is kind of mesmerizing and calming and he watches it for almost four minutes before he snaps out of it.

Okay. If not porn, if not narrative, then bed. And if not bed, then the couch.

And as he lies there on the couch, twisting uncomfortably, he thinks back, remembering the kitchen accident all those years ago, the guy he saw who was on fire. It happened back when he was dishwashing at a crappy family restaurant called the Fairlane, back in Ohio. Something had gone wrong with the Fairlane's rangetops and the owner had tried to save a couple of bucks by calling his uncertified handyman brother in to fix the thing. Billy remembers that guy on his back, visible only as a belly and legs while the rest of his body banged around clumsily inside the half-disassembled stove with a ball-peen hammer in his hand.

Billy can't remember the guy's name but he remembers the fireball that suddenly erupted from under the thing, ignited by an errant spark or by the pilot light from the neighboring rangetop, and he remembers the brother yanking himself out of the blast with his whole head on fire. He remembers what that looked like. What it smelled like. And he thinks about something like that happening to everything in the world. All the people. All the books. All the Brazillian cockroaches, and all the bananas; all the dogs, all the wolves. And then he's asleep.

CHAPTER FIVE

FAILURE OF IMAGINATION

A PHONE IS NOT LIKE A BANANA • LEADING THE BACKLASH •
TRAVELING BOOK HUNTERS • THE WHOLE POINT OF A CLOAK •
SEAFOOD WAREHOUSING • LOOKING HOMELESS • COWARD=ICE
• FLAUBERT • CAFFEINE, MEAT, AND REVENGE • WHAT
STORYTELLERS DO • TO THOUGHTLESSNESS

He wakes up to the sound of his phone buzzing. *It's Denver,* he thinks. Hope muscles him around, pulls him up into action. He slept on the couch last night, though, and so he opens his eyes expecting Loft and instead sees Living Room. There's a disorienting second during which he can't quite figure out which way his head is pointing. Maybe it's just leftover fug from last night's high, but for that second, the apartment seems like some Escher structure he can't orient himself within. God only knows where the phone is.

It buzzes again. Billy makes a valiant go of getting to his feet, but he's slept with one leg jammed underneath himself, and that leg has gone completely numb, useless, transformed from trusty appendage to strange tube packed full of cast-off meats, like a long sack of dog food stuck to his body. He tries to stand and instead he crumples down to the floor, banging his knee on the coffee table's remorseless edge. "Son of a bitch," he says.

The phone buzzes again. Billy kneads his fist vigorously into his inert calf while using his other hand to grope around on the coffee table, knocking a pile of mail onto the floor but not coming upon anything that resembles the phone's familiar shape.

"Damn it," Billy cries. He's blowing his chance. He feels like if he talked to Denver, even just for a second, he'd be able to say the right thing: the thing that would be convincing, that would show her that he can be the man that he presumes she wants him to be. Caring, compassionate, competent, whatever.

He finally finds the phone nine minutes later. It's in the fruit bowl in the kitchen, nestled in the curvature of the bruised banana he brought home two nights ago. Present Moment Billy looks back at Past Billy with bafflement and contempt. Past Billy, thus roused, offers a thin explanation as to why it was a good idea to stick the phone there last night, something about the vaguely satisfying correspondence between the shape of the banana and the shape of the phone. And Present Moment Billy experiences a sudden, acute awareness regarding how he must appear to other people. His puzzlement, his dreaminess, his hapless wonder: How fucking contemptible. It's no wonder Denver is done with him. He'd be done with him, too.

The phone's tiny screen, upon inspection, reveals that it wasn't even Denver who called. It was his dad again. Billy frowns at this: twice in one week is a little odd. It's not in Keith Ridgeway's character to press a book on Billy twice. That's not the way it works between them. Usually when he mentions a book in a voice mail that seems to be enough for him to be able to pretend that Billy will track it down and read it, which means that the book simply never comes up again between them. So a second call from his dad means either that he's pushing two separate books or that something else is going on. *I should call him,* Billy thinks. But not today. Today he has shit to do.

He looks out the window, checks that Brooklyn is not on fire. It seems no more in danger of being on fire than it did yesterday, or the day before that. Some tension he's carried since last night, located somewhere behind his sternum, releases. Someone else is solving the problem. He feels certain of it.

Having freed himself from obligation, he makes some more of the Devil's coffee and eats the spotted banana. He pulls out the big accordion file which contains his recent fiction and starts looking for something that he could read tonight at Barometer. Something good. Something *epiphany-level good*: something that will make the audience sit up and say *Hey, this doesn't come from the ravaged storehouse of tired forms and stale devices. Maybe Anton Cirrus doesn't know what he's talking about. Maybe he's not so smart after all. Maybe he's just an asshole.* People are getting weary of the controlling grip that Bladed Hyacinth has on the literary scene, Billy tells himself, surely they are. Every two-bit tastemaker is eventually felled by a backlash. Billy could be the one to lead that backlash. That could be his Role in the Scene. All he needs to do is find the piece in the file that is so good that it will eliminate all doubt about his talent.

Except there's nothing like that in the file. He flips through five years of recent output and all he can think is *I have wasted my life.* Moving to Brooklyn, with this intention of making his way as a writer: how stupid. He could have done something else. Sometimes he thinks he would have been happiest as a parking lot attendant or a night watchman, something where he would have spent most of his time alone, in a chair, quietly slacking, reading on the job. That might not have been so terrible.

Billy remembers the first long year after he'd failed out of school, remembers that at some point in that year his dad invited him on a trip to Italy, wanting them to go off together, spending six months tracking down some scattered cache of sixteenth-century books. At the time, Billy was trying to hold down a job scanning documents for an insurance conglomerate, and trying to stay sober, and trying to get up early in the mornings to work on an impossibly tangled outline for an ambitious novel that he never actually began writing, and the idea of spending half a year with his frosty, difficult dad seemed not particularly tempting, but in retrospect it seems like a blown opportunity. Instead of being a washed-up nobody he could have been . . . part of a father-son team of traveling book hunters? Right now it seems like it would have been a pretty good way to make a life. Better than this. Better than sifting through half-revised chapters of a weakly conceived novel.

He built this newest manuscript around a braided pair of narratives: one about a married couple who can't stay faithful to one another, and one about their drug dealer, who is involved in a Big Deal Gone Wrong. He had some idea that the book as a whole was thematically about betrayal, that the two plotlines would reflect one another somehow. One printed chapter has "MICROCOSM / MACROCOSM" written across the top in his familiar scrawl. That must have meant something at one time.

The more he reads, the more the very existence of the document perplexes him. He's never been married. His interactions with drug dealers have always been brief and to the point. He's not even sure he even has anything to say about betrayal. Why did he write this? What larger point was he hoping to make? Had he just been streaming a lot of TV about narcotics? Right now, he'd be embarrassed to see this thing in print, even if he were willing to take Lucifer up on his deal.

Even if he were willing. Which he isn't.

He puts the accordion file down and picks up the folder of PowerPoint slides that the Devil left. He looks at the picture of Timothy Ollard and fantasizes, for a moment, about punching him in the face.

"He doesn't look so tough," Billy says.

But then he flips ahead to the picture of the tower. It still looks pants-shittingly scary even in printout form. But what did Lucifer say? The whole thing was a front, designed to terrify people into not seeing it? He flips to the map, scrutinizes the address. He doesn't get up to Chelsea very often but he's pretty sure he's been by this place at least once in the last decade. It's under a cloak? Last night, while high, Billy was pretty ready to roll with it, but in the glare of day it just sounds like bullshit. Infinite fire? The end of the world? Come on.

But he wants something to do other than look at this folder full of failure. And it couldn't hurt, Billy thinks, to shoot over there and see what's at this address. There's plenty of time before the reading; he can bring the accordion file and look through stuff on the train. He could just go. Just to take a look. Just to know if cloaks are real.

And so then he's in Chelsea, standing at an intersection, peering down at Lucifer's printout. Cold November wind whips around him, threatens to snap the paper out of his hand. According to the map he's at the right corner, but he doesn't see any cloaked building.

Well of course you don't see it, he thinks. *That's the whole point of a cloak. Isn't it? Is it?* Maybe he's been punk'd after all.

Directly across the street from him is a junk-metal yard, blocked from view by tall walls of corrugated iron, lashed and bolted together. It has a foreboding, ramshackle nature that reminds him of the tower, and warlockish clangs and rumbles emit from its depths. He's looked at it from twenty different angles now, trying to catch some sort of change in its nature, but so far, nothing.

Behind him is a gallery space: through the window he can see eight lacy forms made out of what appear to be lathe-cut blocks of industrial Styrofoam. Billy's pretty sure that if you were trying to hide something in Manhattan you wouldn't disguise it as interesting art, although he can hear the Ghoul's voice in his head, making some crack about how people tune out nothing faster, these days, than an artist asking for attention.

Across the way there's an unassuming-looking brick building that takes up most of the block. He hasn't really checked it out that deeply, distracted as he has been by the metal yard and the Styrofoam, but now he gives it a second look. Painted directly on the brick of the building's western face are the faded words SEAFOOD WAREHOUSING.

He reads them for a second time, really tries to think about the business model implied there.

He looks at the map, looks at exactly which corner Lucifer has pinpointed.

He crosses the street.

Tentatively, he puts out his hand and touches the building. It feels like a building. He's not sure what he expected.

He looks both ways along the building's front for a window that he can peek into, but there are no windows at street level, just some ornamental concrete buttresses.

There is also no door.

Interesting, Billy thinks. *So, let's say I'm a customer.* He turns right, heading for the corner. *Let's say I have some seafood I need warehoused. I go over here, to the southern side—*

He rounds the corner. The southern side is a long expanse of brick. More buttresses. No loading dock. No door.

Okay, then, Billy thinks, making the long trek along the southern side. The building nearly abuts another one at its southeast corner, so the eastern face is inaccessible. Billy peers into the thin, trash-choked gap between the two buildings: there's not even enough space to fit his fist in there. So the north side is the only side left. He hurries back the way he came, and it turns out that there's no north side either; it's directly up against another giant brick building on that side, without even an alley to look down.

So. Two sides. No windows. No loading dock. No door.

I got you, you bastard, Billy thinks.

He crosses back over to the gallery so that he can get more of the warehouse in his view. It sits there, impassive.

Billy stands on the sidewalk for a full minute, legs apart, hands balled in fists at his sides, goggling at the building. He is rapt with concentration. He is fully focused; fully focused except the part of him that is remarking on how much he has begun to resemble homeless dudes who he's seen staring intensely at everyday shit with a stance and demeanor oddly identical to his own. He imagines, briefly, what wonders they have seen.

In the end, it works with something like an autostereogram effect: he loosens the convergence of his eyes a little and the warehouse slowly separates into two warehouses. And there, between those wavering visions, he can see it. The horrible tower. The dread castle. Spiny bits and tar-black bones. The ornamental buttresses are still there, only they appear to writhe subtly. They heave like lungs. And right in the center of the mess is a single bloodred door, crawling with calligraphic glyphs.

He blinks and the whole thing snaps back into a warehouse again. He makes himself go walleyed and Warlock House wavers back into view.

He wishes his phone had a camera in it, although he kind of doubts that the effect could be captured photographically.

He tries to imagine what it would be like to go up to the door, go into the place, make good on Lucifer's deal. And he suffers a complete failure of imagination. He can't see himself going into a building that looks like that. He can't see himself even taking one step toward the objective. He literally won't cross the street now, even though the building looks like a warehouse again.

You'd be protected, Billy reminds himself. *The Devil said you'd be protected, that he'd protect you with a ward or something.*

But he doesn't care. He doesn't know what a ward is or how it works, but he has absolutely no certainty that a bunch of mystical hand-waving could protect him against whatever would happen to him in there. Better to stay out here. On the safe side of the street. Let somebody else be the hero.

He does something then. He calls himself a coward. Like this: *You fucking coward.*

This could be it. This could be your Moment. All you have to do is one daring thing and you'd get what you want. You could feel like you accomplished what you came out here to do. You could finally rest. All you have to do is just, for once, be brave.

No, he tells himself. *I can't. Besides*—and at this point he's begun to work up a little thunderhead of righteousness—*if you really want what you want, if you really want to get your damn book published, you don't do it this way. You don't act as the Devil's stooge. You do the damn work. You sit down. You write. You try to write well. You finish the thing. You—you do what Flaubert said—you live a life that is steady and well-ordered so that you can be fierce and original in the work. You don't run around busting into magical fortresses and call that bravery and let somebody else do the hard work for you.*

He pauses there, waiting for the retort, and then it comes: *You ain't exactly Flaubert.*

He turns from the warehouse and walks away.

Billy doesn't know where he's headed. The parts of his brain that were engaged in internal debate have ceased their crowing, opting now to simply choke one another to death. He just keeps walking, grateful at least that the city has retained its capacity to absorb a person who has no particular destination in mind, a person who needs an hour or two to be nothing more than a mote, twisting through space.

At the end of his mote-time he finds himself in the Village, which he normally takes strenuous pains to avoid, standing in front of a display of touristy junk, hemmed in by excitable schoolkids. He's actually physically handling a twenty-dollar hat, a fake fur thing with pointy wolf-ears, trying to decide if it would make an appropriate gift for Denver. *She'd look cute in it.*

Oh, for fuck's sake. He drops the hat, disgusted at it, at himself. First of all, there is no way in hell that she would ever consent to wear such a thing. And second of all, there aren't going to *be* any more gifts for Denver, because he and Denver are finished, even if it turns out that the world isn't going to end. It's been, what, eight days since they last spoke? Surely at this point he should be considering himself well and truly dumped. *Pull yourself together*, he tells himself.

You need protein, some inner voice tells him. And so he hits the nearest diner and devours an enormous burger, ordered rare. He feels a little more stable with some blood in his mouth. He gets his pen and a napkin. *Okay*, he tells himself, with the greatest calm he can muster. *You're going to make a list. A list of all of your problems. And then, underneath each item on the list, you're going to list one Action Item that you can do to address that problem.* This seems reasonable.

Your first problem, he thinks, *is that you're a coward.*

And dutifully, he writes down:

COWARD

Then, on something of a roll, he writes:

FUCK-UP

"No," he says. This is not going to work. He draws an X through each word. Even then the thing is a little depressing to look at: he looks around for a garbage can. Finding none, he folds the note into quarters and sticks it in his pocket.

Action Items. He has a goddamn Action Item: Flaubert's advice. *Be fierce and original.* He pulls the accordion file out of his backpack and starts spreading possible reading pieces out on the table. If he can just find some piece in there that demonstrates his ferocity and originality—that would show everyone. The desire for revenge rises within him, resplendent and gauche, like the phoenix on the hood of a Trans Am. He just needs to find the right piece. If not the novel then maybe the short stories?

After two minutes of reading what he thought was his best shot—a story with no characters at all, told from the point of view of various apartments that had been inhabited *by* characters—he's back to the problem he was having this morning. There *is* no right piece. Nothing he has written in the last decade is good enough to justify the personality flaws that he'd been justifying by telling everyone that he was a writer.

Fuck it. He downs a third cup of coffee. He sweeps everything back into the file. He has an idea. He's going to wing it. He's going to get up there on stage and ad-lib. He can tell a story that way, just by getting up there and opening up the fecund little grotto that houses his creative unconscious. He knows he can do it. He's a fucking storyteller and that's the kind of shit that storytellers do: they tell goddamn stories. He will be bold and daring; he will confirm that he is not a coward and not a fuck-up; he will be epiphany-level good. And maybe the world won't end.

Billy pays the bill and heads north toward Union Square, and jumps on the L, heading toward Williamsburg.

The reading's not supposed to happen until seven, and the train will put him at Bedford just before five. From there it's like a ten-minute walk to Barometer, so he'll be early. But that's okay. He figures he'll sit at the bar, have a shot or two to keep the courage going, center himself, and do a little more preliminary thinking on his plan. Like: Will he tell a real-life anecdote or try to make up something fictional?

He surfaces at Bedford. It's not yet five but it's cold and dark already: fucking November. He pulls his army jacket tighter around him, but it's too thin to do much.

He hurries to the bar, and when he gets there he is greeted by an impassive rolling gate, corrugated metal, pulled all the way down.

"You gotta be kidding me," he says, out loud.

"I think they open at six," says a young woman who is standing off to the side. Billy looks over but can't really see her face, as it is hidden by wild coils of long black hair springing out from under the constraint of a fur-lined aviator hat.

"Six?" Billy says. "What about people who want a drink right after they get off from work?"

"I think this place makes their money more off the nightlife kind of crowd," says the woman. She taps a cigarette out of her pack and lights it off of one that she's already got going.

"Nightlife!" Billy says, mock-contemptuous. "What about people who need a drink in the middle of the day? Someone needs to think about the high-functioning alcoholics."

The woman releases breath in a way that's almost a laugh. He gives another look over as she leans her head back to take another drag. It's the lips that grab him: they're full without being cartoonish, and she's got a little rhinestone punched right where a beauty spot might normally be. A piece of flash, designed to draw attention—in his heart, Billy knows this, but he's never seen the harm in letting himself be drawn wherever women want to lead him. She catches him looking, though, and shoots him an impatient glare. He admires her sleepy eyes, smearily made up, before he looks away, flustered. He stares at his shoes for a second and then something clicks. He actually snaps his fingers.

"You're the poet," he says. "Mastic. Elisa Mastic."

She looks at him again, less impatient this time. Takes a three-second drag on her cigarette, holds it, exhales. "Oh my God," she says, a little drily. "I just got street-recognized. That's the first time that's ever happened to me."

"Yeah, I saw—" Billy begins. He wants to say *your author site* but then he realizes it might sound a little stalkery. He doesn't want her to know that he looked her up online, even if he could pass it off as being in a strictly professional capacity. "I'm Billy Ridgeway," he says, extending his hand. "I'm the, uh, the fiction writer of the evening."

"Well," she says, "okay." She gives his hand a squeeze, meets his eyes, and smiles. Something stirs in Billy for a second, and then she lets go and it's gone.

"I *like* being street-recognized," she says. "It feels good! As a poet, you know, you're not sure that you're ever going to get that."

"You know what they say," Billy says, absently, still spinning a bit. "In the future, everyone will be famous to fifteen people."

"That's good," Elisa says. "I like that. Anyway, you made me feel better about the—the thing." She turns her hand in the air.

"The thing?"

"You know," Elisa says. "The fuckwit."

"The Bladed Hyacinth—"

"Yes," she says. "Don't even say it. I can't even stand the name of the thing."

"So you saw it."

"Yeah," she says. "I saw it. I didn't feel great about it—"

"No," Billy says. "Me either." *Neither?*

"Well, anyway," she says. "Point is: you helped me to feel better."

"Glad to be of service," Billy says, and for a minute they stand there in the cold, wind snapping around them, neither one of them looking at the other or saying anything. Billy doesn't want to let the conversation die, though. He wants to be daring and bold. By this point, conveniently, he's forgotten that Flaubert was talking about the work.

"I read one of your poems, you know," he hazards. "On—your author site."

"Which poem?" Elisa asks. Her eyes are on him, suspicion awakened in them.

"Uh," Billy says. "The first one? I can't remember the name? But there was a line in it that I liked. About the *deleted world*."

"Oh please," Elisa says. "That one—ugh, it's the worst one. I keep begging my press to put *any* other poem up there."

"Pshaw," Billy says, and then realizes with horror that he's saying stuff like *pshaw*. He forges on, though: "I liked it."

Elisa pauses. "You didn't read a second one, though, did you?" she asks.

"I did not," Billy admits, freely.

"Well. At least you're honest."

She walks to the edge of the sidewalk, cranes her head out into the street like she's looking for a cab.

"I see a bar," she says. "You'll be glad to know that it looks open. You want to get out of this cold?"

Of course he does.

They each have a shot and then they each order a second one. Talk thereupon quickly returns to the gripe they have in common, the Hyacinth piece.

"It got me so shook up," Billy says, "that I don't actually want to read, like, *any* of my preexisting work."

"I know," says Elisa. "I was up half the night writing six new poems. They could be good, they could be crap, I don't even know anymore. But I figure, fuck it. It's something different."

"Exactly," Billy says. "Something different. That's the key. I'm half thinking that I'm not going to read anything at all but instead do like a piece of, I don't know, oral storytelling."

"Well, if it's good enough for The Moth, it'll work here."

"Oh yeah," Billy says. He'd forgotten about The Moth. Somehow that shakes his confidence in the violent originality of his idea. A bit. Just a bit.

They seem to have exhausted this line of conversation. She looks at him and he at her. The second round of shots arrives.

"Cheers," she says, and they down them with all due haste.

Seconds pass. She looks at him. He can see the intelligence in her eyes at work, making some set of complex assessments. She leans in incrementally and her nostrils flare once: Billy would swear that she was sniffing him, if there was a way that that made any sense at all.

She leans back. "Okay," she says. "I don't know you well, Billy Ridgeway, but you seem like an honest guy, and I like that."

"Thank you," Billy says, and as he says it he realizes that he's starting to *yearn* for Elisa Mastic. Maybe this breakup with Denver—for that is how he is now thinking of it—doesn't have to be a bad thing. Maybe it's a piece of good luck. Maybe it'll be an opportunity: a chance to start over with someone who doesn't know all his flaws.

"I'm going to ask you a question," she says. "And I want you to answer honestly."

"Okay," Billy says. "Is this a test?"

"This is a test," Elisa says.

"I'm ready," Billy says. This is normally the kind of thing that would make him nervous, but the bourbon is helping.

"The question is: What is the worst thing you ever did?"

Billy blinks. He doesn't want to think about whatever might be the worst thing he ever did. And whatever it is, he's certain it's bad, and he doesn't want to let his bad side enter into full display. Absolutely not. The whole point, the whole goddamn *point* of this conversation is to showcase only his *good* side: to be charming and funny and charismatic. He looks around for a story that will highlight those aspects of himself but also maybe seem a little mean or over-the-top. It takes him a minute to find something that qualifies; during that time Elisa calmly examines her hand, all five fingers extended in front of her.

"So I had this girl over," Billy says. This is a Denver story, which gives him a queasy feeling, but he needs something. Elisa raises her eyebrows in a way that conveys a very guarded species of interest.

"We'd been out," he says, "out at some restaurant or having drinks or something, after what had already been a pretty long day, and then we got back to my place, totally exhausted, and I remembered that I didn't have any clean laundry for the next day, and instead of just saying *screw it* I insisted that we go out to the Laundromat. This girl just wanted to lie on the couch and I made her get up and come with me because I wanted the company. I even made her carry a bag with the sheets and pillowcases."

A thin smile from Elisa.

"And so we're at the Laundromat, and it just seems like it's taking *forever*, it's like time has just slowed to a crawl. A fucking *crawl.*

And then after we've spent like a *year* there we have to move everything over to the dryer. *Bam*, another year gone. We're not even talking to one another we're so tired. And so finally everything's clean, and we go back to my place, and she immediately goes up to the loft and curls up on my bed. Just like direct on the mattress: the sheets are still all in the laundry bag. And I'm like *come on, come on, we need to make the bed* and she just, like, grunts. So, thinking I'm funny, I get the fitted sheet out and I just pull it over top of her and tuck it in on all four sides. She starts to giggle a little, so I figure it's okay. So then I put the next sheet on over top of that, and then finally the comforter, and by this point I think she wants to get out, she starts kind of squirming but she's really too tired to figure out how to make her way out of it, and then I start poking her. Like, index finger, right in the ribs. And she says *stop it* but she's laughing at the same time, so I don't stop right away, I poke her a couple more times, and she starts to shriek, cause it tickles her, right?, and finally she starts to thrash her way out of the sheets and she gets her head out at last, and I'm laughing, and even *she's* laughing a little bit, but then it just *tips* somehow and she starts crying. These big, hot, frustrated, tired tears. And—that's it."

Elisa watches him until finally he raises both palms, as if revealing the absence of more to tell.

"What did it feel like?" she asks, softly.

"It felt bad," he says. "I don't like making people cry."

"No, before that."

"Before what?"

"Before she started to cry. When you had her under the sheet and were poking her. What did *that* feel like?"

"I don't know," Billy says. "I thought I was being funny, I guess. I was just playing around."

"The woman in the story. Are you bigger than her?" Elisa asks.

"Yes," Billy says.

"Are you stronger than her?"

Billy doesn't think of himself as *strong*, exactly, but is he stronger than Denver? "Yes."

"And what did *that* feel like?"

"Being bigger and stronger, you mean?"

"Being bigger and stronger. Exerting power. Using it to scare someone."

"I don't think she was scared, exactly."

"Let me tell you something," Elisa says. "If you say *stop it* to someone who is bigger than you? And stronger than you? And they don't stop whatever it is that they're doing? It's scary. Trust me."

"Okay," Billy says. "What are you trying to say here?"

"What I'm trying to say, Billy, is that you seem like a gentle, peaceful guy, a real nice guy, and I think you've worked hard to come across that way, but I think there's a part of you, and maybe it's a part that you don't look at all that closely, that wants to be powerful and that doesn't give a good goddamn about anything else."

Something inside Billy twinges. A flinch moves through his face. Elisa's eyes change character again, communicating some faint satisfaction, an approval, almost, at seeing Billy hit upon something inside himself that may be true.

Billy turns his empty shot glass with his fingers, tries to reflect upon the part of him that likes being bigger and stronger, that likes being powerful. Elisa is right: that part is there. It moves inside him like an animal, cloaked by shadows. He can kind of glimpse its outlines but it moves away from his inspection, not wanting to be fully perceived.

"Thoughts," Elisa says.

"None," Billy says, and he expends some willpower to ensure that that's true.

"All right then."

The third round of shots lands on the table. They raise them.

"To thoughtlessness," Elisa says, and tosses hers back.

"To thoughtlessness," Billy answers, and he does the same.

"You want to know the worst thing *I* ever did?" she says, wiping her mouth with the back of her hand.

"Sure."

"Don't give me that *sure*. Either you want to know or you don't. I'll tell you if you want to know. But you have to understand that this isn't some hipster *game* for me."

"Okay," Billy says. "I get it. I want to know."

Elisa regards him suspiciously.

Billy puts on his most earnest face despite a sinking certainty that it actually makes him look totally goofy and insincere. "You can trust me," he says.

"No, I can't. But I'm going to tell you anyway, as a gesture of my good faith."

"Okay," Billy says.

"I killed a man," Elisa says.

"What?"

"I killed a man," she says again. "It was an accident." She takes a deep breath. "I killed a man," she repeats, like it's something she has to say to herself regularly, "and I was never caught."

Billy scans her face for some sign that she's making a joke, or just fronting like a badass. But she's wearing that same implacable calm. *Wow*, he thinks.

"What were—what were the circumstances?"

Elisa looks away sharply, glancing down at her watch, a heavy beveled thing that looks like you could crack open a nut with it. "It's ten past six," she says.

"Yeah, so?"

"So we should get back over there."

"What? You're gonna just—leave me hanging? You can't do that."

She gives him a look, one which adequately communicates *Don't think you can start telling me what I can and can't do.* "I'll tell you what," she says. "I'll tell you the circumstances the next time we meet."

"Oh," Billy says. He grins. "You think there's going to be a second time?"

"No," Elisa says. "But one should always plan for the unexpected."

A lesser species of disappointment emerges within him, but he says, "I accept these terms."

"You say this," Elisa says, "like you had a choice."

He settles the tab for both of them even though he still doesn't know how he's going to make rent. When he does this, as nonchalant as anything, he can detect her, out of the corner of his eye, watching him.

This could be good, Billy tells himself, as they cross the street. *Just don't fuck it up. Let it be easy.* He doesn't raise the question of whether it's a good idea to get involved with someone who has killed a man.

They reach Barometer's heavy set of doors. He holds one of them open for her in a showy display of half-ironic gallantry, his motions a little broad from the buzz he has going.

See? he thinks. *You can be charming when the situation calls*

89

for it. He watches her enter, permitting himself a glance at the segment of black panty hose he can spot between the hem of her red tartan coat and the top of her boots. Maybe it's more than a glance; maybe it borders on a leer. But he feels like it's the quickest, most subtle leer he can possibly manage with three shots of bourbon floating around in his circulatory system. Still, a little embarrassing.

Don't worry about it, he tells himself, *nobody noticed,* but even as he tells himself this he feels the prickling sensation of disapproving eyes on him, and he tracks over to the source of the sensation, and that's when he sees her, alone at a table for two: Denver.

CHAPTER SIX

LISTEN, AUDIENCE

IMMANENCE • AMBIGUOUS INTRODUCTIONS • I'M NOT SAYING
BUDDY • TOTAL FAILURE OF CHARACTER • ABSOLUTE CORPO-
REALITY • KAFKA TELLS A JOKE • FAMOUS LITERARY BRAWLS •
A STORY ABOUT SOME THINGS • SOULS • STOUT • RHETORIC

There had been a night, at the tail end of summer, when Billy and
Denver had gone out for drinks with Bingxin Ying, a petite gallery
owner with violet lipstick, an asymmetrical haircut, and an intense
manner of aggressively probing the air while she spoke. The out-
ing was in celebration of the closing of a deal: Bingxin was putting
together a new show, *Eidetics*, to run at her gallery for the next
three months, and she'd acquired five of Denver's early shorts. The
conversation, half conducted in art-speak, quickly went over Billy's
head, but he'd been content to lurk in the back of the booth, eat
the skewered selection of fruits that had come with his drink, and
watch Denver glow in reception of what he guessed was a rather
abstract form of effusive praise.

Content for a while, anyway. Then came a moment when
Bingxin made a vigorous stabbing motion with both of her hands
and, over the music, had shouted "What impresses me the most
about your work is its commitment to immanentization of the
ephemeral." Billy had watched Denver beam, had watched her
say "Thank you" with a real sincerity that he wasn't sure he'd ever

successfully invoked, and he actually felt a little jealous. No, more than a little: straight-up capital-J Jealous. He made a mental note of the phrase. *Immanentization of the ephemeral?*

Later that night, in bed, Billy tried it out. "The immanentization of the ephemeral," he said, apropos of nothing.

"I *know*," Denver had said, propping herself up on one elbow. "Didn't you *love* that? Bingxin really gets me."

This was not, ultimately, the reaction that Billy had wanted, and he withdrew into a kind of sulkiness. It took Denver only seconds to notice.

"What," she said.

"I don't *get* it," Billy said. "What does it *mean?*"

Denver clucked her tongue at him. "It's not so complicated, Billy," she said.

"It *sounds* complicated."

"You're a writer," she said, which went some way toward cheering him. "You know what words mean."

"I don't know what *immanentize* means," Billy had said, still in a bit of a pout.

"It means *to make immanent.*"

"I don't know what *that* means."

"Yes you do. Think about it for a second."

But Billy was in no mood.

"It means," she said finally, "to bring into being."

"Okay," Billy said. "I did know that, I guess."

"And the ephemeral?"

"Yeah, okay," Billy said. "I know that one."

"Lay it on me," Denver said.

"It means things that won't last."

"Yeah," Denver said. "And that's the thing about the world

that's so beautiful and so sad. *Everything* is ephemeral. *Nothing* lasts. And that's why I go around, you know, with a stupid camera strapped to my shoulder all the time. Because I want to capture some of those things. I want to bring them back into being. Just to make them last for a little bit longer."

And now, as Billy enters Barometer, the very first thing that he notices is that she isn't wearing her shoulder-mount tonight. Billy looks around on the table in front of her, feeling certain that he'll spot her camera somewhere within reach, but it isn't anywhere. Looks like tonight the ephemeral will go unimmanentized. Fuck.

Nevertheless, he feels determined to open on a positive note, if only to cover for the fact that he's just been caught openly flirting with somebody else. "Denver!" he says. "Hi!" He can feel shit-eatingness creep into his grin.

"Hi," Denver says, with obvious wariness. She looks at Billy, then at Elisa, then back at Billy, some variety of deepening despair taking residence in her expression. Billy's grin gets even wider, to compensate.

"Denver," Billy says, voice buoyant with cheer. "This is Elisa— she's the, uh, the other reader tonight? The poet?"

"Nice to meet you," Denver says, her voice rimed with frost.

"And Elisa," Billy continues, "this is Denver, my—" And right there he chokes. Can't quite bring himself to say *girlfriend.* He'd spent half the day strenuously contemplating the prospect that she might be really and truly gone. Hadn't he? And yet here she is. He's tempted to just call her his *ex,* and he feels a nasty pleasure at the thought that she might feel stung. But that'd burn the bridge, and so he hesitates. *Friend* is right out. He needs some word that's neutral, ambiguous. Because there's Elisa. And he feels like there's no sense in coming across to Elisa as *taken* unless he knows that

Denver is really, well, taking him. So: not *girlfriend*, then—but what? *Partner? Companion? Buddy?*

Of course as soon as the pause lasts more than a second his entire thought process on the matter becomes completely transparent to everyone.

"Nice," says Denver. She looks away, aiming whatever expression she's wearing now at the wall, where Billy no longer has access to it. She takes a long sip from her martini.

"Uh, okay," Elisa says, a barb in it aimed at Denver. She gives Billy a tightly wound smile, the kind of smile that hides a mouth full of clenched teeth. It's a little fearsome, but then she gives him a kindness: she lays her hand on his shoulder. Just for the briefest second. "Good luck tonight," she says, and then she's off to the bar, removing her hand from his person and using it to signal the bartender with one decisive thrust.

Billy watches her go, but only for a second. With Elisa out of the picture he can at least concentrate on the task at hand: damage control. He slumps down into the available chair. Denver casts a flashing look at him then looks at the wall again.

"Really nice," Denver says. "You're a class act, Billy Ridgeway. Would it have killed you to say *girlfriend*?"

"It wouldn't have killed me. I'm just not sure it's *accurate*. You haven't exactly *been there* for me lately," Billy says, clawing desperately for what looks like it might be the moral high ground.

"I'm here, aren't I?" says Denver. She turns back to him. "I'm here; I'm at your reading; I'm being supportive. Pretty much the opposite of what you did the night of the *Eidetics* opening, if you recall *that* night."

Billy does. He passes on the opportunity to comment on it, though, because The Night of the *Eidetics* Opening serves now as shorthand for Total Failure of Character, a pure instance of asshole behavior, a kind of toxic fact which, he has learned, will cause him to immediately lose any argument in which it is admitted as evidence. Instead, he strategically rewinds back to the part of the argument where Denver used the word *supportive*.

"Supportive?" he practically crows. "It's been, what, eight days since you spoke to me? I left you like twenty-five voice messages and you didn't return even one of them. I didn't think I'd ever *see* you again."

"Six," Denver says.

"What?"

"Six. You left me *six* voice messages."

Billy mulls this. "That's still a lot," he says, after a second.

"I think," Denver says, her tone softening a little, "that it was the right number of times, maybe. I thought about this. I decided that it was enough to show me that you were sorry and not so many that you crossed the line into scary."

"Thanks," says Billy, brightening. "I thought about how to strike that balance, you know."

"I believe you," Denver says. "I could sense that you were thinking about that, actually. It's very *you* to do something like that."

"Thanks," Billy says again, although a little unsteadily: he never feels exactly certain that people mean *that's very you* as a compliment when they say it to him.

Silence for a moment.

"I miss you," Denver says.

"Oh," Billy says. He wants to respond sympathetically, although that means having to mask the reflexive pleasure that he takes from what she said. He dithers over a few possible responses and finally fumbles out "That's good, though, right?" which he's pretty sure is the worst of all possible options.

"I miss you," Denver says, ignoring him, "but I'm not sure I *like* you."

"Oh," Billy says, crumpling. "That's—yeah, that's less good." He really wishes he had gotten a drink before sitting down.

"Let me say what I mean," she says. "What I mean is"—she sighs—"what I mean is, you're likable, Billy. You really are. You're clever and you're funny and you're talented and sometimes when you look at me I can see what you must have looked like as a little boy and I just feel like my heart is going to burst."

Billy risks a smile, although he knows that a *but* is coming. His hands start to fidget at the table, as though they're autonomously seeking the drink he has failed to supply them with.

"But," Denver says. She pulls her hair back from her face, holds a hank of it in her fist and pulls in a way that looks like it facilitates some internal tautening necessary to the conversation. "*But*," she continues, "I don't think you're *good for me*. I just think you're never quite *present*."

"I am present!" Billy exclaims, seizing the opening. He raps on his chest with his knuckles, to demonstrate. "Immanent," he says.

Denver gives him a sad smile. "Immanent," she says. "Sure. But I need someone who's going to be present. *For real* present, not just immanent. I've just—I've learned that, about myself, by now. Guys who can't be present? They're often funny, clever, talented guys, Billy—but they're no good for me. And I'm trying—I'm really *trying* not to like guys who are no good for me."

"But," Billy says.

"But what."

"But I want you to like me."

"I know," she says. "And it kills me. It kills me that you want me and it kills me that I want you back. And it kills me that I'm here, overlooking the fact that you're probably bad for me, even though I swore—swore!—to myself that I was done with you. And it kills me that"—she looks inadvertently over to the bar, in the direction Elisa went—"that you're already looking for the Next Thing. That you weren't even present enough in our relationship to be sad when you thought I was gone."

"I was sad," Billy says, miserably. "Really fucking sad."

"Well," Denver says, with a note of bitterness, "then maybe there's hope."

Billy remembers an old joke out of Kafka: *There is hope. Plenty of hope. An infinitude of hope. But not for us.*

And that's when Anil and the Ghoul show up.

"Billy Ridgeway, man of the hour," says Anil, clapping Billy on the back.

"Explain to me why you don't have a drink in your hand right now," says the Ghoul.

"Hey, guys," Billy says.

"Hey, Denver," Anil says. He looks back and forth between Billy and Denver, evidently trying to assess the state of the dynamic. "Um, am I interrupting?"

"No, it's okay," Billy says. "Pull up some chairs." There will be time—he hopes—to continue this conversation with Denver later. There are times when privacy is crucial, and, yes, being in the middle of a tense conversation with an estranged loved one is usually an indicator that you're experiencing one of those times, but Billy really believes that if you're about to get up on stage you shouldn't turn away even a single friend who wants to be by your side. He glances at Denver to see if she's okay with it. Her face bears a practiced blankness, but he catches sight of something unconsoled floating into the depths of her head, where he cannot reach it.

Shit, he thinks.

Everybody looks at one another, deep in their respective bubbles of social calculation, trying to figure out what to say next.

"I am buying you a drink," the Ghoul says, and he slouches off into the darkness.

"So," Billy says to Anil, eager to get a conversation—any conversation—off the ground. "You just get off work?"

"Yeah," Anil says. "And let me tell you. That place." And he's off, telling a story about the latest wackiness to go down at the sandwich shop, Giorgos getting into it with some customer. Denver listens, cracks a fake smile—to front like she's okay, Billy intuits—and then eventually Anil's patter wins her over, and a real smile replaces the fake one. It's the first real smile Billy's seen on her in a long time. He's glad to see it, even if it breaks his heart a little to know that he wasn't the one to pull it out of her. She ends up telling a story, too, about the baroque anthrax paranoias held by one of her old bosses, the guy who supervised her in the hospital mailroom when she was employed there as a glorified letter-opener, in those days right after 9/11, when everything had seemed so fucked.

The Ghoul returns, putting a pint of ale in Billy's hand, and in turn tells a story about one of *his* old bosses. Denver throws her head back and laughs her loveliest laugh and the reaction even gets a rare, thin smile out of the Ghoul. And for a blissfully unbroken stretch of time—maybe fifteen minutes—Billy feels like his life is normal, like everything is going to be okay.

And then Billy's phone starts vibrating. He pulls it out of his pocket and sees that it's his dad again. What is this, three times in as many days? A troubled expression clouds Billy's face. The others, still clowning with one another, don't notice. Something could really be wrong. It occurs to him, with a dollop of alarm, that he still hasn't listened to either of the previous voice mails his father left. He imagines taking the call, screwing a finger in his ear so he could hear his dad over the dull clamor of bar noise; he imagines getting up, taking the phone outside, having a conversation on the curb. Either way he knows that it would pull him out of the pleasurable little pocket-universe that he's been enjoying. He *likes* it in here, in the world where it seems like everything is going to be okay, where there are no family emergencies to worry about. But he makes a promise to himself to listen to the voice mails on the way home after the reading. Or if he's too drunk, or it's too late, or if he needs that time to sort things out with Denver, then he'll listen to the messages in the morning, before he has to drag his ass off to work. Any emergency can wait until then. He feels certain of it.

He's trying to get back into the rhythm of the conversation when they're joined by Laurent, the editor in chief of *The Ingot*, the guy who organized the reading. Laurent is a pale Glaswegian whose freckles and curly sprawl of red hair make it difficult for Billy to imagine him as any older than fifteen. He swims within a massive, cable-knit roll-neck sweater which provides probably half of his mass.

"Glad you could make it; glad you could make it," he says, pumping Billy's hand with enthusiasm.

"Oh, sure," says Billy. He still hasn't come up with a story to tell, and the realization that he still has to triggers a sudden unpleasant tightening in his scrotum. "I . . . wouldn't have missed it."

"Wonderful. Listen, I think we're going to get started in about five minutes. We're going to have you go first, then a short break, and then we'll have Elisa go."

"Okay," Billy says, falsely. A thin line of sweat breaks out on his forehead. "Great."

Laurent claps Billy on both shoulders. "It's good to have you here. On board."

Billy forces a smile, and waits for Laurent to remove his hands. The moment lasts a little longer than it should, and Laurent's face turns somber.

"I wanted to apologize," he says. "About the—the thing."

"The thing?" Billy says.

"You know," Laurent says. "The unpleasantness."

"The Bladed—"

"Yes. Don't even say it. I can't even stand the name of the thing."

"Don't worry about it. It doesn't matter," Billy lies. "It's just one write-up; it doesn't define the evening. It seems like we got a good crowd anyway."

"True, true," says Laurent. His hands are still on Billy's shoulders. "It's just—*Thanks for the invite,* Ingot, *but we find ourselves in a position where we must decline. It's galling.*"

"Whatever," says Billy, eager to end this. "I wouldn't really have wanted him here anyway. If he steers clear then so be it."

"Well, that's the thing," says Laurent. "He *didn't* steer clear. That's him, right over there."

He releases Billy's shoulders at last and points. Everyone's eyes follow. Sure enough, standing alone, with his back against the deep purple wall of the bar, a tall figure with a slate-gray shirt and a mandarin collar, idly reviewing items in a steno notebook. Billy looks at the bony face; the heavy brow; the thick, bookish eyeglasses made out of some kind of horn; the expression of faint boredom; and he thinks one word: *enemy.*

"I'm not sure why he came," Laurent says, "but I know you're going to prove him wrong."

"Uhhh," Billy says. "Yes. Yes, I will prove him wrong."

"I want you to know," Laurent says, "that here at *The Ingot* we really appreciate and believe in your work."

"Um, okay," Billy says. It actually does still mean something to hear somebody say that. He takes the words and mentally fashions them into a tiny badge of honor, which he fastens invisibly over his heart.

"Five minutes," Laurent says. He checks his watch. "Well, three. Okay?"

"Okay," Billy says.

"So that's Anton Cirrus," Anil says, as Laurent heads off toward the stage.

"Yes," Billy says, with contempt. "I've seen his photo before. On Gawker."

"You should go over there and punch him in the face."

For a long moment Billy actually considers this as a viable direction in which the evening could go.

"I think you could take him," says the Ghoul.

"It would be in the tradition of great literary brawls," Anil says. "You know: Hemingway vs. Stevens?"

"Mailer vs. Vidal," adds the Ghoul.

"Ridgeway vs. Cirrus!" Anil exclaims. "Think about it."

"No," Billy says.

"You could impress your woman."

Denver rolls her eyes.

"No," Billy says.

"You could make your reputation."

"The only thing that is going to *make my reputation* tonight is if I read something *good*. Something that will get fucking *Anton Cirrus* to print something about how awesome I am, which will involve getting fucking Anton Cirrus to change his fucking *mind*. To say, *Oh, actually, I was wrong*. How often can you remember that happening?"

None of them can come up with even a single time.

"So," Denver says, to break the deathly silence that has settled over the table. "What *are* you going to read?"

"I had this idea, actually," Billy says. "That I wasn't going to read anything? I was going to get up there and just—improvise something? To tell a story, you know, from within? From the unconscious?"

Everyone stares at him.

"You know," he says. "Like oral storytelling?"

Everyone keeps staring.

"That's what storytellers do?" Billy tries.

"Do something else," Denver says, finally.

"Do anything else," Anil adds.

"This is a horrible idea, isn't it?" Billy says.

No one confirms this, but no one denies it either.

"Shit," Billy says. "All right. I'll just pull something out of the file. But there's nothing in there that's good. Not good enough."

He looks around at the base of the table but can't find his backpack. It occurs to him that he left it behind, at the other bar, down the block. He calculates how long it would take him to run down there, get it, and get back. At least seven to ten minutes. Which he doesn't have. Laurent is already on stage, gleaming white in the spotlight, fiddling with the microphone.

"I don't have the file," Billy says.

"Why not?" Anil says.

"Why not isn't important. What's important is that I need a story. I need a story in the next thirty seconds."

"I'd like to thank everyone for coming—can you all hear me?" Laurent is saying.

"Tell the one about the Devil," Anil says.

"I thought of that," Billy says.

"It's a good story," Anil says.

"It needs a third act."

"It needs a second act. But it's interesting, at least."

"Wait," Denver says. "Which story?"

"The one about the Devil," Billy says. At the periphery of his attention he can hear his biographical details being declaimed on stage by Laurent.

"What devil?" Denver says.

"The Judeo-Christian Devil," Billy says.

"You met the Devil?"

"It's a long story. But you'll hear it in a second. And then after this we'll work everything out. I promise."

And then, fuck it, he goes for the Hail Mary. He looks straight into Denver's eyes and says, "I love you."

Denver responds with a tired smile, a smile that expresses a sense of bitter confirmation rather than actual pleasure. Billy's heart sinks. Laurent, on stage, says, "Please welcome our first reader, Billy Ridgeway."

Light applause. Billy is up, out of his chair, and he walks toward the stage, still kind of half contemplating bolting across the room and punching Anton Cirrus in the face as a way to get out of having to do this. He turns and he looks back at the table: Denver,

Anil, the Ghoul. They look so happy there, without him. It occurs to him just how easily he could be replaced.

He takes the stage, and the room falls into a dull murmur.

It's okay, Billy thinks, *you can do this.* And he speaks: "Hi there," he says. He coughs. "Thanks for coming out. Really. Thank you. Everybody."

He shades his eyes and peers into the bar, trying to cast a pointed look at Anton Cirrus. When he can finally pull Cirrus out of the gloam, though, he sees that Cirrus is not paying any attention whatsoever to the weak taunt embedded in Billy's intro, but rather is looking at his phone, texting something.

Texting something! Goddamn him!

White rage begins to throttle Billy's mind, and his mouth begins to wind down as he watches Anton Cirrus type away. "I'm glad you're all here tonight because I wanted to tell you a story," he says. "A story about . . . some things."

The murmuring audience shifts into hush, but not a good hush, the kind of fixed, uncomfortable hush that people get when they begin to suspect that they're watching someone who may be about to have a public meltdown. Anton Cirrus is still texting. Billy wrenches his gaze away, lets it fall on the table that's closest to the stage.

And who should be sitting there but Lucifer, his eyes meeting Billy's, enacting an emotionless imitation of pleasured recognition. Billy's entire body breaks into a cold sweat. It's one thing to talk about the Prince of Darkness behind his back, but it's another thing entirely to do so when he's sitting three feet from you, staring into your face, prepared, at least potentially, to pitchfork you in the guts or something the second you make a joke at his expense. Billy needs a new idea.

"Yeah," he says. "Some . . . things." The hush redoubles, grows more acute, progresses ever closer to perfect silence. Billy begins to pat at his pockets, in the hope that one of them will yield some fiction. He finds a folded-up napkin in his back pocket, and he pulls it out, and unfolds it, and reads the slashed words he wrote to himself at lunch:

COWARD
FUCK-UP

He looks at this for a long moment.

"So there's this guy," he says, finally, his voice ringing hollowly in the room. "And the guy, he's lived a good life, okay, a mostly good life. He's made some bad decisions here and there. Nothing like—he hasn't killed anybody or anything like that, he's just—he's just fucked up here and there. Like—like you do.

"And it turns out that's okay. When the guy dies, at the end of his long life as a sometimes fuck-up, he doesn't go to Hell. He goes to Heaven. He meets St. Peter there, at the gates, the whole deal.

"And St. Peter says *Welcome, guy, let me show you around.* And he takes the guy on a quick tour around Heaven. The guy gets to meet Aquinas; it's great. But after a couple of hours the guy is feeling pretty bushed, and he says to St. Peter, *I'd kind of like to,* you know, *unwind.*

"And St. Peter says, *Oh, sure, we have your quarters all ready,* and they go to this room which is like, it's like this lavish hotel suite. And the guy is really impressed. He's checking everything out. And he opens the closet and he's stunned! 'Cause in there is every pair of shoes the guy has ever owned. All there like *waiting for him.* From, like, his tiny baby shoes, to the shoes he was buried in at his funeral, all there in a row. So many memories! But the guy turns to St. Peter and says, you know, like *What's the deal? I get to heaven and all my shoes are here?*

"And St. Peter is like, *Yeah, didn't you know? Shoes have souls.*"

He can hear Lucifer give a single great *haw*, but other than that, the room is silent.

I suck, Billy thinks. *Everyone knows that I suck.* Denver, Anton Cirrus, Elisa, Laurent, the fucking bartender, everyone. He tries to come up with something else to say. He can only think of one other joke, about two people who get frozen to death outside of a whorehouse, and he's not telling that one.

Okay, he thinks. *You may be a fuck-up, but you don't have to be a coward. You can tell the story. Don't be scared of the Devil. He can't hurt you.*

He has no idea how he reaches that conclusion, but he's surprised to find that it feels true.

"But seriously," he says. "I want to tell you a different story. I want to tell you the one about the Devil. It just started yesterday, so I didn't have time to write it down. In fact, it's still going on, right now."

He takes a step toward the edge of the stage and points down at Lucifer. Lucifer regards him. His face still holds a laugh formation, left over from the joke, but his eyes are mirthless, flat.

"You see this guy?" Billy says. "Yesterday morning, I woke up, and this guy was in my apartment."

"Adversarial Manifestation!" someone in the audience shouts. Billy and Lucifer turn toward the source. A bearded dude, somebody Billy's never seen before, a few tables away. "Adversarial Manifestation!" dude shouts again, rising from his chair, pointing.

Billy's a little dismayed to be interrupted by what appears to be a crazy person, but at least some of the room's attention is off of him. There's a commotion back at the bar, and someone—a heavyset guy in a tight black T-shirt, probably the bouncer—begins parting the crowd and moving toward the front. Billy assumes the plan is to eject the crazy guy, who is now shouting "Adversarial Manifestation" a third time, practically frothing, but the bouncer moves past that guy and instead stands across from Lucifer, staring him down.

"What?" Lucifer says. He raises his stout. "I'm just here to have a drink and to catch some contemporary fiction and poetry."

The bouncer raises something, aims it at Lucifer, and fires. Lucifer jolts, loses his drink, flails wildly out of his seat, hits the floor. The audience rears back from this. Billy suddenly fears that he's about to witness a stampede. That people could be killed. It would, he realizes, be his fault.

"Lock it down," bellows someone nearby. "We have a Category Six situation here. Repeat: Category Six."

Category Six? Billy doesn't know what that is, but the words have no immediate effect on the crowd, which is surging away from Lucifer's convulsing form. He peers out, tries to catch sight of Denver, but she's lost in the tumult. He looks down at the microphone, still in his hand. He still has the potential to speak to the crowd, to calm them, to direct them usefully. All he needs is to apply his kick-ass rhetorical skills. Does he actually have those?

He holds the mic close to his mouth.

"Audience," he says. "Listen, audience."

And then there's a twinge in his back, and suddenly everything in his body goes rigid as something horrible rips through his nervous system. Like some barbed white demon coming alive within him. He would think *Oh my God I'm dying* except he can't think anything at all; his mind is like a jagged pattern of flashing triangles. It lasts only for a second. A very, very long second. And then he's on the floor.

He blurts out a syllable that is not kick-ass rhetoric. It is not even recognizable language. It is the kind of sound you might make if you were shitting your pants, which Billy is thankfully not doing. He doesn't have the mic anymore. Someone is screaming. He hopes it isn't anyone he loves. Before he has time to figure anything out someone clamps something foul-smelling over his mouth and nose and the world blurs. *It's all going away*, Billy thinks as everything swims into darkness, *someone please help*. But no one does.

CHAPTER SEVEN

DOUCHEBAGS

SUICIDE IS AN OPTION • CHEMICALS AND SEWAGE • EXCELLENT
VERISIMILITUDE • SICK OF WARLOCKS • WHAT HAPPENS TO
PEOPLE WITH FACE TATTOOS • PROBED BY THE INTERNET •
LITERARY FLAIR • WHAT ABOUT GOD (REPRISE)

———————

Some little part of Billy's consciousness wakes up, probes around
tentatively, and learns that it hurts. Head, face, arms, legs, hands,
feet: every part reports in with the same message: *This sucks.*

Some higher-order function comes back on board and tries to
figure out why he hurts.

Someone Tased me, he thinks.

All at once he's not certain he's safe. He yanks himself the rest
of the way awake and lifts his head to get a look around. Inflamed
muscles seize in protest and Billy lets out a low moan.

He's in a jail cell.

Well, Billy thinks, *this can't be good,* although actually? He can
think of ways in which it could be worse.

He lets his head drop back to the plastic pillow. The crinkling
vinyl sounds incredibly loud, painful. He stares up into the dull
fluorescent disk set in the ceiling for a long time, letting his body
throb. Maybe if he waits long enough somebody will come along
to give him some instruction, let him know exactly what he's supposed to do next. Isn't that supposed to be the silver lining to being
in prison? You don't have to make your own decisions?

He pulls himself to a sitting position and he resists the impulse to just drop his head into his hands and leave it there for maybe the rest of his life. Instead he does a quick survey of the cell. Not really much to see. The bunk that he's sitting on. At the opposite end of the cell is an apparatus consisting of two metal bowls attached to a single central column; he guesses that one bowl is a sink and the other a toilet. He has to take a piss but right now getting up and walking three feet exceeds the range of his ambition. There's also a lightweight chair stamped out of one contiguous piece of plastic and a slab extruding from the wall which could maybe be used as a desk.

The other wall has a door set into it, prison bars in the classic style. Beyond them is darkness. Billy wonders briefly why the cell is lit but not the hallway, but, with no answer forthcoming, he lets the question go.

Aside from his shoes, which are missing, he's still in the clothes he wore to the reading. A quick pat-down, however, reveals that everything in his pockets is gone. Phone, wallet, keys. *Fuck*, he thinks. He realizes, distantly, that he was supposed to be at work this morning. He's not sure what time it is or if he still has a chance to save his job, but if he's late, he can't call in with some excuse. He can't call Anil to get him to cover for him.

Anil. It occurs to Billy suddenly that he doesn't know where Anil is or whether he's safe. Billy knows nothing about anything that happened after the Tasing. For all he knows, Anil, the Ghoul, Denver, Elisa, they could all be trampled to death.

Okay, Billy thinks. *That kind of thinking? Not helpful.*

It's your fault if it's true, he thinks. *Everyone was there because of you.*

One thing at a time. He looks under the bunk and finds his

shoes there. They still have laces in them, interesting. So he could at least still kill himself. Not really his number one choice at the moment but it feels good to at least have an option, any option. He looks around, briefly, for a beam he could hang himself from, finds nothing. But still. He feels certain he could make his laces into some kind of noose if he tried hard enough. He looks at the shoes in his lap, mentally unlaces them, tries out patterns of knots in his head, and eventually realizes he has absolutely no idea how he'd go about using his shoelaces to kill himself. He wishes, for a moment, that he had access to the Internet.

He puts his shoes on.

He tries standing. It hurts, but he can do it. Something in his pelvis seems banged out of alignment; he feels like if he twists at the waist something will pop and accord a degree of relief. He attempts a few test pivots but they don't help.

He looks around. Something about the whole cell feels familiar. He can't quite place it. He looks at the combination sink/toilet unit. It's ingeniously designed, in a kind of depressing way, but he has a foggy memory of having marveled at this precise ingenious design at some point in the past. Maybe just from some stock photo of a prison cell, accompanying some article he read once upon a time? He looks back at the sink/toilet unit, and he thinks *I've been here before.*

That can't be right. He's never been in jail. The closest he came was one time that he had to run from the cops: that was also, he remembers, the first night he met Jørgen, three years ago this past summer.

He recalls the story. The Ghoul had somehow fallen in with this group of bored German pyrotechnicians, three guys in town to engineer special effects for an alien invasion movie that was annoying everyone by shutting down streets all over Manhattan. These guys—young, severe-looking guys from Berlin—were really only needed to orchestrate a few big explosions, which had gotten delayed, so they had a lot of time during which they were basically expected to wait around and do nothing. They quickly grew weary of fucking around in their hotel, the Ghoul explained to Billy, so they had begun hanging out in this art space in the Bronx, taking suggestions for things around the city that could be exploded, and then actually going ahead and exploding them, as little under-the-radar art events, or something. Their next event involved plans to detonate a row of chemical toilets at the edge of a torn-up lot down in Brighton. Billy and the Ghoul had been feeling pretty bored themselves that summer, and so when the night came, they went.

They gathered with others in the pleasant early dusk, watching the German guys drill holes and run wires mirthlessly at the row of toilets, trying to make sense of the badly-translated Situationist pamphlets that had been passed out to the crowd, drinking wide-mouths. And this guy Jørgen had come over and engaged Billy in conversation. They got to arguing about the merits of Olde English 800 versus Colt 45, something like that, and by the time the German dudes shrilled upon their whistles to indicate that they were ready, Billy had thought *Hey, maybe I'm making a friend.*

One more whistle blast. Billy, Jørgen, and the Ghoul huddled together behind an army-green plastic tarp. And then the lead German threw a switch and the toilets blew.

It remains a sight that comes to Billy's mind whenever he's trying to define beauty.

He remembers a string of tiny but deafening bangs crisscrossing the base of the toilets, opening a rift through which sluiced out a marvelously disgusting blue-green tide of chemicals and sewage, the sight of which elicited a tremendous collective groan from the audience, who had suddenly become concerned about their footwear, which they hadn't been, just a moment before. One second later the plastic shells of the toilets were sundered by ribbons of terrifying white fire, a fire so hot and bright that it clearly indicated the presence of fantastic military-grade combustibles, the kind of thing that ordinary citizens just should not have. At the heart of the inferno, the toilets held for a second and then simply liquefied, becoming a pool of molten slime, still burning, producing a towering, fetid black cloud. And that's when two cop cars screeched into the lot, their whirling lights suffusing the great, persistent pillar of smoke with color: red and blue, playing together to produce the most lovely range of violets. It seemed maybe like it had been intended as a final touch, and the audience broke into confused applause as the cops began barking imperatives through a megaphone.

"We should go," said Jørgen, as a third cop car arrived. This one parked itself lengthwise, blocking the lot's wide gate, and Billy had been about to panic when Jørgen touched him on the shoulder and said "This way," and hustled them back through a hole in the perimeter fence that was hidden by a heaped pile of pallets. On the other side of the fence was a van, what Billy would soon come to forever think of as Jørgen's Trusty Econoline Van, and they piled in and peeled out, and Billy didn't have to go to jail, and his friendship with Jørgen was pretty much locked at that point.

He wonders where Jørgen is, anyway, and he feels a sudden, sharp regret at not having been more concerned at Jørgen's long disappearance. Not that there's anything he can do about that now, not from jail.

He can't really do anything about anything. He can maybe,

at best, take a piss. He looks again at the combination sink/toilet thing.

He has his pants unbuttoned and is about to get down to it when he feels a sudden concern about privacy. He looks back at the bars and the darkness beyond. Can people see into his cell? When he's facing the toilet his back is to the door, so it's not exactly like people can see his junk straight-on, but what is going to happen when he has to take a shit? He tries to imagine sitting there, trying to *do his business* while some Aryan Nations dude is staring him in the face. He knew prison was supposed to be tough but he didn't quite realize that every crap he'd take would be within view of prying eyes.

He approaches the bars and peers into the darkness. It's hard to tell what's going on out there. He doesn't see another cell or even a hallway. All he can sense behind the bars is a large, open space of undefined dimensions. He can see shapes and forms but he can't quite make out what they are. When he moves his head he catches something gleaming glassily. Where the fuck is he?

He presses his face up to the bars, shields his eyes with cupped hands, willing them to adjust to the darkness. Eventually he begins to make out the shapes with greater distinction. He sees cameras. Not surveillance-style cameras but movie cameras, on big dollies.

The cell is a set.

And then he realizes why it seems familiar. It's a set from *Argentium Astrum*, the supernatural police procedural. It's the cell of Gorbok the Mad, the tongueless cultist that the team brings into custody in the first episode, hoping to get him to spill his terrible secrets!

Okay, he wasn't expecting that.

He tries the door. The lock is real enough. *Verisimilitude*, he notes, vaguely impressed. But this has to be an improvement. It's better to be locked into a film set than into a prison; he doesn't know what's going on, but he finds that he can at least believe that. He looks at the walls, wondering if he could break them down if he shouldered them hard enough.

Instead he just calls to the darkness: "Hello?"

He hears a voice, somewhere out in the dark studio space, say "He's up," followed by an electronic *bleep* that he recognizes as being the sign-off call of a walkie-talkie.

Interesting, Billy thinks. But not interesting in a good way. He has a sudden feeling that he's going to be interrogated before the morning is out, aggressively interrogated. His testicles shrink a little.

Before long, he sees a figure walking briskly toward him, through the gloom. He recognizes the spray of curly hair. It's Laurent, the editor in chief of *The Ingot*.

Okay, he wasn't expecting that, either.

"Billy," Laurent says, warmly. "Good to see you. Good to have you on board." He sticks his hand through the bars of the cell for Billy to shake. Billy shakes it, a little uncertainly.

"So," Billy says. "You're still alive." One fact at a time seems to be the order of the day here.

"I am," Laurent says, beaming a bit. "That got a little rough last night, there, a little rough."

"You're telling me," Billy says. "Who got hurt? Anybody?"

"Audience members are all okay," Laurent says. "We had to do a bit of, what would you call it, *cleanup* on them, but they're none the worse for wear. As for the readers: well, there's you: you got a little zap, not too much fun there, but you're okay, we've got you now, and that's good. Elisa, the poet: less happy story, frankly, we lost tabs on her, but we're guessing she'll turn up. It's not good for her to be off radar right now, though, not good at all. Of course, the one who took the brunt of the damage dealt out last night was the Adversarial Manifestation, can't say he came out too well at the end of all the excitement."

"Lucifer?" Billy asks.

"The Manifestation," Laurent says.

"He's dead?" Billy feels an unexpected pang of loss.

"It doesn't exactly work that way," Laurent says. "The Adversary isn't *alive* or *dead* as you and I think about it. His manifestation was dispelled last night, though. And if you stick with us, he won't be contacting you again."

Billy frowns. He's not sure why, but he feels bummed by this. It's not exactly like he lost a friend, but more like he embarrassed himself in front of someone he thought might make a good contact.

He looks at Laurent. "Who the fuck are you?" he asks. "I thought you were the editor of a literary magazine. But you know about all this stuff and somehow you're involved with *Argentium Astrum* and—"

Suddenly it clicks. "You're a warlock," he says.

Laurent smiles broadly. "Yes!" he exclaims. Billy, for his part, has to restrain a sigh. He's starting to get sick of warlocks.

"In fact," Laurent says, "I serve as the Executive Director of Cultural Production for the Northeast Regional Office of the Right-Hand Path, an international organization of witches and warlocks."

"Wait," Billy says. "So—is Ollard one of you?"

"Ollard?"

"Timothy Ollard? Guy who wants to burn up the world?"

"Timothy Ollard," Laurent says, "is someone who you should not even know about. But, to answer your question: No. He is not one of us. He is—well, he is a problem, a problem we are actively engaged with and working on. Let me put it to you this way, Billy. Ollard is a bad guy. And we're the good guys."

"The good guys," Billy repeats.

"Yes!" Laurent says.

For some reason this puts Billy in mind of the Office of Homeland Security, which he actually always thought of as a group of extralegal thugs. He narrows his eyes.

"Last night," he asks, "did you Tase me?"

Laurent glances down to the floor and presses a knuckle into his upper lip for a long second, apparently contemplating how to phrase the answer.

"You did!" Billy says. "You fucking Tased me!"

"Yes," Laurent says, looking up with an expression of pity. "I Tased you. If it's any consolation, I did it with great reservation, a really strong, profound reservation. But the important point is not that. That's behind us. That's in the past. The important point is that you're with us now."

"It really fucking hurt, you know," Billy says. "It's not *in the past* until I stop fucking *hurting*."

Billy glares at Laurent while Laurent maintains a hopeful smile.

"Did you say you had to do *cleanup* on my friends?" Billy says, eventually.

"Yes."

"What exactly does that mean?"

"Well," Laurent says, "surely you understand that we can't have people running around talking about having witnessed the dispersal of an Adversarial Manifestation. The results would be—a mess. Just a mess. So we had our team psychic—Gloria, we'll introduce you to her in a bit—we had Gloria go in and make a couple of tweaks to their memories of the event."

"Tweaks?"

"Yep," Laurent says, proudly. "Just a couple of tweaks."

"Without their consent?" Billy says.

A tiny line creases Laurent's brow. "It's not the kind of thing for which one typically asks consent," he says.

"I dunno," Billy says. "Lucifer asked for my consent before he started messing with my brain."

"That may be," Laurent says. "But—"

"So wait a second," Billy says. "What exactly do my friends think went down last night?"

Laurent gives him a look, as though this entire line of conversation is somewhat distasteful. "You remember you told a joke? About shoes?"

"Who could forget that," Billy says, in a low and rueful voice.

"Well," Laurent continues, "in their recollection, you finish the joke, thank the audience, and head backstage. And then the reading ends and everyone heads home."

Billy's ears begin to burn with shame. "Elisa doesn't read?"

"We lost track of her," Laurent says.

"I don't return to hanging out with my friends?" Billy says. "I freaking disappear?"

"It's just a tweak," Laurent says, a little defensively. "Our aim is minimal effective alteration: M.E.A. It's not our aim to, you know, *write fiction* in which you emerge as the star. We're the good guys."

"So I hear," Billy says. He tries to think about how it might have appeared to everyone. He gets up there, he bombs in front of his small band of supporters. In front of Anton Cirrus. He winces to think of it. After bombing, he disappears backstage, doesn't return. Elisa Mastic, the poet who he conspicuously arrived with, disappears. It's not hard to imagine how this might have appeared to Denver. By now she either thinks he's dead, or she thinks he's an asshole, or she thinks he's fucking someone else. He winces again: really at this stage it turns into a full-blown grimace.

"I need my phone," Billy says. "I gotta sort this shit out right now."

"Oh, no," Laurent says. "That's not possible. We had to dispose of your phone."

"Yeah but—what?" Billy says, dismayed.

"Your phone, your wallet, your keys—anything connected to your former identity—all of it, for our purposes, has to be treated as compromised."

"*Former* identity?" Billy repeats.

"Forgive me," Laurent says, spreading his hands apologetically. "I fear that I haven't done the best job in this conversation of explaining the exact details of the protocol we follow in cases like yours. You know how it is, when you're so involved with something, you kind of forget that people on the outside might not intuitively *grasp* all the *nuance* of a situation?"

"Look," Billy says. "I'm starting not to give so much of a fuck about the *nuance* of the *situation*. You say you're the good guys, and I want to believe you. I really do. But so far what I know about you is that you wiped my friends' brains, you got me in trouble with my girlfriend, you trashed my stuff, and you're keeping me *in a cage* against my will. You don't seem like the good guys. Frankly, you seem like a bunch of douchebags."

Laurent steeples his fingers and brings them to his lips, and appears to be considering this.

"If I let you out of the cell," he says. "You have to promise that you'll hear me out. You're right that we can't hold you here against your will—"

"Because it would be wrong," Billy says.

"Absolutely!" Laurent says. "One hundred percent wrong. But if I let you out, you must give me your word that you will hear what I have to say. We believe that you are in great danger, and we believe that the Right-Hand Path is the organization that can best protect you from that danger."

"Check," Billy says. "You got my word."

"Okay," Laurent says. He turns and hollers into the darkness: "Barry! Keys!"

Billy can hear the shuffle of someone's approach, and the janitorial clinking of keys. He squints into the darkness, then starts back when he lays eyes on the massive lumbering form of Gorbok the Mad. Hulking, broad, heavy-browed: a scary square ton of man. On the show he wears a kind of elaborate leather diaper and has a terrifying serpent tattooed across his face. In real life, Billy sees now, he's wearing a broad violet button-down shirt and a rather stylish porkpie hat. He still has the serpent facial tattoo though. *Maybe this is what happens to you, if you get a tattoo on your face,* Billy thinks. Once you've pushed yourself out of polite society, beyond the point where you could still get a job at, say, Whole Foods. You end up having to work for the occult underground. "Hi," says Barry, his voice high-pitched and soft. "I'm Barry."

"I'm Billy," says Billy. He wonders for a second whether Barry was someone else, once upon a time, someone whose former identity got compromised. *Note to self,* Billy thinks, *don't let identity get compromised.* Or is it already too late?

"I know who you are," says Barry, and he opens the door.

"Let's walk," says Laurent, clasping his hands behind him. "Could you hit the lights, Barry?"

"Sure," says Barry, slouching off into the darkness again.

Billy steps out of the cage, enjoys a brief shiver of relief, and then instantly remembers that he never took a piss. He looks lingeringly back at the sink/toilet combination unit until he's interrupted by the loud *chung* of an industrial breaker being thrown. Banks of heavy overhead lights begin to stutter on. Billy marvels briefly at the size of the space. It's only about half the size of a suburban supermarket, but to someone like Billy, who spends most of his time in a cramped kitchen with Anil, anything larger than a squash court qualifies as cavernous.

Laurent starts off, and Billy hurries to catch up. The two of them move through a gangway lined densely on both sides with film production equipment: cameras on dollies, complicated rigs of theatrical lighting. Billy has to be careful to not snare his ankles on the big bundles of cables that run through the gangway like fat river snakes.

Laurent is talking. "As you correctly discerned, this is where we produce *Argentium Astrum.* It's our first foray into televisual cultural production, and we're very pleased with the results, very pleased."

"It's a ... good show?" Billy says. He's a little at sea in this conversation, but he means the praise honestly. "I gotta tell you, though, the last couple of times I tried to watch it, it just kind of degenerated into, like, weird symbols and blocks of color and stuff."

"Yes!" Laurent says. They're crossing in front of the main set now, a hemispherical mock-up of an open-plan police station. Billy recognizes all the different desks in their familiar arrangement; he enjoys a little fanboyish frisson which distracts him, for a moment, from the oddity of Laurent's answer.

"Yes?" Billy says, finally.

"Yes," Laurent confirms. He turns and grips Billy's deltoid muscle in a way that is probably designed to generate a pleasant fellow feeling, although in actuality all it does is make Billy want to squirm free. "See, Billy, one of the things we do here is we maintain a device we call the Board. The Board provides us with a very large, very thorough listing of people who have some degree of supernatural *attention* circulating around them. Persons who are, for one reason or another, *of interest* to figures in the occult community."

"So, what, it's like a magical No Fly List?"

"Ha ha!" Laurent barks. "Very good, Billy, very good." He wipes at the corner of his eye with a finger. "But, no, not like that. Our use of the Board is benign. Our intentions are not to *interfere* but rather simply to monitor, to observe. A sort of process of *keeping tabs on*."

"Okay," Billy says, tentatively.

"Needless to say," Laurent continues, "you are on the Board."

"I am?"

"You are. You have been on the Board for some time now. Many years."

"But why?" Billy says.

The tiny crease in Laurent's forehead appears again. "I don't know," he says. "The Board only indicates that someone with some degree of magical power has taken an interest in you. It doesn't indicate who, or why."

"Huh," says Billy.

"What the Board *does* indicate is when attention begins to shift," Laurent continues. "When someone begins to attract a lot more attention than they'd attracted in the past, they kind of light up on the Board. And two weeks ago you started to light up, quite dramatically."

Laurent releases Billy's shoulder. Billy rubs at it, absently.

"We were fortunate," Laurent says, "in that, at that time, we already knew a few things about you. We knew, for instance, that you were already a consumer of some of our programming, specifically *Argentium Astrum* here."

Laurent gestures around the set. He concludes the gesture by clamping both hands on the back of one of the fancy office chairs and kind of inspecting the mesh with his fingers.

"Why don't you have a seat?" he asks Billy. "Take a load off, as they say?"

"Uh, sure," Billy says. He's a little disturbed that Laurent somehow knew that he was watching the show. He wonders what else from his search history is known to these dudes. He remembers looking at porn the other night, remembers the names of the sites he visited: ultimately they are not units of language that he would prefer to be publicly associated with. He settles into the chair that on the show belongs to Detective Greco, the pallid cop with the haunted look, the one whose wife is lost in some kind of shadowy nether dimension. Billy notices that Laurent has his hands on the chair that belongs to Chief Boudreaux, the show's gruff but lovable patriarch.

"So," Laurent says, his fingers digging rhythmically into mesh, "we waited for you to log in and watch the show, and when you did, you opened an attention conduit, which we were able to use to probe you."

"You probed me?" Billy says.

"Yes," Laurent says.

"You probed me with the Internet?" Billy says.

"No," Laurent says. "We used magic. The Internet isn't the important part, you see, Billy. The important part is that we had your attention. That's what Cultural Production—my department!—is all about. People who are on the Board tend to have somewhat . . . predictable tastes. We generate content that strives to appeal to those tastes. When *your* attention is on *our* content it opens up a conduit that we can use for certain ends. Including, well, probing."

"Wait, though, you *probed* me?"

"Think of it as a diagnostic. We were able to run some checks on you, basic, very basic. We were able to establish that we weren't dealing with a possession scenario or a black curse. Once we ruled those things out we decided that it was important to meet you in person, see if we could figure out exactly what was going on with your position on the Board. You presented us with quite an opportunity, Billy, quite an opportunity. We needed to—branch out. To diversify! To create something, or at least the appearance of something, with a little bit more literary flair. Think of it as our way of trying to get to know you a little better."

"*The Ingot.* The reading," Billy says.

"Correct," Laurent says. He taps his nose once, mirthfully. Something begins to curdle within Billy.

"So *The Ingot* doesn't exist?"

Laurent shrugs. "It exists as much as any literary magazine that hasn't brought an issue to press can be said to exist. You could approach it as a philosophical question, very philosophical."

"So the reading? You set that up to—lure me in?"

"To observe you," Laurent says. "We didn't realize, though, that the supernatural attention around you was approaching a major spike. A Category Six Adversarial Manifestation? That's just . . . that's just off the charts, really."

"So you didn't invite me because you thought I was a good writer? Because you were . . . a believer? In my work?"

"Billy," Laurent says. "I'm sure your work is fine. But clearly there are more important things operating at the moment than your respective level of talent or lack thereof."

"So, wait," Billy says. He clenches his eyes shut and presses on them with his fingers. "You're telling me you didn't even *read* my work?"

"Not read as such," Laurent says. "No."

Billy can feel the little badge of honor, the one he affixed over his heart last night, being pried away. It hurts. Even on top of everything else, that still manages to hurt.

"Well," he says, "at least you're honest." *Only not really very honest*, he thinks to himself, and at that moment he makes up his mind to go. He has a life that needs fixing.

"I want my stuff," he says.

"I can't do that," Laurent says.

"You can."

"I can't."

"Why not?"

"We threw it away."

"You threw it—? Where? Here?"

"Not here," Laurent says. "You have to understand that it would be foolish to retain those materials here, on-site. Their presence would—"

"Shut up," Billy says. "Just tell me where."

"Our team probably put them right in the Dumpster. Behind Barometer."

"I have to get over there."

"By now," Laurent says, "I'm sure they're—"

"Shut up," says Billy, staggering to his feet. "How do I get out of here?"

"You said you'd hear me out," Laurent says.

"I've heard enough," Billy says. "Thanks, but I really do believe that I have."

He looks around for an exit. He spots a glowing red sign; he spots a door set into a cinder-block wall, and he sets off toward it.

"We won't keep you here against your will," Laurent calls after him.

"Because it would be wrong," Billy says.

"We won't keep you here against your will," Laurent continues, "but I want to be clear that it's not safe for you out there. The Adversary has an interest in you and we don't know why. He'll come after you again. He won't stop until he's gotten what he wants. Don't make the mistake of thinking that you can bargain with him. The only thing you can do is hide, and the only place you can hide is with us. We have a secure room. We could make you comfortable in there until we get your new identity set up—"

"I don't want a new identity," Billy says, turning to look Laurent in the face. "I *like* my life. Or at least I did, before you clowns started to mess with it."

He is a little bit surprised to realize that he means this.

Laurent regards him with a look of inconsolable disappointment. Billy turns to go. He has his hand on the door when one final question occurs to him.

"Actually," Billy says.

"Yes?" Laurent says, eagerly.

"What about God?" Billy asks. "If the Devil exists, that implies the existence of God, right? And you guys know about the Devil, you have fancy names for when he appears and all that, so: What about God? Do you know about God?"

"I'm glad you asked that, Billy," Laurent says. "We have some of our best people working on that problem, the Absent Benefactor problem. We have a machine. It's got these meters on it, lights, it's fantastic, just fantastic."

"A God machine?" Billy says.

"A God *detector*," Laurent says. "Banks of lights. I think there's, I don't know, 777 LEDs. Magnificent to behold. It's on constantly. Staffed round the clock. It's designed so that if we detect Benefactor activity the thing will go off like a Christmas tree, if you'll pardon the joke. I can take you up there, if you want, it's on three, in our secure room. You could have a look."

"Does it ever—has it ever lit up?"

Laurent's smile fades. "No," he says.

"Then it's just a box, isn't it?" Billy says, with no small sadness.

Neither of them says anything for a moment. Finally Billy turns again, to go, this time for real.

"At least take my card," Laurent says. "So that when things get really bad you have a way to get in touch with me."

"I don't want your card," Billy says. "I just want cab fare."

"I'll give you one if you take the other."

And this, at last, is a proposition to which Billy can agree.

CHAPTER EIGHT

THIRD-GUESSING

WHEN NOT TO TIP • LEAVING YOUR MARK • YOUR DIGGING
THROUGH GARBAGE GAME • DESTROY ALL GOLFERS •
BEAUTIFUL MACHINES • SIMPLE PLANS • MAGIC VS. SHOTGUNS
• COMPOST FLAVOR • GOING TO FLORIDA • NOT GOING
HOME • INTO THE VESTIBULE

Before long Billy's back in Brooklyn, at Barometer. He opts not to tip his cabbie, which he feels pretty bad about, but at least it leaves him with three bucks in his pocket. Three bucks is not really enough to do much on if he can't find his shit, but he'll at least be able to get a MetroCard, or use a pay phone: reach someone, begin explaining things.

The numbers of everyone he knows, of course, are stored in his phone.

As he hurries around to the weedy alley behind Barometer, hobbled by the insistent pressure of his bladder, he tries desperately to remember Denver's number. He cycles through all the Queens exchanges he can recall in the hopes that one might jog his memory. 264? 267? For some reason, the number that keeps bobbing up, unbidden, is the Ghoul's: it has a certain playful rhythmic character that keeps it bouncing around in Billy's skull, like a billiard ball ricocheting around a china shop, annihilating every other phone number Billy has ever known.

Once he's marginally shielded from the street, he's finally able to take that piss. He luxuriates in the experience. It may be the grandest piss he's ever taken. In a burst of exuberance he opts to write his name in giant cursive across the pavement: he gets all the way through BILLY and about halfway through a magnificent R before he finally empties out. *Mine*, he thinks with satisfaction, as he looks over the result.

Okay: Take a Piss is officially off his list. Now for everything else. Let's see: Denver hates him, everyone else thinks he sucks, he's losing his job probably *right now*, he's locked out of his apartment, he can't afford his rent, Jørgen's still missing, and, oh yeah, the world is still supposed to perish by fire.

First things first. Phone, wallet, keys. *Hope you brought your Digging Through Garbage game*, he tells himself grimly as he advances on the Dumpster, *you're going to need it.*

He doesn't actually need it, he quickly learns, because a long iron security bar prevents the Dumpster's lid from being opened more than a single inch, keeping out the curious, the needy, and the desperate alike. Turns out Billy actually needed to bring his Lock-Picking game. He doesn't, of course, have any Lock-Picking game to bring.

He tries to open up the Dumpster again. He checks the lock, as if he'll notice something about it he didn't notice the first time. He considers going around to ask someone from the Barometer staff, explaining the situation, asking whether he can use their key, until he remembers that they don't open until six.

Fuck it, he thinks, not for the first time today. *I'll just wait.* Some kind of Plan B dimly takes shape in his mind, wherein he hauls ass across town and shows up to work, but the idea of showing up to work three hours late and out of uniform just to find out whether or not he's been fired is too demoralizing to really constitute an option.

So. He looks for a place to sit, a milk crate or a cardboard box, and, finding nothing, he just leans up against a utility pole.

He stands. He waits. He shuffles. He longs yearningly for the distraction of a cigarette. After three minutes, he's cold and bored, wishing for something to happen.

And that's when the Devil appears at the mouth of the alley, wearing a hefty black peacoat over a vivid shirt of electric blue, an acute contrast against the grays of the November morning. For a moment Billy is actually glad to see him, an impression that is dispelled the second Lucifer throws his arms wide in a gesture that strikes Billy as being about as welcoming as a carnivorous plant slowly peeling itself open.

"Billy!" Lucifer says. "Good morning!"

He strides into the alley, takes three steps and then pauses at Billy's signature, written in cooling piss. He stares blankly at it, as if it is a message that he cannot quite decide whether to decode. Eventually he takes a cautious step around it and proceeds on.

Once he's close enough, he repeats the arms-thrown-wide gesture. It does not improve with proximity. Billy edges away a bit. Lucifer holds the gesture for a second, then lets it devolve into an elaborate shrug, and from there into a tiny act of grooming: he picks a fleck of ash from the peacoat's heavy cuff.

"Hi," Billy says, when he's through.

"It is good to see you again, Billy Ridgeway," Lucifer says. "How *are* you?"

"Kinda shitty, actually," Billy says.

"Oh?" Lucifer says, although he sounds bored, and his gaze flicks away to something else. "What is the trouble?"

"Well, let me see," Billy says. "Oh, yeah, I was Tased last night, for starters," he says, although as this complaint leaves his mouth he recalls that Lucifer was Tased last night, too, and doesn't seem inclined to whine about it. He wonders, briefly and unhappily, whether the Devil is a better man than he.

"Ah, yes, *that*," Lucifer says. "The Right-Hand Path does enjoy its little toys, it is true. A nasty assortment of people. You know what they did to me last night, after they had me down?"

"No?" Billy says.

"They burned me alive. In the basement. A classic Manifestation Disruption maneuver, really, right out of their manual, but I would have liked to have pointed out to them that there's a way to do it without savoring the ghoulish aspects with such evident relish."

Billy blinks. "You seem to have recovered well."

"We must not dwell on the past," says Lucifer. "Let us look forward instead. You'll recall that you pledged to have developed a response to my proposition by this morning."

"Oh, yeah," Billy says, frowning. He always forgets that his stalling mechanisms have a finite life span.

"I think," Lucifer says, and then he pauses, composing the utterance. "I think that we have reached a rather specific point, Billy Ridgeway, a juncture, if you will. At this point, you must look within yourself, deeply, and ask yourself which future you want. A future in which—"

Billy doesn't need to hear the rest. He has an answer. He hasn't looked within himself all that deeply, not deeply at all, really, but he can find this answer in the shallows, and he feels certain that he won't get a better answer at the end of a more careful and sustained reflection.

"I just want my life back," Billy answers. "Future? Shit, at this point I'd be happiest if I just got to go back to what my life was three days ago. Where I don't have to deal with Timothy Ollard, or the Right-Hand Path, or, well, or you. Where I have a job, and some friends, and my *wallet*, and my *keys*, and maybe a girlfriend if I play my cards right, and don't have to worry about everyone in the world being *burned alive*. So if there's some funky satanic thing you can do with time, I'm going to ask you to do it, cause I just want to go *back*."

Lucifer gives him a long look. "No you *don't*," he finally says.

"I beg your pardon?" Billy says. For all Lucifer's odd misrecognition of certain social graces, this is the first thing he's said that Billy's actually taken some level of offense to.

"You *think* you want to go back to that life," Lucifer says. "It seems safe and familiar. But Billy." He leans down a little, gets his face closer to Billy's, and begins to speak more softly. "I want you to really *think* for a minute, about what you really wanted for yourself, once upon a time, before you told yourself that it wasn't possible, before you tamed your hope and your ambition."

"Okay?" Billy says, and his mind goes completely blank.

"You're not doing it," Lucifer says. "I can tell, just from looking at you."

"Sorry?"

"Billy. I want you to think. I want you to think back. Not back to three days ago, but back to when you were sixteen. In Ohio. I want you to remember your first job. What was your first job. Tell me."

"My first job," Billy says. "I worked at the driving range."

"You worked at the driving range," Lucifer says. "What were your job duties?"

"My—job duties? Uh. I drove a golf cart back and forth, collecting balls. For like hours at a time. It was a pretty shitty job."

"That's right, Billy," Lucifer says. "It was a *shitty job*. You didn't even like golf."

"No. I hated golf. And I hated golfers. I used permanent marker to make a T-shirt that said DESTROY ALL GOLFERS. And they didn't like me either. They used to aim for my cart while I was driving around out there."

"Of course they did," Lucifer says. "My point here, Billy, is not to ask you to relive whatever you suffered at the slings and arrows of the ignorant, but rather to remind you of the reward that awaited you at the end of that summer. Your girlfriend of the time was saving up to take a trip to Zurich and your best friend was saving up to buy his first used car. You were also saving your money, Billy. Do you remember? Do you remember what those long hours on the golf course bought you?"

"Yes," Billy says, quietly, after a minute of looking down at his battered canvas sneakers.

"What was it?" Lucifer says, his voice almost a whisper now.

"It was an Olivetti Valentine S," Billy says.

"An Olivetti Valentine S," Lucifer repeats. "A typewriter. You didn't need a typewriter. Your family had a computer. So why did you buy an Olivetti?"

"It was—" Billy says, his mood sullen, complexly tangled. "It was a beautiful machine."

"That's not why," Lucifer says. "If you wanted a beautiful machine you could have saved for a Harley-Davidson. You could have saved for a Braun stereo. But instead you saved for an Olivetti typewriter. Tell me why, Billy."

"Because it's—"

"Tell me."

"Because," Billy says, "because real writers used typewriters."

"That's right," says Lucifer.

Billy remembers the draft of an early first novel that he wrote on that typewriter, his senior year of high school and first year of college, this thing about the murder of a young man in a quiet rural town. He still has it in a box somewhere, terrible, probably, but he finished it, three hundred pages hammered out on that Olivetti, and he remembers the feeling of confidence and authority that came from using that machine to make marks on paper. It's been a long time since he's been able to produce those feelings so sustainably.

"You envisioned a future for yourself, then, didn't you?" Lucifer says.

Billy had. That senior year of high school was when he first started drinking coffee, and he remembers hooking up a Mr. Coffee in his room at home, up on the third floor, and he would wake on cold mornings before the sun was up, before he'd need to trudge to where the school bus would pick him up, and he would sit at his desk, in a ratty plum-colored bathrobe, drinking coffee and smoking his first-ever cigarettes and clacking out pages, and he would feel certain that, in some important way, he was making a template for the rest of his life.

He also remembers selling that typewriter, five years ago, on eBay, a hard month, between jobs, remembers the good feeling of an extra hundred and fifty dollars in the bank, even though it disappeared quickly into a few overdue bills, a new shirt for a job interview, groceries, beer, condoms, smokes, a couple of books.

Lucifer goes on: "You aren't allowing yourself to feel that hope again, that ambition, Billy. I promise you the kind of future you really want and you throw it away in favor of *take me back to three days ago*? What did you have three days ago that you won't have in the future that I'm offering you? A *job*? Another shitty job? Your *wallet*? Your *keys*? These things are all replaceable: a few days' hassle, nothing more. Your friends? You're thirty years old, Billy Ridgeway, you don't get to be thirty years old without passing through times when your friends are mad at you. It's passed before and it'll pass now. A girlfriend? Denver? You think she won't *come back to you* when your novel gets published?"

"Maybe not," Billy says.

"Maybe not," Lucifer says, his voice down to a soft hiss, almost drowned out by the rumbling traffic nearby. "But don't you think you would be able to find someone *better*? Do you think you don't *deserve* someone better?"

"I like Denver," Billy says. He does not say *love*.

"Think, though, Billy, think about other women. Think about the women you didn't pursue in the past because you thought they were *out of your league*. Think about being in the league that they're in."

"That's—" Billy says. "That seems creepy and wrong."

"Wrong? You deserve it, Billy. You deserve to be *up a notch* by now."

"I don't," Billy says. "I don't deserve it. I didn't do the work." He remembers the speech he gave himself yesterday. "If I want that? The future you're describing? With the book, and the—the women and stuff? If I want that future, I have to get there on my own."

"No one gets there on their own, Billy," Lucifer says, his normal tone of voice returning. He draws back from Billy, hooks his thumbs into the heavy lapels of the peacoat. "That's not how it works."

Billy considers this.

"Besides," Lucifer says. "If you do this, you'll have saved the world. I would hope that you could categorize whatever ancillary benefits might emerge as things you had *earned*."

"Maybe," Billy says. "But what exactly would I be doing? I still don't get that part. How exactly would I be getting the thing from the dude?"

"Let's get off the street," Lucifer says. An expression of deep appetite spreads across his features. "Have you had breakfast? I know a place."

They end up taking a quick cab to an Algerian creperie. They settle in on tufted ottomans and a lean man with the most impeccably groomed mustache Billy has ever seen brings them an octagonal tin samovar of what Billy can immediately tell is really good coffee. After his first sip, Lucifer begins speaking with more animation than Billy's ever seen in him.

"Until Ollard dispels all the seals," Lucifer says, "the Neko still, in some real sense, *belongs* to me. I can *sense* it. I can't tell you exactly where it is, but I can tell you that it is likely underground."

"Like buried?" Billy says.

"Not buried," Lucifer says. "More like in a basement. So you won't need to waste time going through the upper levels of the tower. You get in, you go down."

"How am I even going to *get in* in the first place? If I were, in fact, to actually agree to go in."

"What do you mean?" Lucifer says. "You've seen through the cloak. You go in through the door."

"Okay, but, seriously, am I crazy to think that Ollard might just not, you know, be a hundred percent cool with me just walking in there and taking his cat?"

"My cat," Lucifer says. "But no, he probably won't be."

"So what do I do? When he tries to stop me?"

Lucifer shrugs. "You fight him."

"I *fight* him?"

"You fight him like the fate of the world depended on it."

"You have the wrong guy," Billy says. "I haven't thrown a punch in, like, ever."

"This might help," Lucifer says. He reaches into the pocket of his coat and takes out a little cylinder of self-defense spray, which he slides across the table. It has a key ring on it.

"This?" Billy says. "Is it magical?"

"No," Lucifer says.

"So, really? That's the entire plan? Walk in the front door, pepper-spray Ollard, grab the cat and run?"

"Billy," Lucifer says. "It is dangerous to overplan. Plans, by definition, are rigid, and it is to our advantage to remain as fluid as possible. Thus, as you said: you walk in the front door. You find the Neko. If you need to, you fight Ollard. If you encounter any difficulties, simply retreat, and you and I will make a new plan that accounts for whatever difficulty we have encountered. That is the plan. Simplicity, Billy. The great virtue of a simple plan is that it leaves one with fewer, far fewer, things to fuck up. You can do this. Now: eat."

Billy's savory lamb crepes hit the table, and he wolfs them down. They are the best thing he's eaten in days, weeks maybe, and he feels a sudden swell of gratitude. He remembers Anil's gag from the other night: *a small, good thing in a time like this*. But there's something to that. Good food: that alone maybe makes the world worth saving. His mood picks up a little. Maybe the Devil is right; maybe he can do this. He stifles a belch with his napkin.

"Okay. Okay," he says, in a very small voice. "I have to tell you, though: I'm *scared*. I saw that tower. It's scary."

"Well," says Lucifer. He takes a sip of coffee. "It's designed to look scary. It's an illusion."

"It's a really fucking good illusion," Billy says.

"Yes," Lucifer says, "because Timothy Ollard is a really fucking good illusionist."

Billy frowns, tries out an alternate wording, frowns again. He takes the tiny pepper-spray canister into his hand.

"You're afraid," Lucifer says, after watching this for a minute, "that Ollard is going to kill you."

"Yes," Billy says, a little relieved to have it out there, on the table.

"The You Getting Killed part," Lucifer says. "You see? I remembered that."

"Awesome?" Billy says.

"Ollard will not attempt to kill you. It's a delicate time for him; while he works on the Neko he needs to lie as low as possible. Using magic to take a human life is—attention-getting. Disruptive. Sloppy."

"But what if he doesn't use magic? What if he uses, like, a shotgun?"

"Even sloppier," Lucifer says.

"Sloppy but possible."

"Not possible," Lucifer says. "You have forgotten the details of our arrangement. You will be provided with a ward that will leave Ollard unable to harm you, by magical means or otherwise. Speaking of which."

Lucifer downs the last of his coffee, and then reaches into the inside pocket of his peacoat and draws out a cigar tube.

"Here," Lucifer says, unscrewing the end of the tube. He draws out the cigar and steers it firmly into Billy's mouth. Billy sputters a bit around it, pulls it out and weighs it in his hand. It's hefty, like something a billionaire might light with a bundle of money. It has no band or other identifying mark.

"You'll want to smoke that," Lucifer says, rising, using the edge of his hand to smooth the front of his shirt.

"What, why?" Billy says, looking from the cigar to Lucifer and back again.

"The ward requires a variety of herbs and other assorted components to be transmuted by fire, the ceremonial smoke entering the body of the individual to be warded. The traditional swinging thurible is a little conspicuous, as I'm sure you'd agree."

"A giant *cigar* is conspicuous. It's *illegal* for me to smoke that in a restaurant; maybe you didn't get the memo."

"This place has a back room we can use," Lucifer says. "That's part of why I wanted to come here." He drops some bills on the table and calls to the proprietor: "Hadadj! Back room?"

"For you," the lean man replies drily from the front counter, "anything." He is punching numbers into a calculator. He does not look up.

"Follow me," Lucifer says to Billy. Billy pushes himself off the ottoman clumsily and follows Lucifer through a beaded curtain. They pass the restrooms and open a door bearing an EMPLOYEES ONLY placard. Behind it is a small, harshly-lit office almost entirely taken up by a steel desk and a filing cabinet, both of which are obscured under the burden of slumping piles of three-ringed notebooks. A portly man wearing a gold chain and white earbuds sits at the desk, leafing through what appears to be a catalog of men's shoes. He looks up at Lucifer and glares with contempt and distaste. Lucifer ignores him, doesn't even spare him a look, and instead crosses the room and opens another door.

Billy follows briskly. The back room is a cramped, dim space, smelling strongly of lentils. Two overstuffed recliners marred with what Billy hopes are soup spillages squat on a dingy Persian rug, with an elaborate brass hookah placed between them. The chairs face a flat-screen TV, which has a stack of Algerian-market VHS cassettes and Xbox games heaped in front of it like an offering. Lucifer takes up one of the hoses from the hookah, sniffs it, makes an assessing face, and then replaces it.

"Sit," Lucifer says. Billy sits, the cigar still in his hand. Lucifer takes the cigar, lops one end off it with a handheld cutter that he's produced from somewhere, and directs it back into Billy's mouth, whereupon Billy promptly takes it out again.

"I still haven't said that I'm doing this," Billy says.

"I understand," Lucifer says. "Nonetheless, I see no reason to postpone your preparation. It is my sincerest belief that once the pieces are all in place you will act with no further hesitation. Regardless, it is probably a good idea for you to receive the ward: now that more people know that you and I are . . . affiliated, word may get to Ollard before too long, which will put you at risk, risk that this ward will mitigate."

"Affiliated?" Billy says. "We're not affiliated."

"Shall we commence?" Lucifer says.

He points at the cigar with a tiny, steel lighter which has somehow surreptitiously replaced his handheld cutter, and then he points the lighter at his own face, encouraging Billy to mirror the gesture by lifting the cigar to his mouth. Which he does.

"Very good," says Lucifer, in a tone one might use to speak to a dog. He leans in and presses a button on the lighter, which emits a blue flame with no perceptible sound. Billy awkwardly angles the cigar into the flame, and takes a long pull, which immediately dispels whatever goodwill toward the world the lamb crepes and coffee had helped him to muster.

"Oh," Billy says, a huge cloud of rank smoke rolling out of his mouth. "That's bad."

"My apologies," says Lucifer.

"It's like smoking compost."

Lucifer regards him.

"It's like smoking compost through a raccoon," Billy says. He sticks out his tongue, scrapes it against his upper row of teeth in an attempt to scour off the dank, fungal taste. "It's like you put a fur-lined shit in my mouth."

"It will keep you alive," Lucifer says.

And with that, he struggles his way through the rest of the cigar. He doesn't feel like a billionaire. He doesn't feel like some badass toughening up before a combat mission. He feels like a kid who got caught smoking a cigarette and was forced to finish the whole pack. The decorative pattern in the rug begins to swim and waver disorientingly. Billy stares through watering eyes behind the TV at a poster that he hadn't noticed when they first came in, depicting the full roster of the New York Mets. Their faces appear sallow, dead-eyed, cheerless. Billy blinks repeatedly, as though if he exerts enough willpower he can make them resolve instead into happy Yankees. Another long suck on the cigar and some violet form begins to bloom in his head, like ink blossoming in water. He hears a voice, distant, drowned in buzzing, as though reaching him only through a thick curtain of flies: he turns his head and sees Lucifer talking on the phone, saying words, words that sound somehow familiar, that Billy feels like he should be able to parse. After a minute of turning them over in his mind, Billy manages to make the syllables resolve into an address, the address of the tower, in Chelsea.

"I've arranged for a cab," Lucifer says to Billy, placing the phone back in his pocket. The words wind their way through Billy's consciousness, only slowly, fighting through the thicket of noise. Less flies now. More like the massed baying of wolves.

Before Billy's head fully clears, Lucifer has marched him out of the tiny room, back through the office and corridor and restaurant, past Hadadj and out onto the street again. The cab arrives and Lucifer pops the door open, steers Billy into the seat.

"Just—wait—just do me one thing," Billy says groggily. "You can change my mind about stuff, right? You can—what was it you said?—simple binary beliefs? You can change those?"

"I can," Lucifer says, looking down at him.

"Well—can you—can you just change it so that I think that I'm making the right decision here? I'd really feel a lot better going into this if I knew I wasn't—fucking up."

"I don't think you're a fuck-up, Billy," Lucifer says, with what sounds like real sincerity.

"No?" Billy says.

"No," Lucifer says. "So rather than inscribe more beliefs into your tender brain, I want to simply urge you to stop second-guessing yourself, for once. If you look at your life, you'll see that it's never been your *decisions* that have pointed you in the wrong direction, but rather your *resistance* to your decisions. Every time. So: Trust yourself. And watch your fingers."

And with that, Lucifer slams the door, and thumps a palm on the trunk of the cab, and Billy's off, headed toward Chelsea.

Billy spends the ride looking out the window and mulling over what the Devil said. *It's never been your decisions, but your resistance to your decisions?* It had a sort of horoscopy applicability that made it ring true at first, but the more Billy subjects it to careful scrutiny, the less he thinks it actually makes sense.

Stop second-guessing! says the part of him that really wants to latch on to the Devil's diagnosis.

But that's just it, says the more rational part of him. *Wasn't your first instinct to just say no to the Devil? So agreeing, today:* that *would be the part where you're second-guessing yourself. And that would make* this *batch of reservations technically third-guessing. The Devil didn't say don't* third-guess *yourself.*

Well, he has to admit, *that's true.*

"Okay," says the driver, pulling up on the curb next to the gallery with the Styrofoam shapes in the window. "Here we are."

Billy peers miserably out at the Seafood Warehousing building, which looks dense and imposing even when it's not in its Warlock House form. He makes no move to get out of the cab.

"Hey," he says to the cabbie, suddenly. "That guy I was with: he's paying for this ride, right?"

"Yep," says the cabbie.

"So if I wanted to go somewhere else? If I wanted to have you drop me off in Queens, instead?"

"Yeah, whatever, buddy," says the cabbie. "I'll take you all the way to Florida, just say the word."

Florida! thinks Billy, for a second. *That could be good!* But no. Instead he thinks of Denver. *You could go to her. You could go to her, and apologize, and explain. She would understand.*

Or you could go through with this plan, says his internal counterpoint. He's not sure if this counts as second-guessing, or third-guessing, or fifth-guessing. *You could save the world. Be a real writer. Have a different life.*

He remembers Lucifer saying *Do you think you don't deserve someone better?*

But I don't want someone better, he thinks. *I want Denver.*

Then go to her, he tells himself.

And he's about to tell the cabbie to take him to Queens when someone he recognizes walks by outside. Of all people. It's Anton Cirrus, marching along with a businesslike stride, his trench coat billowing in the wind. Billy's blood begins moving. He thinks the same word he thought last night at Barometer: *enemy.* He feels a sudden urge to confront Cirrus, to engage him in argument, to come out on top in some exchange of verbal jabs. To *win,* for once.

"One second," Billy says to the cabbie. And he lets himself out.

"Cirrus!" Billy shouts at Cirrus's back, which has gotten a good ten paces ahead of Billy by this point. "Anton Cirrus!"

Anton stops and turns, and when he sees Billy he wrinkles his face into a mask of distaste, as though Billy has just opened the conversation with a robust fart.

"Do I know you?" he asks.

"Do you—" Billy begins, incredulous, and then rage throttles his voice and he goes silent. *I'm going to kill you,* he thinks. *I'm simply going to kill you.* "Yeah, you know me, you fuck," he finally manages. "The storehouse of tired forms and stale devices?"

"Well," Anton says. He manifests a plainly insincere smile.

"This *is* a pleasure. The great Billy Ridgeway, fresh off his triumphant Barometer reading, deigns to make a street appearance to the humble critic."

Billy's face burns at the mention of the reading. "I was interrupted," Billy says. "It was just about to get interesting."

"Please," says Anton. "The story of how you met the Devil? Everybody has a story about how they met the Devil."

Billy opens his mouth to reply, and then he pauses. He gnaws on Anton's response for a second. Something seems off about it. Laurent said that the audience didn't remember anything past the punch line of Billy's joke. Therefore, Anton shouldn't remember that Billy had even mentioned the Devil. And if Anton does know that Billy spoke about the Devil, then he must not have had his memory wiped. Which means—which means what?

Billy has no idea. But the discrepancy provides some kind of opening, in any case, so he lunges into it, making his voice go all fake casual: "Oh, you remember that? That's very interesting. Not too many people remember that, I hear."

Anton looks quizzically at Billy for a second, but then Billy gets to watch him have the realization that he's tipped his hand somehow: he looks away, clicking his tongue minutely against the roof of his mouth, annoyed over having revealed—something. Billy's still not sure what, exactly, he's revealed, but seeing Anton pissed at himself is a little more information, a second slip, in a way, and Billy revels in receipt of it, finally having the opportunity to look stupid Anton Cirrus right in his stupid face and think *Not so goddamn smart now, are you?*

So, Billy thinks, his interpretation shifting into overdrive, if Anton Cirrus didn't have his memory wiped, that means—he's working with the Right-Hand Path? But that doesn't make sense:

Why would Anton Cirrus have preemptively panned the reading if he were working for the very people who set the reading up in the first place?

So if he's not working with the Right-Hand Path—the so-called good guys—that means that maybe he's—with the bad guy? With Ollard. Which squares all too nicely with why Anton Cirrus would be here, randomly outside of the magical tower that no one is supposed to know about.

Before Billy can get any further with this line of thought, Anton reaches into his pocket, gets his phone out, and begins working at the screen. Texting again, it seems, which makes anger flare up in Billy. Right at the moment when he's about to tell Anton to knock it the fuck off Anton pockets the phone and speaks: "It was pretty stupid of you, you know, to point out the Adversary in a room full of Right-Hand Path goons."

"You call it stupid," Billy says, groping, a little out of his element. "I call it—unpredictable?"

Anton looks up, as if trying to tell whether or not Billy is for real. "Yes, well," Anton says. He rocks back on his heels. "We'll see where your unpredictability gets you. I got twenty bucks that says that in the end it will be indistinguishable from stupidity."

"You're on," Billy says.

"Super," Anton says.

They stand there, regarding one another silently, in a stalemate. Anton has about five inches on Billy, which gives his gaze a permanent sense of disdain; Billy tries to counter that with a particular jut of his chin that he hopes looks pugnacious. They hold their respective poses until the cabbie, having grown impatient with idling at the curb, leans on the horn. They both jolt. Billy wheels around and holds up a finger—*one minute*—and returns his attention to Anton, who lets out a long, elaborate sigh.

"What are you doing here, Billy?" he asks, wearily.

"I could ask the same of you," Billy says.

"You could," Anton says. "Except there's an important difference between you and me: I know what I'm doing here. And you clearly don't."

"Don't I?" Billy says.

"No. You don't. Go home, Billy. Go home and work on your shitty novel or your terrible short stories or whatever it is you're working on."

But I'm locked out, Billy thinks, although he doesn't say this. The cabbie gives a short, curt blast of the horn; Billy ignores it, keeping his eyes on Anton.

"Go home," Anton says, a note of real entreaty entering his voice, "and be happy with your tiny little life. Because I guarantee you that if you continue with whatever it is you think you're doing, your life is going to get a whole lot worse."

"Uh." Billy turns, the temptation to check on the cab having grown too great, and he watches it pull away from the curb, roll slowly around the corner, and disappear. "That's what your mom said?" he rejoinders, distracted.

Anton Cirrus gives the long sigh again. Billy didn't notice, last night, just how sad Anton's eyes look behind the designer glasses. "I gave you my advice," he says. "Do what you want; my conscience is clear." He turns into the chilly wind and continues his brisk departure.

"Hey," Billy shouts. "Hey, I'm not through with you." But Anton doesn't look back, and when Billy looks deep within himself to try to find the winning taunt, he comes up with absolutely nothing at all.

So then Billy is alone, standing on the sidewalk in front of Warlock House, doing the trick that allows him to see the single red door, wreathed in calligraphy. All he has to do is just take three steps, turn the doorknob, and let himself in.

Go home, he thinks to himself, echoing Anton. *Just go home.*

You know what? Fuck Anton Cirrus.

He takes one step forward.

Your life is going to get a whole lot worse.

But maybe not. Maybe this is the point where his life gets better. He has a ward that protects him. He has a simple plan, unfuckable by design.

One way or another, my life will be different.

He takes another step forward, grips the knob, turns it. The door, not locked, opens out, revealing a tiny, grim vestibule, the size of a closet, with some ordinary street dirt and paper trash collected in its corners. Set into the far wall is another door, this one lacking the ornate trappings of the outer one: no bloodred paint, no crawling glyphs, just a plain metal door. Not so scary.

And if you go through there and never come out? Billy asks himself. He contemplates the prospect for a minute, tries to figure whether anyone would really even miss him. His dad, maybe. Everyone else? Denver? Anil and the Ghoul? Maybe he's just depressed, but he can't see them still thinking of him at all after a few weeks, a month or two at best. Springtime will return to the city, and as the snow recedes and drains away so will their memories of him; years from now maybe they'll have a dim remembrance of a funny guy who maybe showed some signs of talent on occasion but never really pulled it together, who hung out with them for a while and got them to crack a smile every now and then, but not really the type of person who you miss, once he's gone.

Okay, Billy thinks. *You can do this.* Something rises inside him. Maybe it's that animal part of him, the part that likes being bigger and stronger, that likes being powerful. Maybe he's ready, at long last, for a fight. He takes a final step, into the vestibule. And then he crosses it, without hesitation, opens the metal door, and enters.

CHAPTER NINE

THE LOOSENING

WELCOME TO STARBUCKS • CAHOOTS • THE PROBLEM WITH
HARD-ASSES • WHEN NOT TO TIP • NOT OKAY • SOOTHING
VOICE: ON • GROWING UP FASTER • HUMAN CUISINE IN TOTAL
• NO MORE ORGASMS • PANDAS ARE BORING •
CONNOISSEUR OF PAIN

He's in a Starbucks.

Billy frowns. He double-checks, just for the sake of his sanity, looking back through the metal door he's just passed through: he can see the dirty vestibule, and then the red door that leads back out to Chelsea. It's still open a crack; he can still see a little sliver of street. And he looks back at the Starbucks. It looks exactly like every other Starbucks he's ever seen: a counter with an aproned staff working behind it, busying themselves at various beverage-producing apparatuses. It has the same impulse items flanking the register: mints, CDs, individually wrapped madeleines that Billy has always been pretty sure are only there because someone in Starbucks's upper echelons thinks that the Proust reference is clever. Soul music sung by a white British person comes out through unobtrusive speakers.

He turns and looks at the tables, to check out whether there's a clientele in here or what. And sitting there in one of the big overstuffed leather chairs, dressed in a tawny corduroy suit, holding what appears to be a Caramel Macchiato, staring right into Billy, is Timothy Ollard. Billy jumps.

Ollard smiles slightly, places the macchiato on the table, wipes one palm with the other, then rises. He does not advance, a fact for which Billy is incredibly grateful.

"Billy *Ridgeway*," Ollard says, rocking back on his heels. "I've been expecting you."

"How is that possible?" Billy blurts, dismayed that he doesn't even have whatever questionable advantage might be conferred by the element of surprise. "Have you been reading my mind? 'Cause at this point I'd kind of prefer for people to just stay out of there, thank you very much."

Ollard surveys Billy's perturbed demeanor. "Billy," he says. "One thing you should have learned by now. You don't need to reach for a complicated answer when a simple one will do." He reaches into the breast pocket of the suit and pulls out a phone, activates it with a finger-swipe. "I got a text," he says. "FYI," he reads from the screen, "Ridgeway is here."

Billy remembers Anton Cirrus, outside, fiddling with his phone while they argued.

"So," Billy says, trying to add it all up in his mind. "Cirrus."

"Yes," Ollard says.

"You and Cirrus."

"Yes."

"You're . . . in cahoots?"

"Cahoots?" Ollard says, amusement ringing faintly in his voice. Billy feels fury swell within him; language is supposed to be the thing he's good at. He almost pulls out the spray to give Ollard a good blast of it just on principle. "Not *cahoots*," Ollard says, finally. "Think of him as an *independent contractor*. You could say a *gun for hire* if you wanted something with a little more *pizzazz*. With the Right-Hand Path setting up their little literary production it's useful to know someone like Anton, who can knock it right back down again."

"Why would he help you?"

"I sought him out. I showed him that partnering with me would provide him with certain advantages. Men like Cirrus enjoy advantages. Maybe to a fault."

"Does he know," Billy says, "that you're planning to burn up the world?"

"He knows that I have the Neko," Ollard says, showing no surprise that Billy is familiar with his plan. "He knows that it is a source of plentiful energy. He knows it's unique and valuable and that important people are interested in it, and I think that represents a line beyond which Cirrus cannot see very clearly. The crest of the hill, in a way. See, that's the thing about men like Cirrus—"

"Look," Billy says, "I don't really care about men like Cirrus." He says this, although if he were being totally honest he would have to admit that something in him seizes greedily at the prospect that Cirrus's takedown of him on Bladed Hyacinth was maybe less about the merits of his writing, or lack thereof, and more about some kind of chess move against the Right-Hand Path. "I'm here for the Neko. Where is it?"

Ollard looks flatly at Billy for a long moment. "Why don't you get yourself a drink?" he asks.

"I don't want a drink."

"Billy," says Ollard. "I've only just met you, but I can tell that this hard-ass routine doesn't suit you. It's fake."

Billy feels a bit stung by this, and Ollard must notice, because he holds up a finger in a wait-one-moment-before-you-react gesture. "Hard-asses," he says, "are boring. They see one route toward what they want, and barrel straight at it. It's embarrassing. They're easy to sidestep, easy to trip up. They don't make satisfying opponents. If you're not a hard-ass it means that there's some small hope that you'll be intelligent. And an intelligent opponent gives me at least something to savor."

"Maybe the most intelligent thing an opponent could do, though," Billy says, "is to *pretend* that they're a hard-ass, to . . . *lull* you . . . into . . . a false sense of security."

"You're not doing a very good job of pretending, if that's your strategy."

"Maybe my *strategy* . . . is to *pretend* to be doing a bad job of pretending, so that you'll *think* I'm pretending, when in *reality* I'm actually . . . *smarter* than that."

"Well," Ollard says, a little wearily, "yes, that would be one strategy. But if you're such a master strategist, you can sit with me, and drink some coffee, and we can talk. Intelligently."

Billy considers this. He takes a step backward toward the counter and waits a second to see if Ollard takes this opportunity to spring across the space separating them. He sort of half expects Ollard to sprout giant razored talons or something. But all Ollard does is wave Billy toward the counter with his fingertips, settle back into the armchair, and sip from his macchiato.

Well, Billy thinks, *okay*. If there's been one good thing that's come out of this week it's been all the coffee. He approaches the counter.

"Welcome to Starbucks," says the young man stationed there. "May I take your order?" The man's voice is cheerful but there's something strangulated in it that startles Billy, gets him to pay a little more attention. He looks the Starbucks Guy in the face. The guy—a blond kid, can't be a day over twenty-one, wispy hints of a starter goatee around his mouth—is smiling at him expectantly, but something in the smile looks fixed, knocking Billy from *alert* to *on edge*.

"Uh, sure," says Billy, suspiciously. "Can I get a … Grande Americano?"

"Grande Americano!" the kid hollers to one of the other workers back there, a woman, who jerks into motion with the gracelessness of a dusty animatronic figure, a robotic Abe Lincoln in a forgotten Hall of Presidents.

Billy looks into the kid's puffy, red-rimmed eyes and spots the raw terror in them. They come so close to screaming *Call the police* that Billy reflexively pats his pockets, looking for his phone, which of course is still in a Dumpster somewhere.

The guy rattles off how much Billy owes, and Billy looks over his shoulder to see if Ollard is going to offer to pick up the tab on this. Billy figures that if you have your own personal Starbucks with the employees held in some kind of terrifying mystic bondage then you might as well make all the coffee complimentary. After all, you can't exactly be expecting the place to meet a quarterly profit projection. But Ollard is paying no attention: he's gazing out the windows. *Out* is perhaps the wrong way to put it: it's really more *at*, because the windows are great panes of solid blackness.

Billy pulls the three dollars out of his pocket, unfolds them, and hands them off to the terrorized-looking kid, who returns him a handful of change. Billy considers dropping the coins in the tip jar but he has the sense that no one working here is going to get around to spending their tips anytime soon. He makes eye contact with the cashier for a second in which both of them understand that their transaction has concluded, that there is nothing more that Billy can or will do for this kid right now. Billy's the one to break the glance, and as he pockets his change he's scorched by a rising shame.

"Grande Americano at the bar," shouts the young woman at the other end of the counter, with that same fracturing cheer. Billy makes the mistake of looking in her eyes as she slides his drink across to him, checking in the hope that maybe the kid was a one-off, but no: she has the exact same *please-help-me* look, the exact same fake frozen smile.

Billy wonders for a moment whether his ward protects him against this kind of enslavement. Tries to remember exactly what Lucifer said. Ollard is unable to harm him—what was it—through magical means or otherwise? The Starbucks workers don't seem *harmed*, exactly, but it certainly looks like their experience is sucking. Maybe he should just get out of here while he can?

But when Billy turns to face Ollard again all he sees is a guy, just sitting there in his corduroy suit. He looks placid, really, almost bland. Pasty. Wan. It's hard for Billy to feel like he's actually in danger. So Billy goes and sits in the other overstuffed chair, which leaves him positioned at about a forty-five degree angle to Ollard. He puts his Americano on a little round table. Knowing that it was served to him by zomboid slaves makes it seem a little creepy. So instead of drinking it, he just sits there, looking at the black panes, waiting for Ollard to speak. The two of them sit side by side, staring. At blackness. This lasts for about a second before Billy begins to find it disturbing.

"So," Billy says, groping around for a way to kick-start the conversation. "You must really . . . like Starbucks, I guess?"

Ollard shows no signs of having heard the question, for a long minute. The song by the British soul singer ends, and then it begins again, a second time.

"I think better when I'm in here," Ollard says, finally. "I've spent most of the last year in one Starbucks or another, thinking. They're all over the city, now, did you know that?"

"Um," Billy says. "Yes, I guess I did."

"I used to alternate between seven different Starbucks," Ollard says. "A different one for each day of the week. Of course, now that I have the Neko, I haven't been able to get out. It's not . . . safe for me outside any longer. So I decided to set one up here." He turns toward Billy and smiles weakly.

"Starbucks every day, huh?" Billy says.

"For hours. Hours every day."

"That's a lot of thinking."

"It is. That's the thing I'm good at. Thinking. That's all there is left to do, really."

"Yeah, um." Billy's still trying to find his grounding in this conversation. He feels a bit like he's on an awkward date. He has begun to detect an odor, like meat left out in the sun, which he assumes is coming from Ollard, and he notices that the corduroy suit, which looked so sharp from a distance, is actually quite dirty, filthy even, going nearly translucent in spots from grease and wear.

"So," Billy tries. "What do you think about?"

Ollard makes a sucking sound with his mouth before he answers. "What do I think about," he says. "I think about the world. The world and all that is in it."

"Okay," Billy says. "That's cool."

"Is it?"

"Sure."

"I don't think so," Ollard says. "I don't think the world is cool."

"No?"

"No. I think—and I have considered the problem at some length—that the world, ultimately, is repulsive."

"Okay," Billy says.

"It's not okay," Ollard says. "I am grateful to this place, though. To Starbucks. It helped me to think, during this time. It helped me to *focus*. It *reminded* me. Every day. Of the world. Of just how little the world has to offer."

His expression suddenly cracks. His eyes clench shut; a network of deep lines emerges across his forehead; his mouth tenses, widening into a distorted black hole, rimmed with bad teeth. You'd think if you were an all-powerful magician who'd been alive for a century you'd at least be able to take the time to fix your terrible teeth.

"Hey," Billy says, in a voice that he hopes is therapeutic. He momentarily considers reaching out, putting a hand on Ollard's shoulder, although the idea creeps him out too much for him to get far with it.

"Ollard," Billy says, expending enormous effort to sound very calm. At this point he's past thinking that this conversation is like an awkward date; he's instead realized that it's more like a hostage negotiation. He tries to remember anything he knows about hostage negotiation, any movie where a hostage negotiation situation was handled effectively. He gets a vision of Denzel Washington, stern and commanding, but he can't come up with any immediate way to put it to use.

"Timothy," he tries, with his soothing voice still on. "Where is the Neko?"

"I'm so tired," Ollard says. He presses the heels of his hands into his face, as though he's stuffing thoughts back into his head. "I'm tired," he says again.

"We're all tired," Billy says. "Take me to the Neko."

Ollard draws a long, shuddering breath, and then looks back at Billy, his face having regained some of its composure. "You want to see the Neko?" he says.

"Well, yeah," Billy says. "I mean. Eventually. We can keep talking for a bit if you want."

"It doesn't matter," Ollard says, rising. "We can talk on the way."

"All right then. Let's go." Billy claps his hands on his thighs and gets out of the chair, leaving the creepy Americano on the little round table, untouched. They walk behind the counter, weaving between the three workers, who are involved in polishing nonexistent spots off the machines at the bar. Ollard hooks around into the supply room, and just past the big industrial refrigerator and the sinks, right in the spot where labor practices posters should be hanging in mandatory display, the Starbucks abruptly opens into a long corridor, grim and dingy, its walls a sort of dulled avocado, gone rippled from layers upon layers of paint. It has a dusty whiff about it, like a rarely visited back wing of an underfunded natural history museum, like a stuffed bison slowly rotting in an alcove.

"I've been alive for a long time," Ollard says, as the two of them enter the corridor. His voice wavers.

"I'd heard that," Billy says. They're passing doors on either side; Billy wonders what he'd find if he opened them. "Lucifer said you'd been alive for like eighty years or something?"

"Oh, longer than that," Ollard says. "Before that I was just off the radar, I guess. I was . . . very subtle."

"It's a good trick," Billy says, encouragingly. He looks over his shoulder, back down the hallway, making sure that he can still see the Starbucks supply room. If he can make it back there he can make it back to the door that leads out to the street, and for some reason he believes that if he makes it back out to the street, he'll be safe.

"A good trick," Ollard says. "Is it?"

"Sure," Billy says. "Staying young? You could make a million bucks if you figured out a way to teach people how to do it."

"I'll tell you how to do it," Ollard says.

"Okay," Billy says. Against his better judgment his interest is piqued.

"You learn how to *take*," Ollard says. "That's all there is to it, really."

"Uh," Billy says.

"That was what I wanted," Ollard says, "as soon as I was old enough to really be aware that *I would die*. As soon as I became aware that I would die I also became aware that there were people *younger than me*. They were—further away from death than I was. And I decided that I wanted what they had. Their youth: I wanted to take it. And I had to figure it out. How to take it. You can do it subtly. Small doses. I take a year from someone; I gain a year. It's only a year. Sometimes you can take a few at once. Young people hardly even notice. Most of them want to grow up faster anyway. You have to be careful, though. You take too many years at once and you create—aberrations."

Billy doesn't want to hear about aberrant children. He wants to get the Neko and get the hell out of here. They reach the end of the corridor, which terminates in a heavy metal door. Through a tiny window, crisscrossed with safety wire, Billy can see a stairwell.

"Regardless," Ollard says. He yanks on the door handle and the door squeals open. "It was, for some years, a satisfying puzzle to work on, the puzzle of getting more life. And as you can see, I've gotten very good at it."

"Too bad about the aberrations, though," Billy says, uneasily, as they enter the stairwell. Raw brick here, the steps metal grates.

"They're not the problem," Ollard says, as he begins to descend. "I mean, yes, they are a problem. An unpleasantness for others to deal with. But they're not *my* problem."

"Okay, I'll bite. What is *your* problem?"

"My problem, Billy, is with the world. There's enough in it to be interesting for a lifetime. Maybe a hundred years' worth of interest in total. Puzzles to solve. Satisfying activities. But after that, something happens. You get bored. You detect the larger patterns, the cycles. The repetition. Everything repeats. You have to *eat* every day. Three times a day. Can you imagine that? For two hundred years? It becomes oppressive. You begin to recognize that every variation—everything that constitutes human cuisine in total—is just an attempt to use novelty to disguise the repulsive *oppression* inherent to it."

Billy thinks of the lamb crepes, of wanting to save the world because they were so damn tasty. He opens his mouth to object, but Ollard just keeps rolling on: "You can amass more *knowledge*— there's always more knowledge—but there's no longer an *end* to put it toward. Most people bother to amass knowledge for very basic reasons, you know. To convert it into *power*. To flatter one's own *vanity*. To impress a potential *sexual partner*." They've reached the bottom of the stairwell, and Ollard hauls open another metal door. Billy follows him down a narrow aisle between banks of grey utility shelving heaped with disintegrating wood-grain-print file boxes, and begins to formally worry about the distance between him and the street now.

"But if you live long enough," Ollard says, "you see that even these ends are worthless."

"I don't know," Billy says. "Sex is pretty good." *Except when it's not*, he thinks, and with this thought comes a jolt of renewed regret at having failed to set up the Nice Evening with Denver; it would be good to have a really memorable recent sexual experience to fall back on in this conversation. It would be one more cause for hope, which seems to be in increasingly short supply as they go deeper and deeper into the tower.

"Sex?" Ollard says. "Are you kidding me? A jumble of thrashing flesh. And an orgasm? What is that? Cheap stimulation of your own mind's pleasure center. My final orgasm was in 1969."

Well, Billy thinks, *that explains something*.

Ollard stops, turns to Billy, beginning to tremble as the strains of outrage and disbelief in his voice redouble. "I even tried being *good* for a while," he says. "I thought, well, *there's* something I haven't done. Maybe being *good* has its own interesting aspects. Intrinsic rewards? I'd heard of them. So. Ten years I spent. I cloaked a couple of acres of mountain valley in China, found a couple of *pandas* the world didn't already know about, started up my own little private conservancy. I thought, now here's a thing that will—just a thing that will make me *happy*, in this godforsaken world. I even got them to put out a couple of cubs. But you know what? It was *boring*. Turns out pandas are incredibly boring. I would go there—I had some stupid idea that it would serve as a retreat, a place where I could go to *quietly reflect* or something equally pointless—and so I would go there and watch these idiot Ailuropods shamble about, and it just got to the point where I felt *contempt* for them, nothing but the deepest *contempt*. And so I killed them."

Billy's been doing his best, through this monologue, to keep his facial expression neutral, but at this he can feel a look of dismay crack through.

161

"Oh yes," Ollard says. "I slit their throats with a ceremonial blade. And then I set the valley ablaze and watched it die. And that? Watching my verdant mountaintop be scoured clean by fire? *That*, Billy Ridgeway, felt good. And that's when I knew that there was one last satisfying puzzle for me. The puzzle of how to make that experience be the *only* experience. For me, for everyone. The puzzle of how to burn the world."

They're both silent for the rest of their progress through the aisle. At the end of the aisle is another large door, this one painted red and lacking the little safety window.

"Every puzzle has its solution," Ollard says, pausing in front of the door. "And so here we are. The Neko of Infinite Equilibrium. The tiny machine that just gets hotter and hotter. The Little Engine That Could. You wanted to see it? Here it is."

He pulls open the door and enters the room. It's about the size of a suburban garage. The floor is ashily chalked with a set of concentric rings, and at the center of those rings sits a pair of sawhorses, and suspended between the sawhorses is the feline form of the Neko. Red ears, red collar, deep and expressive eyes. It beckons benignly. Surrounding the Neko is a kind of iridescent globe, like a huge, perfect soap bubble, only giving off an aura of timeless indestructibility, not exactly what soap bubbles are known for.

Billy squints at the shimmering sphere.

"One seal," says Ollard. "The only seal that remains between the Neko and this world. The five others have fallen before me. This final one is—interesting. A diabolical intelligence lurks in its architecture. It almost makes me believe that Lucifer and I could have been friends, if circumstances had been different. That might have been nice. I could have used a friend."

"Uh-huh," says Billy. He's not really listening anymore. He's become distracted by the realization that this is the moment: all he has to do is give Ollard a quick squirt of chemicals in the face, grab the Neko, and tear ass out of here. *You can do this*, he tells himself. He curls his fingers around the pepper spray in his pocket, flips the flip-top with his sweaty thumb. And he yanks the canister out and aims it—

It turns into a live dove in his hand.

He releases it with an inadvertent flourish, and it flutters out into the room, wheels in a circle, and is out the door and gone. Ollard watches it go.

"Billy," he says, piteously.

Shit, Billy thinks.

Ollard contorts his left hand into some gnarled position, like he's throwing a gang sign, and Billy is lifted off the ground, about three feet into the air.

This can't be good, Billy thinks, although he retains some degree of faith in Lucifer's ward: he is, after all, not in pain. Not yet.

"See, Billy, this is what I was saying about hard-asses," Ollard says, calmly. "Hard-asses just charge on ahead, trying only the most obvious methods. You think I would have taken you down here and shown you the Neko if there were any chance, any chance at all, that you could have pulled a cheap snatch-and-grab on me?"

He walks in a half circle around Billy, gets in close to Billy's ear, and drops his voice. "I am *disappointed*, actually, a little disappointed," he says. "You almost had me convinced that you were a person pretending very sophisticatedly to be a person who was pretending very poorly to be a hard-ass. But no. No, it turns out you were a hard-ass after all, just a very very bad one, which at least has the merit of being a strategy I haven't seen before."

"You can't hurt me," Billy says, with a bravery that he doesn't actually feel. His facial muscles—all his muscles, actually—have gone slack and jellylike; he feels like he has the physical coordination of an infant. He can't quite manage to fully close his mouth again after he speaks. A thin string of drool hangs off of his lip; he can't reach for it to wipe it away. This is starting to suck.

"I noticed that, actually," Ollard says. "It is curious."

Billy is about to crow triumphantly about the ward, as triumphantly as he can manage through his rubbery mouth, but then he realizes that the less Ollard knows in this particular situation, the better, and he should just shut up now, thanks very much.

"Let's run a little diagnostic," Ollard says. He turns to a rack of gray utility shelving at the wall and busies himself there for a minute, leaving Billy hanging in space. When he returns, he has a kind of leather holster slung at his hip; emerging from the holster are six or seven slender rods. Some are gnarled branchlike things and others are smooth, polished, ebon cylinders. Magic wands?

Ollard draws one out of the holster: it's about fourteen inches long, mahogany-colored, tapering to a point no larger than the pink eraser on the end of a pencil. He holds it up to Billy's face.

"Fuck you, Dumbledore," Billy says, his mouth all slack, drool running down to his chin. Ollard's eyes narrow and flash with what Billy recognizes as genuine hatred.

"Okay," Ollard says. "Let's see."

He places the tip of the wand just inside the rim of Billy's nostril. Billy tries to rear back but ends up just squirming in the air, splaying his limbs helplessly. Ollard pushes the wand in maybe another half an inch and something seems to happen to it; it seems to develop distinct segments, *points of articulation*, and then it begins *moving*, it begins to goddamn *wriggle* in his nose, chitinous and feelered, like a centipede, burrowing deeper into his nasal cavity. He suddenly remembers a grubby, friendless kid from his high school years who had to undergo merciless abuse because, as the rumor went, he had once been taken to the hospital to get a cockroach removed from his ear canal. For the first time, he understands that kid as someone who deserved his truest sympathies.

"Ngh," Billy says. Ollard's face is fixed with an expression of deep focus, a certain grim contemplation that is not quite perplexity, the sort of expression one might wear if one found a dead bird on one's doorstep. He holds that expression for a long moment and then finally it gives way to a sly grin.

"Very clever," says Ollard. "He's given you a Model Eight Demonic Ward. Not a bad choice, actually. Tough to detect; effective; tricky to get rid of because of its mercurial spin. Tricky, but not impossible. Let's just get that dispelled—now."

The wand up Billy's nose seems to fatten and discharge, and Billy feels a sensation like something intricate exploding in his head, a Christmas ornament shattering in his brain, dusting his consciousness with silvery particles, sharp and toxic. He feels the urge to sneeze, and he simultaneously feels a dawning awareness that he's about to die.

"Wait," Ollard says. His face reverts to the nearly-perplexed expression. "There's something else. Older. Deeper." The centipede scuttles a bit further in. "A second ward."

A second ward? That doesn't make a ton of sense to Billy, but he doesn't really have the mental real estate to attempt to figure out what it might mean, as he's too busy thinking about dying. He thinks about the book he'll never get to see finished. The first box of books he'd get from the publisher. Cutting it open. Inhaling the smell. Seeing his name on the cover. Giving the first copy to Denver. He would have liked to be able to do that.

"It's strange," Ollard says, in the slightly absented voice of someone working through a crossword. "It has a signature that I don't recognize. It's sophisticated, but it doesn't resemble most traditional wards. It seems . . . handcrafted. I don't quite get what it's *for* but I should still be able to remove it—let's see, here."

He slowly draws the wand back out of Billy's nostril, and something distressing happens deep in Billy's head. The sensation reminds him of how it felt to have his braces pulled off by his orthodontist, back when he was fifteen. The event is happening in his brain instead of his mouth, but otherwise it's identical: a series of wrenching pops, wired together; a relief of an old restraint; a kind of forceful, violent loosening. Finally the wand is all the way out of his nose. Billy feels completely drained.

"So how about now," Ollard says, almost murmuring. "Can I hurt you now?"

He draws a longer wand out of the holster, a twisted black number studded with thorns, and gently touches it to Billy's sternum. Billy's body jerks as tendrils of pain loop and coil through his chest. It doesn't quite hurt as much as getting Tased last night— he's still able to think—but it still hurts like hell. He makes a mental note to kick Lucifer in the balls if he ever sees him again, for getting him involved in this bullshit. Assuming he survives. Which he probably won't.

Ollard lifts the wand away from Billy, and Billy sucks air like a flopping fish.

"Please don't kill me," Billy says, miserably.

"Oh, Billy," Ollard says. "I don't want to kill you. I want to kill everyone."

Billy whimpers. He'd like to think that the sound he makes is more noble than that; he'd like to think that he's trying to make *a grunt of resistance* or something, but he hears it come out of him and he knows it's a whimper.

"I do intend, though, to make you suffer," Ollard says. "You see, Billy, I learned something when I was inside your head, a minute ago. I learned that you are a man who is governed by fear."

"I'm not a coward."

"I think you are, actually. I looked around in your head just now. So many fears in there. That's why you were never a great man, Billy; you were scared of the world. So I think it's fitting that when I send you away I send you to the place that you fear the most."

The place I fear the most? Billy thinks. He tries to summon it up. Hell? Afghanistan? He has trouble thinking of a place *anywhere* that scares him more than the bowels of this tower, right now. He wonders for a moment if he can't get out of this by pulling some Brer Rabbit shit.

"You know what really scares me?" Billy says, slowly. "My apartment. That place—I just never liked it. It just always creeped the fuck out of me. I'd wake up at night, rigid with terror."

"Very funny," Ollard says. "But I already know where you're going. Its coordinates blaze deep in your mind. Buried in your memory: the locus of your most profound fears."

"Give me a hint," Billy says. "What *kind* of place is it?"

"I don't know," says Ollard. "I don't care. I only know it is a place where you once pledged, out of fear, to never return. A fitting place for you to end your days."

"I don't like you," Billy says. "Really, no one likes you."

"Yes," Ollard says. "That's true."

"Fuck you," Billy tries to say, but he only gets as far as *fuck* and then he's gone.

CHAPTER TEN

AWAY

THE CAVE OF DENIAL • MUD/SHIT RATIO • NOT KNOWN FOR
FOLIAGE • NEVER LIKED GOATS • SQUARE PUPILS • SOMETHING
CRACKED • TOTALLY FUCKABLE • FRIENDS VS. ASSOCIATES •
TOO MUCH NOTHING • AMONG THE DAMNED • NEEDING AN
ANIMAL • WANTING YOUR MOTHER

Billy appears somewhere, still hanging in space, three feet above the ground, only now that he's away from Ollard there's no magic holding him in place anymore, so he falls down. He lands in mud, cold mud; he produces the squelch that is produced when a great volume of the stuff is displaced at great speed to accommodate the arrival of a plummeting body. Beneath the mud is something harder, clay maybe, perhaps a layer of rock, but definitely something that stops his fall, firmly, without friendliness.

He groans. He feels broken and sick, his pummeled muscles and guts still shot through with awful magic. He keeps his eyes closed. Unless he's actively under attack, he doesn't feel any special need to immediately reacquaint himself with the spot that's the locus of his most profound fears. Quite the contrary. When he considers all his options, he feels like ultimately he'd maybe be better off lying here, in the mud, with his eyes clenched shut, in a dark little cave of denial.

Despite these wishes, bits of the world gradually trickle in.

He can tell that he's outside. He can feel chilly wind stream across his face; he can hear the dry shush of that wind shifting masses of nearby autumn leaves. A crow, not far off, caws. He can smell the pungent kick of animal shit. This introduces a gram of worry about the ratio of mud to shit in the immediate area of where he's fallen. With that said, being covered in shit no longer seems like it will constitute a significant reduction of dignity, given everything that's happened to him in the last twenty-four hours or so.

He hears the bleat of some nearby mammal. Almost against his will he opens his eyes. He's in a muddy outdoor pen, three feet from a mottled goat which observes him vacantly.

Beyond the fence at the pen's perimeter he can see trees, a row of deciduous trees in the full blaze of fall. So he's probably not in Afghanistan, at least: although he's not a hundred percent sure what the tree situation is in Afghanistan, he does know that it's not a place that's exactly renowned for its scenic foliage. And didn't Ollard say that this was a place he'd been before? Plus it doesn't seem all that scary, although it is true that he's never liked goats.

He cranes his head around, sees a barn of a decidedly North American typology and a huddle of sheep. For one moment he feels the uncharacteristic desire to eat them; he clears it with a vigorous shaking of his head.

He frowns at a few gumball-type vending machines that are loaded up with corn and sunflower seeds. Something about this place does seem familiar. And then he figures it out. It's the Apple Cheeks Farm Stand and Petting Zoo in Ohio, about an hour from where he grew up.

He laughs. Ollard behaved rashly: sent him someplace harmless. Ollard made a mistake. Fuck, he had Billy hanging in the air like a trussed deer: he could have cut any one of Billy's prominent veins and just let him bleed out. Although maybe not: Billy remembers that Lucifer seemed to think that Ollard wouldn't have killed him, even without the ward. Or wards, plural, whatever that's about.

He looks at the vending machines and remembers the day he swore never to return here. His smile fades a little.

His parents had brought him. He was maybe six. They purchased a handful of grains out of one of those very vending machines, a quarter's worth, and Wee Billy toddled off eagerly, ready to find some kindly fauna to feed. What Wee Billy didn't know was that one handful of grain doesn't last all that long when you're up against the single-mindedness of the average farm animal. It all disappeared into the maw of one goat, an animal that Wee Billy experienced not as some harmless Disney critter, all shy smiles and eyelashes, but rather as a kind of frightening machine designed for gnashing. Something in the ballpark of an industrial thresher. Billy remembers looking into its otherworldly eye, with its diabolical-looking square pupil, and in there he found it, the terror, the terror at being up close with something that wasn't human, that could not be reasoned with, that could not possibly be understood as good or kind.

Billy remembers wanting his mother. As the goat moved on to chewing wetly on the sleeve of Wee Billy's shirt, he wanted his mother in a way that he had never wanted her before. There had been many times in his infancy and early childhood that he had wanted his mother to pick him up, to hold him, to feed him, to have her face fill his field of vision. Times when he had wanted her to tell him a story, something with mead halls and hunting horns, phrases that he didn't understand but that she spoke with such delectation that he felt in her thrall, and felt comfortable there. But this time was different, fundamentally different. This was the first time he had wanted his mother to rescue him from Evil.

The goat had worked its way up Wee Billy's sleeve until it finally began to nibble at the rim of his ear. His sniveling turned into open shrieking. He had needed his mother to rescue him from Evil and she wasn't there. No one was there.

She had never been far, of course, nor had his father, and they rescued him a second later and took him home, stopping at an ice cream stand for soft serve vanilla with a sweet orange shell, but something in Billy's world had cracked a bit. He learned that day that he was not fully under anyone's protection, that there were bad things out there, things that don't understand mercy, and ultimately, he would have to face those things by himself, whether equipped for the task or not. And on this cold morning, his mission failed, fucked in more ways than he can count, Billy has, once again, been reminded of precisely how ill-equipped he is, most of the time.

He thinks of Ollard's rotting teeth, of the stink that bloomed from his mouth.

He sits there, in the mud, trying futilely to come up with a next move. The planet is slated to die and he's in Ohio, of all places. He's cold. He's alone. Apple Cheeks seems to be closed for the season, or something; he doesn't see anybody else around: no farmers, no members of the public, nothing but goats and sheep. If he could get to his dad's place—easily forty-five minutes away even if he had a car—then maybe he could . . . borrow some cash? That would be a good start. But then what?

Billy feels a hot flush of frustration surge into his face, threatening to squirt out into big stupid tears. Ollard didn't make a *mistake*. He was right not to care where he sent Billy off to because in the end it doesn't matter. Ollard didn't need to kill him, all he needed to do was flick him away and he would no longer count.

He wants his mother.

He lies back down.

He's been lying there for a few minutes watching clouds scud across the sky when he hears approaching footsteps crunching through the rutted dirt. Billy tries to prepare an explanation for the proprietor of Apple Cheeks, some plausible narrative explaining how and why he came to be lying in this field. He's a fiction writer, ostensibly; he should be able to come up with something.

But there's no need. It's not the proprietor. It's Lucifer. He looks down at Billy with some admixture of pity and consternation, with the latter seeming more genuine than the former.

"What are you doing?" Lucifer says.

"Just—" Billy says, trying to figure it out, exactly. "Just lying here? Feeling sorry for myself?"

"Well, stop it," Lucifer says. "We have things to do."

Billy considers this. He considers the alternative. After a moment of this, he gets up, knocks the biggest clumps of dirt off of his coat with the heel of his hand.

"You're a real asshole, you know that?" Billy says.

"Perhaps."

"I promised myself I would kick you in the nuts the next time I saw you."

"But why?"

"Why?" Billy says. "I'll tell you why. You said your plan was unfuckable by design. But let me tell you: it was fuckable. Totally fuckable." That sounds wrong.

"Slow down, Billy," Lucifer says. "Tell me what happened."

"I'll tell you what happened. I got *tortured*."

"But—the ward," Lucifer says, in a manner that seems to convey exactly no surprise.

"Yeah, the ward didn't work worth a crap," Billy says. "You told me it would protect me, but Ollard was just able to, just, dispel it or rip it away or something."

"Ah," Lucifer says. "But, you see, that's good."

Billy stops knocking mud and shit off of himself. Instead, he gives over all his energies to try to make any sense at all of that utterance. "That's *good*? How on earth is that *good*?"

"Well," Lucifer says blandly, "it was what I expected would happen."

"It was—? Let me get this straight. You *expected* that Ollard would be able to dispel the ward that you put on me to *protect* me?"

"Correct," says Lucifer.

"You didn't tell me that."

"Correct."

Billy lets this sink in.

"You really are an asshole," he says.

"Let me ask you something," Lucifer says, ignoring the invective. "Did Ollard find the second ward? The *older* ward?"

"Yes?" Billy says, not at all certain that he should be answering this question honestly.

"And he dispelled that one, too?"

"Maybe?"

"I was *hoping* that would happen," Lucifer says. He swells his chest proudly. "I *knew* he wouldn't be able to resist, once he got into your head; he's gotten careless in his confidence. I *knew* he'd go through there and just scrape you clean. So, you see, Billy, you see the genius in this? You see the real purpose of the ward I put on you? Not to *protect* you but to draw Ollard's attention, to get you free, at last, of that accursed *older* ward. A thing I could not do myself. And now we're ready. Now we can move into Phase Two."

"Wait, wait, wait," Billy says. "I don't get it. This older ward? What the hell was it even *for*?"

Lucifer grins. "The older ward." He emits a chuckle. "What was it *for*. Well, a couple of things, actually, but in part the older ward was designed to protect you from *me*."

Something drops in Billy's stomach. He takes a step back.

"But," he says. "But, why would I need that? You and I— we're, we're, like, friends."

"Associates," Lucifer suggests.

"Pals," Billy insists.

"Coconspirators," Lucifer tries.

"Yeah, sure, coconspirators. But the point—the *point* is, you don't want to hurt me. It makes no sense."

"It makes some sense."

"What sense? We're on the same goddamn side!"

"Be honest, Billy," Lucifer says, quietly. "You're really on your own side."

"That's not true. I want to—I want to save the world and shit, same as you."

Lucifer weighs this. "Very well. Let's say that we're on the same side. But in order for *our side* to be victorious, I need *you* to be— let's say, more *efficient* as an ally. You require certain—modifications."

Modifications? Billy remembers Lucifer's fingers in his brain on Thursday morning, making tweaks, adjusting things. He remembers falling, distressed, into a huddle. He's not really up for more of that right now, even if Lucifer can rejigger his identity to make him resemble some kind of Special Forces dude, someone more mentally capable of completing an objective. "I don't think I like the sound of that," Billy says.

"No, no," Lucifer says, "I didn't expect that you would. And if you still had the protections of the older ward, I would require your consent. But now the older ward is gone. And here we are."

Billy can't make sense of it. Why did he even have an older ward in the first place? Who put it on him? Who would find him worthy of protecting? He thinks again of his mother: her face, filling his field of vision.

"So," Lucifer says. He looks around, faint distaste curling his lips. "I'd like to take this elsewhere. Shall we adjourn?"

"No," Billy says, "I think, for now, we should stay right here." He eyes the tree line beyond the fence, tries to figure out how far he could get if he loped into it at top speed.

"Billy," Lucifer says. "I hate to put it this way, but you don't have a choice."

Billy opens his mouth to protest.

Lucifer raises his hand and snaps, once, only instead of a snapping sound his fingers make the pungent ashy burst-noise of an old-timey flashbulb, complete with the crinkle of tiny glass collapsing. And, just as if the Devil has popped a flashbulb in his face, everything goes white.

He waits for his vision to clear. Waits for the world to come back. But nothing. Everything stays white.

Oh shit, he thinks. *I've gone blind.*

Except he hasn't gone blind. He looks down and he sees his hands, his torso, his legs. But there's nothing beneath his feet. No Ohio mud. Nothing. Whiteness. He suddenly has to fight back the sense that he's not standing, but falling, plummeting through empty space. He looks around, helplessly hoping to find a point he can use to orient himself, but there's nothing.

He clenches his eyes shut and waits there in self-imposed darkness for a second, until the wave of rising nausea passes. A vast silence roars around him.

Eyes still closed, he drops into a crouch, reaches down, touches whatever it is that is supporting his feet, reaffirms the presence of resistance. So, okay, there's that at least.

He slowly rises to standing again, opens his eyes, lets the whiteness rush in. He turns a full circle, hoping to find something behind him, but there's just more nothing. He would have thought, when he woke up this morning, that *nothingness* was not really a thing that could be meaningfully modified with terms like *more* or *less*, but there behind him is definitely *more nothingness*, definitely, in fact, *too much nothingness*. It's like he's mainlining pure oppression directly into his eyeballs. It's like all his senses are being smothered to death under a pillow.

And it is then that Billy thinks, with a sickening jolt: *Oh, shit. I'm not blind. I'm dead.*

No, he tells himself. *No. I can't be dead.*

Why not? You could die. People do die. Why not you? This could be Hell. The Devil killed you and sent you to Hell.

Is this Hell? This combination: consciousness plus nothingness? It's not what he imagined but he feels certain that remaining in this place, alone, will cause him to suffer, as surely as if he were writhing within a lake of fire.

He pats down his pockets, finds the loose change from the Americano, and throws it out into the void, hoping that just seeing something, anything, will help to quell the panic. The coins fall in the arc dictated by Newtonian physics, bounce, scatter out, help to define a plane that Billy can think of as *the ground*. It's not much but it helps to orient him a little bit.

He sits and thinks. There has to be a way out of this.

After a few moments pass, his thoughts turn instead to Denver. He allows himself to regret the fact that he died with Denver thinking that he was a flake. A cheating flake. An asshole. A cheating flake asshole. He wishes he could have proven to her that he could be a person who was, what was it, *fully present*. He won't be getting any more present now, that's for sure.

He takes a moment to try to envision what his funeral will be like, tries to work up a gratifying image of his friends, grief-stricken at his graveside, rending their garments and such. But all he can envision is them at the table at Barometer last night, all together, laughing, having a good time, without him.

Fuck.

He wonders how long it will be before he goes insane. He gives himself maybe an hour.

No, he thinks, closing his eyes again to block out the nothingness. *It doesn't make sense. The Devil double-crossed you for some reason. And that reason wasn't to kill you. He talked about a plan. He talked about a Phase Two.*

A Phase Two is at least something, not nothing, and as such Billy clutches at it with hope.

A Phase Two might not, of course, be anything good.

He recounts the one thing he knows. The older ward—wherever it came from, whoever put it on him—protected him against the Devil, and now it's gone. The Devil expended some effort—some *trickery*—to get it dispelled. That must mean the Devil intends to harm him. To *modify* him. To modify him *without consent*. That just sounds *bad*. He wonders whether he's just going to have his free will sluiced away, be turned into some kind of foot soldier for Satan.

So, okay, he doesn't want to get modified, he can pretty much take that as a given. The solution is: run away. Get to safety. But he really has no idea where safety might be, or if any spot in the blank expanse is different from any other. Does it even make sense to run?

It may not make sense, he decides, but at least it's a course of action. He's trying to think of himself as a Man of Action today.

He wonders if there's still any chance that he's going to get a book published at the end of all this.

He opens his eyes. Whiteness, check. He climbs to his feet. He takes a tentative step forward. And then another.

He turns around to see if the coins are still there. If the coins are still there he can at least feel confident that he can find his way back to where he started, if for some reason he needs to.

The coins are still there. There's also a door there. It's an ordinary-looking door, beige, free of adornment, set in a frame. It wasn't there a minute ago.

Well, he thinks. He's pretty sure that the implicit suggestion here is for him to go ahead and go through the door. He's also pretty sure that doing that will mean that he is playing right into Lucifer's, whatever, clutches.

This is what Lucifer does, he thinks, turning away from the door. *He tempts people. And when you have nothing, what's more tempting than something?*

He chooses a random direction and marches off, into the void. He goes for less than a minute before being seized with a certainty that the door is no longer behind him, that by spurning it he's lost his chance. He whirls to look, terror clawing at the base of his brain. The door, mercifully, is still there.

Fine, he thinks. *Let's get this over with.* He advances to the door, puts his hand on the knob, and finds it cool to the touch—this goes a little way toward allaying his unvoiced suspicion that on the other side of the door he'll find nothing but hellfire.

He turns the knob and the door opens onto a corridor, a corridor within what appears to be a moderately-priced chain hotel.

He steps through, scopes out the scene. The walls are some noncolor, some color positioned midway between peach and beige, a color chosen by a decorator for whom the choice of either peach or beige would have been just too bold. There are doors on both sides, with the usual numerical placards. Room 2001 on the left and 2002 on the right. So Billy's either on the second floor or the twentieth floor or maybe the two hundredth, for all he knows.

Well, he thinks, *it could be worse.*

He closes the door behind him, leaving his loose change in the void. All he has to do is find an elevator or one of those fire plan signs and he can beat it out of here. He sees no reason not to go, so he goes, off down the hall. It comes to a T end and he looks to the left and the right. More corridor. No elevator, no helpful signage. He notes that to his left the corridor terminates in some sort of open nook—a lobby, maybe?—so he heads that way. As he gets closer he sees that it's not a lobby but rather a little institutional lounge, with a few bistro-style tables and chairs, a few sad-looking plants, and a little kitchen station: a coffee service, a Plexiglas case containing an array of baked goods.

He also notices that there's a woman sitting at one of the tables, her back to him. Maybe she knows the way out of here.

"Hey," Billy says, hurrying toward her. "Excuse me!"

She turns, and Billy stops where he stands. It's Elisa Mastic, author of *Sanguinities*, MIA since last night's reading. She's not wearing makeup, and she's in yoga pants and a Duran Duran *Rio* T-shirt instead of the skirt and coat that Billy remembers her in, but it's definitely her. He also takes the time to notice that she's not wearing a bra.

She recognizes him, too: he watches the surprise flood into her face, matched, he's certain, by the surprise that's flooding into his own.

"What are *you* doing here?" Billy says.

"I could ask you the same thing," Elisa says. A pissed-off look wipes away the surprised expression. "Are you friends with that guy?"

"What guy?"

"That guy from the reading last night."

"Wait a second—you *remember* that guy?"

"*Remember* him? Are you kidding? He's been *stalking me* for two *weeks* now. When you pointed him out in the audience last night I was like *Oh shit, he's here* and then I went outside to figure out what the fuck I was going to do, like whether I was going to go through with the reading or just take off or—I don't know what. And then I could hear shit just start to go crazy in there, like a brawl going down or something, and I was like *Fuck this, I'm out of here.* You said you knew him. That guy's not your *friend*, is he?"

"No," Billy says. "I don't think so."

"Good," Elisa says, "because that guy fucking abducted me."

His brain gives up on trying to make sense of Elisa's appearance here, opts instead to crumple into a dull headache. He eyes the coffee station warily: he has his doubts about exactly how good this coffee will be, but he feels like his mind would benefit from some sharpening right now, so he pours himself a cup, sits down across from Elisa.

"He abducted you?" Billy repeats. He blows across the top of the coffee hopefully.

"Yeah," Elisa says. "But I first met him like two weeks ago when he showed up *in my apartment.* I woke up in bed and he's there *in my bedroom.* Said he had a proposition for me, wanted me to look at something on his computer or some shit."

"What did you do?" Billy asks.

"What the fuck do you think I did?" Elisa says. "I told him to get out, and I called 911."

"Oh," Billy says. "Yeah. That would have been smart."

Elisa goes on: "It scared him off. I thought. But the guy wouldn't leave me alone. He'd disappear for a couple of days, then I'd be walking down the street on my way to pick up my mother-fucking laundry and he'd pull up alongside me in this stranger-danger van, leaning out the window, trying to convince me to get in. He kept saying that he could—that he could explain something that was going on with me. I'm like, *Yeah, no thanks, I know what happens to women who get into vans with random guys.* It was freaking me out—but every time I'd tell him to fuck off he'd always leave, and he'd always be like superpolite about it— which actually almost freaked me out more; I mean, if the guy is a raving psycho I at least know how to deal with that. It was almost as if he thought that I might come around eventually, decide on my own to get in the van, which I found—creepy. Like *profoundly* so."

Billy takes a sip of the coffee, swallows, and immediately hisses with reflexive, lizard-brain distaste. He notes that the longer this adventure of his goes on, the worse the coffee seems to get. That bodes poorly. He wishes he'd drunk the Americano of Evil back when he had it.

Elisa continues: "But then today—I don't know, I can't really explain what happened today. I was doing my yoga DVD and there's a knock at the door—I remember looking through the peephole and seeing him—I know I didn't open the door, I wouldn't, there's just no way—but then somehow he was talking to me—he must have drugged me, I guess, 'cause the next thing I know I was here? And, I gotta tell you, this place is awfully weird, 'cause I've been wandering around for like two hours and I can't find the way out."

"I have something to tell you," Billy says.

He takes another sip of the wretched, brackish coffee, grimaces again, wonders if the powdered whitener would improve it in any demonstrable way. "This is going to sound crazy but—fuck it— I'm just going to put all of the cards on the table. I think that guy is the Devil. Like, I really believe that. I know how that sounds, but—"

To his surprise, Elisa is looking at him straight-facedly, as though she does not find what he has said to be even the slightest bit absurd.

Emboldened, Billy continues: "I think that guy is the Devil, and I think you and I are in Hell. And I think—I think something is going to happen to us. Something maybe—something bad."

"Let's figure this shit out," Elisa says. "You want all the cards on the table? I have a question for you. Is there anything unique about you? Anything that you've never told anybody before? Anything that if you said out loud everybody would think you were crazy?"

"I don't know?" says Billy. "I have a ward on me? Or had? I guess? A—magical thing?"

Elisa peers at him, frowns, and then lets out a little, exasperated laugh, shaking her head. "Okay, Ridgeway, I gotta hand it to you, that was *not* what I expected that you were going to say."

"Well," Billy says, "what about you? Do you have something that *you* never told anybody before? That makes *you* unique in some kind of crazy way?"

"Yeah, no, we're not going there," says Elisa.

"Come on," Billy says. "You said you wanted all the cards on the table."

"*You* said that."

"Look, are we going to help one another or not?"

"Okay," Elisa says, "yes. But I need a little more from you. I'm angry and scared and pissed off and all I really know is that I'm somewhere I don't want to be, and the guy who put me there is somebody you know. So go ahead, Billy, illuminate me. Tell me a story. Tell me the one about the Devil."

It's right then that the lights dim for a moment, as though some leviathan-sized appliance in a subbasement has just kicked on, sucking down a massive allotment of juice. A faint hum he wasn't aware of before clicks off for a moment and then seems to click back on, its frequency adjusted minutely.

Elisa sighs. "Or not," she says.

Billy begins to feel strange. He feels dizzy. Some fluish wave passes across him and he starts to feel sweaty at the same time that his body spasms with chills.

"Something's happening," Billy says.

"No shit, Sherlock," says Elisa. For some reason she steps out of her slippers. "Tell me honestly: has this ever happened to you before?"

"I don't know. I feel sick. I've been sick before—"

"This isn't being sick," Elisa says. "This is something different."

He tries to take his final sip of coffee but his hands seem wired all wrong: the cup falls to the floor and the coffee spills out into the carpet's unholy design.

He looks at his hands. His hands don't look right. He remembers the first time he took acid, with Anil, remembers Anil saying *Whatever you do, don't look at your hands; I can't stress that enough.* And of course as soon as he started peaking Billy couldn't resist looking at his hands, and sure enough they looked really strange, and then he thought too much about the connection between his hands and his brain and promptly had a panic attack, and Anil had to swaddle him in up to his neck in blankets and give him a stuffed raccoon to cuddle until he calmed back down. This is worse than that. He needs a stuffed raccoon and one is not available.

"Okay," Elisa says. "Take off your clothes."

"What?"

"We don't have time for questions," Elisa says. "You just have to trust me. You're going to want to take off your clothes."

As she says this, she slides her yoga pants down over her hips, steps out of them. She has nice legs but Billy's not really in a position to enjoy looking right now.

"You're not listening," she says.

"Okay," he says. He kicks off his shoes.

"One last thing," she says. "This is maybe going to sound alarming but I think I should tell you." She pauses, winces. "If what I think is happening is happening, I'm going to want you to fuck me."

"I beg your pardon?" Billy says.

"You heard me," Elisa says. She pulls her shirt off over her head. Before Billy really gets a chance to check her out, he jolts and falls out of his chair, needs to use his hands to catch himself. It feels more natural, suddenly, to be on all fours.

Something is happening to his face. That's no good. He kind of likes his face, his boyish good looks. And then he vomits, a hot torrent of slime ejecting out of him. He experiences one acute moment of embarrassment, at having thrown up in front of Elisa, who he thinks is probably not going to want to fuck him now, but then the embarrassment is erased, wiped away, replaced by pain, the pain of his bones beginning to change shape. It sounds like kindling, crackling in fire, and it feels, well, it feels like shit.

His spine extends and his shoulders broaden. He gains mass. His shirt and jacket split across the back. He tears through his pants also. Turns out Elisa was right: he should have taken off his clothes.

He is growing what can only be described as a pelt.

As his jaw extends and his teeth begin to change, Billy finds himself wanting his mother. Not for the first time today. He wants her there, by his side, her swords at the ready, in full fighting stance, ready to fuck somebody up.

His skull extends uncontrollably, his ears flaring back and out, his bristling face exploding into a muzzle. The world of smells opens up to him. He can smell the coffee he spilled on the carpet, and the acrylic fiber of the carpet itself, and the dull note of industrial rubber that lies beneath. He can smell the shit on his torn clothes; he can smell microscopic particulates of goat from Apple Cheeks Farm.

And he can smell Elisa.

She smells like an animal.

He turns his head to look but she is gone. In her place is a wolf: a massive wolf, her coat so black it's almost blue.

Maybe he should feel afraid, but then, his very capacity to think or feel anything is disrupted as something happens to his brain.

It's as though his id and his ego are changing positions in some kind of Freudian square dance. Normally the part of him that is *Billy*—the part that is clever and funny and talented and distractible—remains front and center, merrily overriding the part of him that is *something else*—the wants and appetites, drives and instincts. The animal part. But now it's the reverse. He can still hear his voice in his brain, frightened, trapped in some dark oubliette, repeating *Your name is William Harrison Ridgeway*, as though he might lose even that.

Your name is William Harrison Ridgeway, he thinks, helplessly. *You prefer to be called Billy. You live in New York City. You are a human being. You are not a wolf.*

Except a wolf is exactly what he is.

CHAPTER ELEVEN

SOCIAL ANIMALS

NO LONGER FRAIL • FUCKING AND WINNING • MONSTROUS
BEHAVIOR • GRECO-ROMAN EMBRACES • SNEAKERS WITHOUT
SOCKS • BIBLES, MOLESKINES • OLD DUDES AND SEX MAGIC •
MINIBARS IN HELL • MISUNDERSTOOD

Billy doesn't think anything for a while. Because his brain belongs
to the animal now.

The animal is not afraid, and the animal is not in doubt, and
the animal doesn't want a book deal or to save the world or to rec-
oncile with its girlfriend or even to be cared for by its mother. The
animal only wants what an animal wants. To eat. To fuck.

He looks at the dark wolf and the dark wolf looks back at him.

She begins to walk a circle around him, rubbing her flank
against his. He growls, low, and with pleasure.

The pain of the transformation is gone. He no longer hurts.
In fact he feels good. In fact being a wolf feels better, a hundred
times better, than being a human being, riddled with human frail-
ties. His heart is stronger. He can hear more things than he could
before. His dick is bigger.

The female wolf completes her circle, brings her head next to
his, snaps her jaws playfully, a bid for his attention. As though she
didn't already have it, every iota of it. And then she steps in front
of him and he sees her hindquarters and they do something crazy
to him. He wants her. The force with which he wants her is a force

he has never known before, not with his human mind, not with his human body. It is like a living cord that runs down his center is being yanked.

He does what he wants to do, what she wants him to do. He gets up on her, slots his forelegs in front of her hind legs, uses the leverage to pull himself up.

He feels the yanking cord again; he thrusts. His heart pulses faster and faster. His whole body surges up into her and there is only the smell of her in his long nose and the sensation of being inside her, which might as well be destroying the world and everything in it because it's the only thing he knows at this second. He thrusts, and a throbbing grows, deep in his groin, and it builds and doubles and then an orgasm jets into her and the wanting disintegrates and then there is a long still peaceful moment during which he does nothing but breathe her in and feel content, at long last, finally, content.

And then the dark wolf pulls away from him and yanks her head with animal alarm to look at something in the hall.

Billy can smell what she's looking at before he turns his head to follow her gaze: it's another wolf. A male. Massive, stark white, grizzled, glaring at them.

It smells familiar. But Billy doesn't really have time to reflect on this, because the white wolf bares its teeth and he launches himself at Billy.

The collision knocks Billy to his side, smashing him into one of the bistro tables, toppling it, and he has to kick up into the throat of the white wolf with all four of his feet to block it from biting him while he's down.

If Billy—the old Billy, the human Billy—were in charge here, he would be thinking *This is it. This is the part where I die.*

But Human Billy's not in charge. Human Billy's locked in the trunk somewhere with a gag stuffed in his mouth while the wolf drives. And Wolf Billy knows how to fight.

He slithers out to the side while the white wolf tries to stand on his chest. The white one loses its balance and falls over and gets trapped between Billy's uprighted body and the edge of the toppled table. Now Billy's on top and he bites down into his enemy's face. The first time Billy lunges in, the white wolf jerks away just in time and Billy gnashes air. The second time he gets that son of a bitch's ear in his teeth and he locks down onto it like a rawhide strip and jerks it hard. Just jerks the fuck out of it. He wants to feel it detach from the other wolf's skull. He wants blood in his mouth.

Billy clenches and feels the ear perforate in his jaws, and the white wolf's guttural growls give way to distressed yelping, and then, abruptly, that's it. It's over. He won. Billy feels a sense of satisfaction switch on, and it's like a breaker coming down on his aggression. He lets go. He backs off a step, lets the defeated white wolf right itself, slink around the overturned chair, curl up in the corner, cowed.

And then something happens. Billy's body begins to change again; it begins to soften. His snout and ears begin to retract. His paws are turning back into hands. He's losing his tail. And his consciousness begins to reassert itself, to take over the forefront of his mind again.

His first instinct is to panic. He wonders whether the white wolf is just catching its breath, getting ready to come back at Billy twice as hard. For that matter, it occurs to him, the dark wolf formerly known as Elisa might also opt to eat him. But before his imagination even really gets around to detailing these gruesome visions, he notes that he might be safe after all, for he can see that the other wolves are undergoing a transformation as well: they're also twisting and shrinking, also becoming human before his eyes.

Elisa is the first to return fully to human form, and she sits up, cracks her neck with a sudden, swift jerk to the left, and folds her arms across her tits. She heaves a sigh, gathers up her clothes from a loose pile on the floor, turns around, and begins to get dressed. As Billy's skull snaps back into shape he thinks: *You cheated on Denver. You cheated on Denver and it wasn't even really with another woman, but with an animal. You're a monster.* And yet, even as he's hating himself, he sneaks a look at Elisa's ass, and allows himself to enjoy its admittedly fine qualities.

And then he looks over at the other wolf, and sees who that wolf has become.

It's his roommate. His missing roommate. Jørgen. Big, hairy Jørgen, rising, naked, in all his wide-bellied Northern European resplendence.

Despite everything, Billy grins: Jørgen is here, and he's all right, or at least as all right as one can be, in Hell. Jørgen spots Billy, and grins back, and lifts him up into a great embrace. Both of them are still naked, so maybe this should be awkward, but Billy decides to think of it as Greco-Roman and just roll with it. It's not the only thing he needs to just *go with* at the moment. Fuck, he doesn't understand a single thing that's happened in the last hour. He's still half operating under the principle that maybe he's dead, and that this is the beginning of some kind of long review of every person he's ever met in his entire life.

When he's released from the crushing hug he gets a look at Jørgen's ear, which looks, well, which looks like someone bit the fuck out of it. He remembers doing it; he remembers liking it, in the same way he liked fucking Elisa. And he remembers what Elisa said, in the gloom of last night's bar, after she weighed him in her mind: *There's a part of you that wants to be powerful and that doesn't give a good goddamn about anything else.*

"Shit, man," is the first thing Billy says. "I'm sorry about your ear."

Jørgen touches it absently. "It will heal," he says, after a moment.

"I'm so—I'm so glad to see you," Billy says. "How long have you been stuck here?"

"Almost two weeks," says Jørgen. "I think. Telling time here is—difficult."

"I'm sorry, man," Billy says. "If I'd known, I'd—"

Billy tries to figure out what exactly he could have done.

"So you two know one another?" Elisa, now dressed, says. Introductions are made, a little awkwardly. Elisa won't quite look Billy in the face, and he wonders what she thinks about what they did. Whether she enjoyed it. Whether she feels sorry. Whether she would do it again. They didn't even use a condom, Billy realizes. But reflecting on *what just happened*, reminds him of the fact of the moment, that all three of them, a minute ago, were all turned into animals—godforsaken *animals*. Billy gets an upsurge of raw existential confusion, rising like a wave of nausea. His legs go weak.

"What the fuck," Billy says. He uprights the chair and sits down on it heavily. "I mean—what the fuck?"

Elisa and Jørgen, who are managing somehow to come across to Billy as actually *calm*, exchange a look.

"I understand your distress," Jørgen says, finally. "Follow me, and we will talk. I have a room. My clothes are there. I will dress, and I will try to explain."

"Okay," Billy says. He breathes hard, tries not to hyperventilate. "Okay. Let me—let me get my clothes."

But his clothes are ruined. He tries to see if he could salvage them, but they're totally shredded, not even enough left to make a loincloth. He takes a second to mourn his army jacket, which he loved, mud-and-shit-covered though it had become during the day's indignities. Deep in the pockets of his burst pants he finds a wadded-up napkin. He knows the words that are written down on it and he opts to leave it behind. He also finds Laurent's card. The guy is an asshole, but Billy folds the card into his sweaty palm nevertheless: he has a feeling, right now, like any ally might be a good ally.

His socks are gone but his sneakers are intact at least, and he's seen *Die Hard* enough times that he knows that it's probably a good idea to put them on.

"Elisa says there's no way out of here," Billy says, as he and Elisa follow Jørgen down the hall.

"She is correct," Jørgen says.

Billy falls into a worried silence that seems shared by the others. Eventually they reach a door with a broken lock, and Jørgen pushes it open. Inside it looks like any other hotel room: king-size bed, tiny desk, bad art. Billy wonders whether the end table contains a Bible.

Jørgen gathers the sheet off the bed and offers it to Billy, who throws it over himself like an enormous drape. His legs still feel weak, and he collapses into the armchair in the corner. "Okay," he says, and the questions rush out of him. "Where the fuck are we, and why are we *here*? Is this Hell? Are we dead? Did we live terrible lives and we're now dead and stuck here forever? Oh, and, also, am I the only person who is going to mention that we all changed into fucking *wolves* a minute ago?"

"That is not exactly right," Jørgen says, zipping up his jeans.

"Did you *see us* a minute ago?" Billy says.

"Yes, my friend." Jørgen gathers up an undershirt, pulls it on over his enormous, squarish head. "But we weren't changed *a minute ago*. We were *never* changed. We were *born* this way."

"But," Billy says. He looks from Elisa to Jørgen and back again. "That doesn't make sense. I've never *turned into a wolf* before."

"I have," Elisa says.

"As have I," Jørgen admits, scratching his blond beard. "Many times."

Billy grips his head. "We've been roommates for two and a half *years*," he says. "How could I not have *noticed* that you were on occasion *turning into a wolf*?"

"I was out at night a lot," Jørgen says, looking a little pained.

"You were in the music scene," Billy says. "You told me you were going to shows!"

"Yes," Jørgen says, remorsefully. "Yes, and for this? I apologize. I had intended to tell you the truth earlier."

"I would have liked that," Billy says. "You're saying that you knew that I was . . . like this, too?"

"I did," Jørgen says. He shakes his head sadly. "I knew it the first night we met, the night the toilets exploded."

Elisa arches an eyebrow at this.

"I could smell it in you. I thought we could learn things from one another."

"But you didn't learn anything from me," Billy protests. "I mean, I didn't have anything to teach you. I didn't even know that I was . . . this. Whatever it is that I am. That we are. How is that even possible? How could I be, like, a *wolfman* and not know it?"

"You didn't know it," Jørgen says, settling his weight down onto the edge of the bed, "because someone—a person, or a group of people—hid it from you."

"Explain," Billy says.

"I cannot fully explain," Jørgen says. "I do not have all the answers. But I have pieced some things together. You remember last year, when I went home, to Norway?"

"I remember," Billy says. "You were gone for a month. You told me you were doing audio engineering for some power electronics band."

"And that was true. But on that trip I also did research. I found people who had some information about a thing, a type of being, called *Fenrissonr*."

"Can you spell that?" says Elisa. She's sitting at the desk and she's jotting things down into a little Moleskine notebook. Jørgen assents to the request.

"*Fenrissonr* are creatures talked about in Norway, Sweden, Finland. But they are not animals. They are not organisms. They are not a thing that belongs on earth."

Elisa pauses in her scribbling. "What the fuck are they, then?"

"They are demons."

"Demons?" Billy says.

"Wolf-demons."

"Hell-wolves," Elisa says.

"If you like," Jørgen says. "And on my trip I spoke to some people, old men, part of the Scandinavian occult underground. They claimed to be eyewitnesses to a ritual that occurred sometime in the early eighties. A sex magic ritual."

"A sex magic ritual?" Billy says.

"Sex, magic, ritual," Elisa says, copying down the phrase. Billy can hear her put a period at the end of it.

"A sex magic ritual," Jørgen says, "presided over by Lucifer himself. And in this ritual, these old men said, three witches were impregnated by three *Fenrissonr*. They say that Lucifer was try-ing to breed a new race of creature. Not ordinary wolves. Wolves with powers. Wolves that could serve as an elite guard for the Devil himself. I think that we, the three of us, were the result of that ritual."

Something starts to spin wildly in Billy's head at this. "But wait a second," he says. "We weren't raised by witches. I mean—we have parents. Real parents."

"I was adopted," Elisa volunteers. Billy whirls, looks at her with wild accusation in his eyes. She lifts her palms and gives him a *what-do-you-want-from-me* expression.

"It is—hard to determine what happened next," Jørgen says. "From what I pieced together, it seems like the operation was sabo-taged by mystic operatives who had infiltrated the coven. The three infants were taken from their witch-mothers, and put under the protection of—"

"Don't say *wards*," Billy says.

"Yes," Jørgen says. "Wards."

"Motherfuck it," Billy says.

"Powerful wards, designed to both contain the wolf part—the *Fenrissonr* part—and to keep Lucifer away from the infants. And then I think the infants were smuggled away, and raised by the operatives, who tried to raise them normally. As normal children."

"And here we are," Elisa says. "Normal as blueberry pie."

"Bullshit," Billy says, his voice going wild and high. He says this less because he's certain it's bullshit and more because it's just too much, finally too much, he can't take on one more world-shattering revelation after every other thing that's happened this week. "I mean, you could *test this theory*, right? Just *ask your parents*?"

"I cannot," Jørgen says. "My parents are gone. Their house burned in an accident, five years ago."

"Shit," Billy says. "I knew that. I'm sorry."

"Do not apologize," Jørgen says, shrugging. "But I should tell you this detail. The first time I ever turned into a wolf was less than one month after they died."

Billy has nothing to say to that, really. He turns to Elisa. "What do you think?"

Elisa claps her notebook shut. "I don't know," she says. "It's pretty fucked up, but some of it fits. I was adopted, like I said. Also, my parents are both dead. They both contracted viral myocarditis two years ago, in Thailand. Aaand, the first time I turned into a wolf? Less than one month after they died. That's a close fucking match."

Billy takes in this information.

"So I might be *adopted*? My mother and father might have been—fucking—mystical *secret agents* or some shit?"

"That is what I am proposing," Jørgen says.

Billy remembers his mother's swords and his father's books. He remembers all the voice mails he never listened to this week. "I should . . . call my dad," Billy says, slowly, trying to remain as calm as possible. "Do either of you have a phone?"

"Well, yeah," says Elisa, "but signal sucks here."

They all sit there for a second in silence.

"I want a cigarette," Elisa says.

"I want a drink," Billy says. He wonders if there's a minibar in this room somewhere. He figures, wearily, that there probably is, only each drink comes with a terrible cost.

"There is one last thing I can't figure out," Jørgen says, to Elisa. "You and I turned into wolves after our parents died. This suggests that our parents were probably maintaining the wards on us, secretly, throughout our lives. But"—he turns to Billy—"your father is still alive—and yet—"

"Yeah, no, the Devil tricked me," Billy says. "He got the ward off me a different way. He—he used Ollard to do it. Which reminds me. Did the Devil fill you in on *that* whole part of the story? The deal with this guy Ollard? The guy who wants to, whatever it is, destroy the world?"

"I'm glad that you mention that, Billy," says Lucifer, who is standing there, in the doorway, watching them. They all jolt and look at him. He's a little dressier than Billy's seen him before: he's wearing a white tuxedo shirt, with French cuffs. Must be a big day. He has a garment bag slung casually over his shoulder.

"It's good to see all three of you together," Lucifer says, "and we'll have ample time to enjoy one another's company later. I hope you'll forgive me for cutting the niceties short for the moment, however, as Mr. Timothy Ollard is still very much a pressing concern. He has dispelled the fifth of the seals that separate the Neko from this world, faster than I expected, and I can feel that he's close to dispelling the sixth. By my sense of things, I would guess that we have less than a day left."

"Fuck," Billy says.

"Fortunately, my little cubs, we don't need a day. We don't need twenty-four hours; we don't need twelve. We simply need to go to Ollard's tower—"

"I can't go back in there," Billy says. "The last time I went in there I got tortured. He could have killed me."

"Billy," Lucifer says. "With all due respect, I would hope that you can see the difference between the last time you went in there, and this forthcoming time. Before you were a scared little man, with your potential tamped down deep within you, jammed in a box you'd never opened. But now—now you are something very different."

"I don't want to be different," Billy says, but Lucifer ignores this, throwing Billy the garment bag.

Billy unzips the bag. Inside is a single-piece jumpsuit, high-visibility orange. Billy half expects to turn it over and see PROPERTY OF HELL stenciled on the back.

"I'm not wearing this," he says, pulling his bedsheet tighter around him.

Lucifer gives Billy a beseeching look, holds it for a good five seconds while Billy watches it impassively. Eventually he drops it.

"Jørgen's van is parked in Lower Manhattan," Lucifer says. "I'm going to take you to the van, and you will drive to Ollard's tower, go into the tower, and do what is expected of you. By doing so, you will save the world. Are we understood?"

"Absolutely not," Billy says.

"Remember, Billy. You no longer have a choice." He raises his hand and snaps his fingers, only instead of the old-timey flashbulb noise there is instead a noise like a peal of thunder, followed by a sharp feedbacking whine that causes everyone except Lucifer to clap their hands over their ears.

"How odd," Lucifer says, when the whine has subsided. An expression of concern crosses his face. "Normally that—goes differently."

He leans out into the hallway.

There is the sound of automatic weapons fire.

Lucifer is blown back into the room; blood gouts from his chest and from a wound in his throat. A great wet plum-colored stain spreads across the tattered front of the tuxedo shirt. Billy,

Jørgen, and Elisa all leap away, horrified. Lucifer stumbles backward, gets tripped up by the desk chair and goes crashing down. Someone screams. Billy realizes that it's him.

Lucifer clamps a hand over the breached artery in his neck, and struggles to speak.

"Ultimately," he says, "should someone choose to write my story, I hope that author will take the time to mention that my entire existence really was characterized by my being profoundly, uniquely misunderstood." This descends into a jag of morbid coughing; blood surges from his mouth in three great waves and then he's still.

Standing in the doorway are two bearded commando-looking dudes, dressed in gray fatigues webbed with meshes of black nylon, holding stubby automatic weapons at their waists. The older one—his beard almost entirely gray—enters the room and prods Lucifer with his boot. The guys smells like hot machine oil and pipe tobacco, a particular type of sweet Virginia tobacco that hits Billy square in the sensorium and unlocks, of all things, a strong memory of childhood. It's the smell of home.

And that's finally the thing that allows Billy to recognize the bearded commando, allows him to realize that he knows him quite well, has in fact known him for his entire life, even though he never expected to see him in this kind of outfit, or in this kind of context.

"Dad?" Billy blurts.

"Put your clothes on, son," says Keith Ridgeway, Billy's father. "We're getting out of here."

CHAPTER TWELVE

BACK TO WORK

CIRCUMSTANCES • ADOLESCENT FEELINGS • GEOMETRY •
RELEASING THE CLUTCH • LIFE IN WISCONSIN • BATSHIT
INSANITY • FINALLY YOU GET TO FULL STOP • CHINESE FOOD
VS. THE VOID • CAN I GET AN AMEN? • A FACT ABOUT OCEANS

"You have got to be fucking kidding me," Billy says, looking into the face of his father. "You're not—I mean are you really—?" He's suffering a surge of astonishment at seeing his father here, standing over the bullet-riddled corpse of the Devil himself, and he can't quite shape it into the form of a question. Just the sight of his bookish father holding a *gun*: just that alone is a shock to his system.

"Billy," Keith says. He takes a pair of his familiar technocratish glasses out of a Velcro pouch lashed up under his armpit, rubs them with the hem of his combat jacket, and dons them. "I'm glad you're all right."

"I'm not all right," Billy says. He feels a little truculent, saying it, 'cause clearly his dad is here to rescue him, and maybe this is the part where he can begin to relax, just lie back and be shunted to safety, but right now all Billy can think is that he has been lied to his entire life, and that kind of crowds out any major feelings of gratitude that he might otherwise be enjoying.

"I understand," Keith says. His eyes, magnified by the wide

lenses of his glasses, look sad, although Billy finds himself doubting the sentiment. "I am sure some of the occurrences of the last week have been—disorienting." And then the sadness gives way to intensity, a completely unfamiliar blast of goddamn *derring-do* or something, and he turns to look at the other commando, a tall, thin man with a West African cast to his features. "Jean," he barks, "get me a reading on these three."

"Already on it," says the other commando, Jean, who has slung his weapon over his shoulder and is poking at some kind of gadget that looks a little like a plastic model of a thighbone. Like Billy's dad, this guy is all done up in paramilitary gear, and he looks like a soldier, his face grease-smeared and sooty, but Billy can't help but wonder whether he has a double identity as a high school principal or a pastry chef or something normal.

The gadget in Jean's hand is flashing red.

"They've been changed," Jean says. "It's hard to tell how recently. We're glitching hard here—this tech was not really cleared for cross-planar function—"

"Are you talking about the wolf thing?" Billy says. " 'Cause you could just, you know, *ask us.*"

At the word *wolf*, a look of deep remorse settles into Keith's face. "I'm sorry, son," he says. "This is not the way that I'd hoped you'd learn about your unfortunate circumstance—"

"My *unfortunate circumstance?*" Billy shouts, finally having had enough. "Missing your bus is an unfortunate circumstance. Throwing up in a cab is an unfortunate circumstance. Being a goddamn *sex-demon wolf thing whose whole life is a lie* is a fucking *existential nightmare.*"

"You know, Billy," Keith snaps, his voice suddenly flinty with annoyance, "maybe you'd have a little bit more information about this situation if you'd just *picked up your phone* sometime in the last *month*."

"If I'd picked up my— You're really going to put this on *me*? You knew about all this wolf shit for thirty *years* and you never told me; I go *a couple of weeks* without calling you back and it's *my* fault that everything goes to Hell?"

Elisa jumps in. "Listen," she says. "You two. Watching you bicker is very illuminating—every unhappy family is unhappy in its own way, as we know?—but I could have sworn that somebody mentioned something about *getting out of here*, and it seems to me that if we can do that—? Then maybe we should do that." She taps a finger on the doorframe once, firmly.

Jean looks at Billy. "She's right," he says. "Get your clothes on. Your dad will explain everything when we're all back safe."

Billy, kind of past caring who sees his ass, drops the sheet, kicks off his shoes, and grudgingly works his legs into the orange jumpsuit. "Safe," he says, as he struggles with the zipper. "Can we really even be *safe*? We're talking about going on the run from the Devil. I kinda doubt that bullets kill him. He's going to come back, and he's going to be pissed. Where can we run?"

"We're going to go to the Manhattan headquarters of a group that can help us," Keith says. "They call themselves the Right-Hand Path."

"No way," Billy says, shaking his head in vigorous denial. "Not those guys."

"Not those guys?"

"Yeah," Billy says. "I met them, they're assholes." He feels a cold wave of dread swell in his gut. "Oh my God, are you one of them?"

"Not formally, no," Keith says. "But they're—allies. They have the resources that we'll need, and they're open to our using them. From their HQ we should be able to hide you from Lucifer, and once he's lost your trail I'll take you all with me back to Ohio; I can reestablish your wards there. That should effectively mean the end of your collective wolf problem. So. Come on."

Billy looks at the ring of faces. Maybe they're right. Maybe he should just go. Maybe he just got off on the wrong foot with the Right-Hand Path; maybe they really are decent guys. He thinks for a moment about how it would feel to have his life back, to be safely removed from the grand design of Lucifer's plan, the full extent of which he still may not know. It sounds good, and yet he balks. He wonders, though, how much of his resistance is just willful perversity. He doesn't want to do what his dad is telling him to do: But how much of that is just because he's being told to do it *by his dad*? Has he just straight-up backslid to being a sulky adolescent?

He looks down at the bloody ruin of Lucifer's most recent manifestation, just a foot from his bare feet, leaking ichor. And he thinks, for just a second, about Lucifer's promise to him. The promise of a book. And he thinks about his mission, and the Neko in the tower, and the world, and the threat that the world would burn. And some impulse in him stirs.

"I hate to be the guy who's going to say this," he says. "But— what about Ollard? I mean, do you think Lucifer could have been *right*? Maybe Timothy Ollard is a dude we should be worrying about. You know he's gotten past five seals of six, right?"

"Who's Ollard?" Elisa asks.

"Billy," says Keith. "Listen to me. The important thing at the moment is that we get out of here. The Right-Hand Path has people working on the Ollard problem. It's not a thing that you need to worry about."

He envisions Laurent and Barry, tries to imagine them up against Ollard. Tries to imagine them triumphant. It's not an image that coalesces easily.

"I just don't—" Billy begins.

"Billy," everyone in the room says at once.

"Fine," Billy says, and he gets his shoes back on and takes his spot at the end of the line, following the rest of them through the doorframe and out into the hallway, leaving Lucifer behind.

"Whoa," Billy can hear Elisa say. And when he gets out there he can see why.

The air in the hallway is split. A great seam open in space, spilling incandescent torrents of light out over them. It gives off a low sound that's half children's choir and half roaring vacuum cleaner. Little susurrating vortices spume off of its edges. Something fascinating is happening inside it, like a set of geometry problems solving themselves very rapidly. Elisa, Jørgen, and Billy all stop in their tracks and just peer into it for a second, transfixed like deer on a rural road, deer who are about to be plowed into by some sports-utility vehicle.

"Don't look at it directly," Keith says to them all, and Billy averts his eyes, opting to honor this recommendation. Despite everything, he does feel humbled by this whirling, thrumming piece of magic; he does feel a little in awe of his father for ripping this magnificent hole into Hell. For the first time, Billy thinks *Maybe it would be cool to learn some magic.* He wonders what was in all those books his dad used to try to get him to read.

"Okay," says Jean, drawing them all into a loose huddle. "This is a Class A Fiat Gate. Basically, it's a portal that will take you more or less anywhere you command it to take you. This works *fantastically*—catch is, you have to maintain an image of the place in your mind. You have to be already familiar with the place where you're going."

"This presents us with a problem," Keith says, regret in his voice.

"What problem?" Billy says.

"The problem is that we want to go to the Right-Hand Path HQ, and unless you've been there before, you'll have to go with a guide. Jean and I can serve as guides, but only for one person apiece, and there're three of you."

"We had bad intel," Jean says, remorsefully. "We thought there were only two."

"Everybody always forgets about the girl," says Elisa.

"So," Keith says, "one of you will have to wait. Then we'll have to *reopen* the Gate and *come back* for whoever stayed behind."

"That'll take time," says Jean, "and the person left behind will be at risk during the time the Gate is closed."

"Well, wait a sec," Billy says, popping up his hand. "I've been to the Right-Hand Path HQ."

Billy's dad frowns at him. "What? When?"

"I told you, I met them. I was with them this morning," Billy says. "So the picture of their HQ in my mind or whatever is pretty fresh."

Keith and Jean exchange looks.

"You can visualize it well enough to manifest yourself there?" Keith says.

"Yeah, sure," Billy says, although he doesn't try to do it. "I even have their address." He fishes Laurent's business card out of his pocket and holds it up. It is bent and moist but still in one piece.

"Yeah, but, Billy, the *address* isn't going to help you," Keith says. "It's not like you're putting it into a GPS. You have to *concentrate* on—"

"Yeah, yeah," Billy says, waving him off. "Maintain an image of it in your mind. I got this."

Billy's dad fixes him with a familiar skeptical look.

"Keith," says Jean. "It's time. Let's go. Doing it in one trip makes sense; it's safer."

Keith frowns, looks at Billy, looks at the portal. His frown deepens.

"It'll be fine," Billy says. A desperation to please that he remembers all too well creeps into him. "Hold an image of the place in your mind. How hard could it be? Is there another, more complicated step, that you're leaving out? Do I have to *release the clutch* at some point?"

"Not really," Keith says, a little grimly.

"Okay, then," Billy says.

"Okay, then," says Jean. "It sounds decided." He reaches out toward Elisa. "We're going."

"Great," Elisa says. She takes Jean's hand. She turns to Billy and offers him an uncertain smile. It's intended to be reassuring, he guesses, but Billy can see the fear in it. It's maybe the most readable expression he's ever seen on her.

"It'll be all right," he says, as Elisa and Jean run into the light. He's not sure if she hears him. They whirl apart into blobs and little flaring squibs and then they're gone.

"Listen to me," says Keith, taking Billy by the shoulders. "A Fiat Gate is serious magic. It can be confusing. Just stay focused on the mental image of the Right-Hand Path headquarters."

"Check," Billy says.

Billy's dad takes Jørgen's hand, makes sure Jørgen is ready, and then the two of them enter the portal, boil away into vectors.

"Don't let them wipe your memory," Billy says, to the empty hallway.

Billy looks at the portal or gate or whatever, remembers he's not supposed to look directly at it, looks away, looks at it again. He takes a step forward. *Okay*, he thinks. *Let's do this.*

And then he passes through and his mind becomes a mirrored disco ball, glassy and faceted, refracting brilliance in a thousand different directions.

Yikes! Billy thinks.

But even thinking that is a good sign: it means that Billy can at least maintain a thought among the dazzling optics and shrieking noise. Which means—presto—he can visualize the Right-Hand Path headquarters.

The image that comes to mind is the cell he woke up in this morning, which causes him to remember, just for a second, what manipulative dicks they were. This causes him to frown, or it would, if he had a body at the moment, which he doesn't. A frown of the mind. This makes him remember joking about being immanent when Denver said that he hadn't been *present*. Now he's not even immanent: ha ha.

It occurs to him that he could use the warping luminescent matrix that he's falling through to fling himself straight to Denver's apartment, just show up, as he's been longing to do all day. Show up, apologize for everything. He tries to remember her schedule, tries to remember if today is one of the days when she goes in to work at the video archive.

Today's Saturday: she doesn't work; Billy does. Except he probably got fired today. He feels a momentary pang for his life as it was, wishes, for just a single self-pitying second, that none of this had ever happened, and that he was just at work, with Anil, making sandwiches, the same way he's done every Saturday for the past year and a half.

And the light assembles itself into an image, like a melting film in reverse. Only it's not the image of the cell in the basement of the Right-Hand Path headquarters. It's the image of the kitchen at the sandwich shop. Anil is there, working, his hands dipping deftly into steel bins of cut onions and shredded lettuce. And Billy is there. He can kind of see himself from the outside for a second before he realizes that, no, really: he's actually, physically there. Not in the light. In his body. In this kitchen.

"Son of a bitch!" Billy says, presented with one more piece of conclusive evidence about his inability to focus on a goddamn thing for more than one goddamn second. He pounds his fists against his temples, once, solidly, as though attempting to physically drive some sense into his skull.

Anil jumps.

"Billy?" he says, blinking. "What the fuck? Where have you *been*? Everyone has been *freaking out* worried about you."

"Really?" Billy says, a little flattered at this unexpected piece of news.

"Yes!" Anil says. "Well, everyone except Giorgos, he's pissed at you and he says you're fired. But everyone else! You seemed so *out of it* at the reading, and then you fucking wandered off—we thought you might have gone into some kind of fugue state. I expected to hear from you in six months, saying *I live in Wisconsin now. I run a dairy farm with my wife, who is kind, and simple.* You can imagine our dismay."

Billy tries it. "Dismay?" he asks, seeking confirmation.

"Sure," Anil says.

"Even Denver? Would you characterize her reaction as—dismayed?"

"Are you fucking kidding me?" Anil says. "*Denver* thought we should *call the cops* and get them looking for you. I'm happy to say that saner heads prevailed, but, yes, dismay; I would say that that describes it."

Billy takes a moment to enjoy this, but only a moment, and then panic pulls the rug out from under it.

"I fucked up, Anil," he says. "I'm not supposed to be here."

"News flash, Billy," Anil says, "you *are* supposed to be here. You were supposed to be here *five and a half hours ago*. I've been doing this fucking shift by myself. In conclusion: I'm glad you're alive, but you remain a major-league asshole. Put some fucking gloves on and help me with these tickets."

Not certain exactly what else to do, Billy puts on a pair of gloves, and takes his station. He's sliced exactly one baguette in half before he pauses.

"I can't stay here, Anil. He can find me here. He found me in the fucking middle-of-nowhere *Ohio*; he can find me here."

"Oh, Billy," Anil says, arranging roasted red peppers on top of a slice of Gorgonzola, "I *have* missed you. You make no fucking sense whatsoever. Bread. Slice it. While you're doing that, you can explain what it is you're on about."

The extra adrenaline pinging around in his bloodstream makes him a little spasmodic, but Billy picks up his knife again and does his best, mangling a ciabatta roll. "I'm talking about the Devil," he tries.

"Still?" Anil says. "Didn't we decide that was a joke?"

"It's no *joke*," says Billy, plaintively.

Anil claps the top on the sandwich he's making, plates it, puts it on the counter, slaps the bell.

"This may be one of those begin-at-the-beginning type of situations," he says, finally.

"I'll explain it," Billy says. "But quickly. And then I have to get out of here. I'm supposed to meet some people and they're going to be pissed that I'm *here* instead of *there*."

"Well," Anil says, "yes, that sounds like a situation you might find yourself in."

"Ugh," says Billy, trying to review what Anil knows and what he doesn't. "I guess one important thing for you to know is that— that reading last night? It didn't just end with me wandering off. It ended up in like—a riot."

"A riot?"

"A scrum. A stampede. You don't remember because some asshole fucked with your memory."

"I *did* wake up this morning with a *wicked* bruise that I couldn't explain," Anil says, although he seems unconvinced.

"But at least you didn't get Tased," Billy says, and then he just launches in, explaining about the Tasing, about the Right-Hand Path, about Ollard's tower, about the Neko, about the wards, about being a wolf, about his dad. It takes him fifteen minutes and the whole time he is assembling and plating sandwiches at ferocious speed, even though he probably isn't getting paid. Somehow he also manages to gobble down half a pound of roast beef.

"Well, congratulations," Anil says, finally, when he's through. "You and I have been friends for a long time, but that is, without exception, the most batshit insane line of batshit insanity that I've ever heard fall out of your mouth."

"It sounds bad, I know."

"Well, the good news is that it makes a good story. I think you found your second act."

"Yeah, but—what happens in the third act? I think it might be that we all burn and die."

"Burning and dying is bad," says Anil, blithely.

"Yeah, I know," Billy says.

"So what's your plan?"

"I don't know," Billy says. "I'm totally confused. I mean—I look at my dad, and I'm like, *You're my dad, I love you*, right? *I trust you, you seem to know what's going on, I should just throw in with you and maybe it'll all be okay.* But then I think about it and I'm like *Well wait a second, you're not really my dad at all. Plus you lied to me for a long time—remind me why I should be trusting you now?* But I sure as shit don't trust the Devil either—I mean, he's the *Devil.* He's *evil.* Right?"

"Um," Anil says. "Not my particular mythic system, remember?"

"Come on, Anil. Tell me what you think."

"What do *I* think? *I* think you've had a psychotic break," Anil says, and then there's a fire in the kitchen.

It's Lucifer, manifesting himself. For all the times he's popped up, this is the first time Billy's actually seen him appear out of nowhere. Turns out that when it happens, it's accompanied by a huge burst of hellfire. Towering blue plumes *fwump* into existence like someone's fired up a gas burner the size of Venus's half shell. That has ramifications in the space of a tiny New York City kitchen. Fist-sized whorls of flame peel off from the edge of the efflorescent bloom and spin toward Anil. They land on his black work shirt, send tendrils out into the blend of fibers, seeking whatever can be consumed.

"Ahh, fuck—" Anil says. He swats at his sleeves but the flames course away, greedily surge across the back of his shirt, transforming it, in the span of a second, into a curtain of fire.

"Extinguisher!" Billy shouts. The mandated one is right there, mounted on the wall, behind Anil. Billy can't get to it. Both Anil and Lucifer are in the goddamn way.

"Anil! Extinguisher!"

The flames cling to Anil's back, lick at the locks of slightly greasy hair that peek out from under Anil's work-mandated hairnet. *Oh, Anil,* Billy thinks, *fuck the extinguisher; just stop, drop, and roll; every goddamn kid in America knows that that's what you do,* but Anil either doesn't know that or he's forgotten in a moment of panic, and Billy estimates that Anil has maybe two more seconds before the fire eats into his undershirt and then begins to do something bad to the skin underneath.

And that's when something funny happens with time.

It reminds Billy of watching Denver edit video on her Mac, trying to decide where to make a cut. Things on the monitor happen at the normal speed until she adjusts some slider which slows everything down at some rate which exponentially curves very pleasingly until finally she gets to full stop, the point at which flowing experience has become a single soundless image, a thing to reflect upon, a moment about which to make a decision. It's just like that. Anil frozen in space, his hand a good eight inches from the extinguisher; the unflickering flames silent on his back, still, looking delicate yet tangible, like an array of frozen orchids, a thing that could be lifted safely away from him and crumbled to dust.

"So," says Lucifer. "This is an interesting moment." He has his hand held up in the air, two fingers together against his thumb, as though he were holding something tiny and valuable, a diamond, a precious mote, some invisible speck. He's also still wearing the tuxedo shirt he had on earlier, bloody and tattered.

"Help him," Billy says, for it turns out that Billy can still speak, somehow, through the stasis. He isn't entirely sure whether his lips are moving. "You can help him, can't you?"

"I could," Lucifer says. He looks at Anil with a look that seems, to Billy, to be inappropriately dispassionate, given the circumstances.

"Look, you asshole," Billy says. "He's my friend. He has nothing to do with any of this, and you set him *on fire*."

"Yes, well, that was an accident," Lucifer says.

"Then you *apologize*, and you *fix it*," Billy says.

"It was an accident," Lucifer says, "but the situation as it now stands provides me with a certain degree of *leverage*. Leverage in its crudest form—a regrettable form, it must be acknowledged—but leverage nonetheless. We are short on time, Billy Ridgeway, and this requires me to use perhaps more direct means of impelling you than I have in the past."

Billy sputters. "What—" he says, "what is it that you want?"

"The same thing I've always wanted, Billy," Lucifer says. "I want us to be allies against a common enemy."

"But we are."

"Are we?" Lucifer says. He uses his free hand to gesture down at his bloody shirt. "We were all together, all together again after so long, making a plan that would make the best use of the short time this entire planet has remaining, and then some distasteful people intruded upon our conversation and gunned me down. Like an animal. And then you left with those people. You left with those people and hid, leaving me to waste valuable time and resources in order to find you yet again. You'll forgive me, Billy, if this leads me to cast some aspersions upon where your allegiances truly lie."

"Okay," says Billy. "I admit that it looks bad when you put it that way. But honestly? Those people? I was *arguing* with them. I argued with *my own dad* that we should work with you."

"Well, you'll have to forgive me for not noticing that," Lucifer says. "I was, as you'll recall, dead at the time."

"So, look," Billy says, beginning to panic at the thought that he may not be able to convince Lucifer that they're on the same side. At the thought that Lucifer may burn Anil alive as a way of demonstrating the extent of his leverage. "You want to get this thing with Ollard done? Let's do it. I'm ready. I'll help."

"I'm afraid I can't trust you on that point any longer, Billy," Lucifer says. "You've proven to be very reluctant, and I've come to believe that it would be in your character to lie, now, to protect your friend, only to change your mind and abandon our mission at some later point if you thought that it would confer you some more immediate advantage."

"Yeah, but, I wouldn't," Billy says.

"I think you would," Lucifer says. "And we no longer have the time it would require for me to chase you down again. I need to understand that you are fully committed to our task. I can no longer enjoy the luxury of doubt on this front."

"It's not like *I* can trust *you*," Billy says. "You fucking double-crossed me!"

"Billy," says Lucifer. "I never lied to you."

"You didn't tell me things," Billy says. "You left things out. Important things! You made—lies of omission."

"Those aren't really lies, though, are they?" Lucifer says. "I mean, *lie of omission*, you hear the phrase. But they're not really real, are they?"

"Real enough," Billy says.

"Regardless," Lucifer says.

"Okay, fine. You want full commitment from me, you got it. Just tell me—tell me what I have to do to get you to believe me. There has to be something."

"Actually," Lucifer says. "There is."

"Tell me."

"You can kneel before me," Lucifer says.

"Uhhh, yeah?" Billy says, wrinkling up his nose involuntarily.

"Yes. You can kneel before me and swear your undying fealty."

"Fealty?" Billy says. The word just sounds bad. Not the kind of word that sounds like he's agreeing to do one little thing for the Devil, one little thing and then it's over, he walks away in the morning. It sounds particularly bad when you pair it with that other word, *undying*. *Undying fealty* makes it pretty much sound like if he swears this oath he's going to spend the rest of his life floating in the void, or pacing an endless circuit in the infernal hotel, or something else equally bad. Billy's smart enough to know that this sucks way worse than the deal the Devil originally offered him—and he never formally accepted even *that* deal, so he sure as shit doesn't plan to accept this one. In fact, his first instinct is to look Lucifer straight in the face and say *Go fuck yourself*.

Lucifer, perhaps anticipating this, continues: "If you kneel before me and swear your undying fealty, we can get back to the work that awaits us, and I will remove your friend from the hellfire that imperils him. Or you can refuse me. If you refuse me, I will depart, leaving you and your friend to cope with the flame on your own.

He's close to that extinguisher. Reasonably close. He'll be fine. Probably he will be fine."

Billy remembers the guy at the Fairlane, the guy who burned his face off. The brother of the owner. He didn't die. One of the prep cooks hit him with a blast from the extinguisher within maybe five seconds after the explosion but a lot of damage had already been done. Billy remembers what the guy's lips looked like as the EMTs loaded him onto the stretcher. What the guy's eyelids looked like. He remembers the guy screaming.

And he remembers that the owner didn't come back to work for a long time after that; his wife and her sister took over the day-to-day operations of the place instead. Billy wonders what it must have been like for him, the owner, to know that he was at fault—at least partially at fault—for the accident. For putting his brother in the accident's path. Billy wonders how you would live with that.

He looks at Anil, frozen in time. They have ten long years of friendship between them. Billy remembers the long month when he was trying to not get drunk every day; he doesn't really remember it all that well but he does remember it, and what he remembers, mostly, is Anil being there, endlessly being there, bearing huge cartons of greasy Szechuan takeout which Billy would eat like it was the only thing to live for, reading Billy interminable segments of the *Mahabharata*, sitting with Billy at the tiny kitchen table and playing round after round of canasta. Canasta to 50,000 points, to 500,000 points. Epic games that did not ever need to end because the point was not really who was winning. The point, Billy knows, was to get Billy to look away from the void, the sucking void that he had been skirting the edge of for a year, watching in terror as more and more of his life got dragged down into its maw. If he could just look away, it seemed, he could be yanked out of the range of the void's inexorable pull. And he did, and he was, and in his heart he knows that Anil was responsible. Sometimes, in his rare moments of focus and quiet reflection, he thinks *Anil saved my life.* Sometimes he has a feeling that he is maybe obliged to *do something* with the extra life that he was gifted. You get one life for free, to do with what you will. Waste it if you want. But when someone goes to the trouble of helping you get a second life you kind of have an obligation to that person to do something good with it.

This, maybe, is as good a thing to do as anything. Someone saves your life, you save his. It seems fair.

And so he says to Lucifer: "Yeah. Sure."

Lucifer nods the tiniest nod, indicating satisfaction at Billy's choice, maybe even the faintest glimmer of something bordering on respect.

And without further preamble, Billy kneels. It's sort of an astral kneel, or something, because he can't move, because Lucifer is doing his thing with time, but Billy wills himself to kneel and can feel himself psychically go down in submissive prostration.

"Like this?" Billy says.

"That's good," Lucifer says. "Now, repeat after me. I, William Harrison Ridgeway—"

"I prefer Billy," says Billy.

"I know," Lucifer says. "But just this once. It's important."

Billy considers this. Sure. Why the fuck not. "I, William Harrison Ridgeway—"

"Do solemnly swear fealty to Lucifer Morningstar, Lord of Hell—"

"Do solemnly swear fealty to Lucifer Morningstar, Lord of Hell—"

"To whom I cede agency over my will and my being—"

"To whom I cede agency over my will and my being—"

"And whom I agree to serve as my master, and, in doing so, return to the purpose for which I was bred and born."

"And whom I agree to serve as my master, and, in doing so, return to the purpose for which I was bred and born."

"Amen."

"Amen."

And when Billy says that—that satanic amen—he feels something happen in him. There have been times in the past when he's said *I just died a little inside* but he's never actually felt it happen, not for real, not like this: he's never actually felt a whole wing of his spirit—in this case, the entire part of him that wants to kick and fight and resist—just crumble and expire without so much as a gasp. He wants to feel sadness for it but he can't even find the way to that anymore, as it would be in violation of his vow. He has returned to the purpose for which he was bred and born. He serves the Devil. Period. There is no reason to be sad about it. It is simply a valueless fact, like *70 percent of the earth's surface is covered by oceans.*

"So," Lucifer says. "Let's get back to it, shall we?"

He releases the invisible mote of time he'd been holding onto and everything speeds up again. Anil, still ablaze, crashes into the wall. Lucifer slowly closes his open hand into a fist, and completion of the gesture utterly snuffs the hellfire, leaving nothing behind but a heavy pall of sulfuric reek. Anil keeps grappling with the extinguisher in its bracket for a second, not quite realizing that he's safe.

"Anil," Billy says. "It's okay. The fire. It's gone."

Anil pauses, looks back over his shoulder, trying to get a look at the extent of the scorching. His work shirt is ruined, but his undershirt only has a few quarter-sized holes in it, and the skin underneath seems fine. Still, it was close, and Anil's face loses some of its color.

"Motherfucker," he says, softly, sinking down into a crouch, resting his wrists on his knees. He looks like he might vomit.

"Anil," Billy says, "this is Lucifer Morningstar, the Judeo-Christian Devil."

"Nice to meet you," Lucifer says.

Billy interposes himself between the two of them, crouches down to look Anil in the face. "Anil," he says. "I have to go. I hope you could do me one last favor, though."

Anil's eyes are wide, lambent with the gleam of fear. Billy assesses that it will pass. He rummages in the pocket of his jumpsuit and finds Laurent's card. He presses it into Anil's slack hand.

"I need you," he says, "to call the number on this card. Go to the address if you can't get through. My dad should be there. Tell him I went with Lucifer. Tell him not to look for me."

Anil gives one jerking nod.

Billy thinks for a moment. "I guess I have one other favor to ask as well. Sorry to keep adding them on. I'm still an asshole, I guess."

Anil blinks out of his shock long enough to crack a smile. "You are," he says. "But what? What is it?"

"Tell Denver. Tell her—tell her that I'm sorry."

He still doesn't feel any pity for himself—he still feels like his servitude to the Devil is an immutable fact—but he recognizes that sometimes the facts hurt people. *Seventy percent of the earth's surface is covered by oceans.* There's sadness in that, if someone you love has drowned in them.

"Billy," Lucifer says, dropping his hand on Billy's shoulder. "It's time."

"I know," Billy says. He rises.

"Wait," Anil says. "When are you coming back?"

But Billy doesn't answer. He leads Lucifer out through the service entrance and they advance through a greasy back alley lined with rotting produce, making their way magisterially toward the street. Pigeons scatter before them.

Something occurs to Billy. "What about the others?" he says, helpfully. "They went to the Right-Hand Path headquarters. It'll be harder to get them. They're defended against you."

"Billy," Lucifer says. "When the Right-Hand Path catches me by surprise, they may be able to momentarily deter me. But when I come for them? In my full splendor? That is a moment when they stand revealed as the rank novices that they are. You worry about my ability to get the others?"

They emerge from the alley into the slanting sunlight of a late November afternoon.

"I got them first."

And Billy sees, before him, gleaming golden in the light, double-parked on the sidewalk, hazards blinking, attended by a Traffic Enforcement Agent who is already printing a ticket for it, Jørgen's Trusty Econoline Van.

Lucifer pushes the parking agent gently aside with the back of his hand. The agent turns, looking pissed, mouth already forming the first phoneme of what would surely be an impressive string of abuse, but Lucifer fixes him with a stare, a soul-accounting stare, and he is harrowed, shaken into silence. He moves back. He is maybe beginning to cry a little.

Through the windshield Billy can see Jørgen and Elisa. He can see that somehow Lucifer has gotten them to swear fealty as well. Their faces are expressionless, calm. They have a job to do, and that is all.

Lucifer slides open the van's side door. "I will return to you in two hours," he says, placing both hands on Billy's shoulders. "In that time, I task you with retrieving the Neko from Ollard's tower."

"I can do that," Billy says, although he's not actually sure that he can. But he knows this: He will go into the tower. He will fight Ollard. Maybe he will be tortured. Maybe he will be killed. Maybe he will win. The important thing is that he serve Lucifer, as best as he can.

"I believe in you, Billy," Lucifer says. "Now. Go. Jørgen knows the way."

Okay, then, Billy thinks, as he climbs in the van and fastens his seat belt. *Back to work.*

CHAPTER THIRTEEN

KILLING MACHINES

ROOKIE MISTAKES • HOT HITS • A GOOD CALF • GERMAN PUNK
REISSUES • SKEEVED OUT • OPENING A DOOR WITH YOUR EYES
• IGNORING THE NUANCE • NOT KNOWING SHIT ABOUT SHIT •
FORENSICS • ONE LAST THING

———————

Traffic is bad, so it takes a while. Everybody and their sister is try-ing to get to the tunnel. Jørgen sits behind the wheel, plays with the radio, occasionally lets out a judgmental grunt, as though they don't have traffic in Europe and the very manifestation of it is some kind of New World cultural failing.

Elisa joggles the rickety lever that controls the heat.

"Please do not touch that," Jørgen says, tersely.

"I'm cold," Elisa says.

Jørgen works himself out of his heavy leather coat and passes it over to her. She arranges it behind herself, slouches down into it, her head half disappearing into its depths. She sticks one leg out, plants her slippered foot on the windshield. Even from here in the back Billy can see Jørgen kind of tense up with the effort it requires to prevent himself from telling her to sit normally.

"We should have taken the subway," Billy says.

No one answers him.

"The fate of the world hangs in the balance and we decided the best way to spring into action was to crawl across town at five miles an hour?" he says. "Fucking rookie mistake."

"It was Lucifer's idea to drive," Jørgen says.

"Yeah, well, he's not exactly a local, is he," Billy says.

Jørgen sighs and stabs at the radio, going back to Z100 for maybe the fifth time.

Billy slumps back down in his seat, looks out the window at the West Manhattan buildings. He looks at the slate-gray sky, wondering whether it's about to ignite. Everything looks pretty much normal; no ominous portents. So maybe they have time. They'll get there when they get there. He fiddles with a puncture wound in the vinyl of his seat, tries to see if he can fit his finger into it. He may have sworn fealty to the Devil, but the act seems to have left much of his personality more or less untouched, which means that he seems to be as free as ever to be distractible, fidgety, restless. He looks up at Elisa's foot, at her ankle, at her calf. It's a good calf. He finds himself kind of turned on.

Wow, he thinks, as if realizing it for the first time. *I had sex with her.* He goes up a notch in his own estimation of himself. He knows he shouldn't really feel good about it, given the fact that he's technically still involved with Denver, sort of, maybe, maybe not—but, fuck it, after the day he's had he feels like he wants just one moment to bask in the sensation of pure self-congratulation. The way things are going, it may be the last time he ever has the experience.

The only problem is, Billy's not really very good at the self-congratulatory mode. He's just not capable of looking at an attractive woman and thinking *that's right, she digs me.* He's just not that particular kind of dude. He can always find some way to doubt it.

In this case, of course, it's easy. The sex he had with Elisa doesn't really fit with the kind of sex he usually has. The lead-up was all wrong. He and Elisa did not enjoy a meaningful gaze across a heap of half-consumed tapas dishes, no furtive hand-holding at the IFC theater, no lingering kiss at the steps of someone's brownstone. It was just straight to the fucking. Hardcore animal fucking, in point of fact, which makes it all the easier to believe that he didn't actually have sex with her. Not, like, her, For Real Her. *You had sex with some kind of hell-wolf thing that she was stuck inside*, he tells himself.

He notes that she hasn't really spoken to him since.

He leans forward, sticking his head over the back of her seat.

"Hey," he says. "Hey."

"What," she says. She does not turn around.

"Are we cool?"

"Are we cool?" Elisa repeats, soiling it somewhat with a note of incredulity. "What do you mean?"

"I don't know," Billy says. "We kind of—had a moment back there, and I was—"

"A moment?" Elisa says, the note of incredulity becoming more pronounced. "We didn't have a *moment*. We fucked."

Jørgen turns up the radio incrementally.

"Yeah, I know, I was there," Billy says. "I just—I just wanted to make sure that—that it was okay."

Elisa cranes around in her seat to look at him finally.

"Yeah," she says, "Of course it's okay. I told you before we changed that I was going to want to fuck you. And then we changed, and we fucked. End of story."

Billy frowns. "But—" he says. He lowers his voice to a hush. "How did you *know* you were going to want to fuck me?"

"Because that's the way it is, when you change," she says. "You changed, you remember what it was like. It gets you turned on. It makes you feel like fucking is goddamn Job One. Now imagine having that experience every *month* for two *years*, every time the moon gets full, and not ever having another hell-wolf around. You climb the damn walls. Pretty much literally. I can show you claw marks in my apartment. So I knew that if you were going to change I was going to want to fuck you. It's not because you're *you* or anything. I mean, you're fine and all, but that's not why I let you fuck me. I let you fuck me because you were the first other wolf to come along."

This stings Billy, lacerates his attempt at self-congratulation pretty much completely.

"That seems wrong," he says.

"*Wrong.*" Elisa pronounces the word like it's only vaguely familiar. "Come on, Billy. That's the thing about being a wolf, or a hell-wolf, or whatever the fuck it is that we are. You don't give a shit about what's right or what's wrong. You just do what you *want*. You've been there. You know it."

"I only changed once," Billy says. "I don't know what it's *like* or what it's *not like*. I don't know shit."

Something in Elisa's face relaxes a little, and she gives a half laugh. "Okay," she says. "I keep forgetting you're new to this. So you want to know what it's like? What it's really like? I'll tell you a story. I owe it to you anyway."

She gets up, clambers over the seat into the back. Jørgen seems to breathe a sigh of relief, focuses again on the road.

"It's kind of a long story," she says. "But we have some time, it looks like. There was this guy, Joseph. I met Joseph when I still lived in Philly. Six years ago now. I was at Penn at that time, and I was burning out. Just like *done*. I wasn't even sure I was going to graduate. And then along came Joseph. We met on this post-punk forum. He'd dropped out of Princeton, was working as a shift supervisor at some record shop over in Jersey. And he was funny and smart but like totally decoupled from the whole academic treadmill—he just didn't give a shit about it and that was so refreshing to me, at that time, like I was really hungry to hear that you could have a pretty cool life without being academically successful. So my final year at Penn I'm driving out to Jersey every weekend, hanging out with Joseph in his shitbox apartment which is crammed with records and lunchboxes and whatever else, and we're getting high and listening to German punk reissues and reading our god-awful *poetry* to one another. And then I sleep on the couch. Because, I don't know, Joseph is cool, I really did think he was cool, but at the same time he's like super skinny and has this kind of dorky haircut and bad glasses and is just, like, not a guy who gives off much in the way of sexual confidence. And I start to feel *guilty*, actually guilty, about not fucking him, 'cause I can pretty much tell that he wants it to happen, and I even start telling *myself* that I want it to happen, like during the week, I'm at Penn, telling myself, all week, *this weekend, you have to do it, you have to fuck Joseph.* But then I get out there and I think about doing it and I'm just like *Ugh. No.*

"So then eventually there's this one night, and he's got some good news, he just got promoted at the store, he's now assistant manager, something like that, and in addition to getting high we drink like an entire bottle of vodka, and I'm thinking *This is it, this is the time that I'll fuck him*, but I still don't want to, and eventually I stumble over to my normal spot on the sofa and I crash out. And when I wake up in the morning he's on the couch with me, kind of crammed in behind me, and our clothes are all still on but he has his hands up my shirt and on my tits. And I kinda pull myself out of there and am just like *Goddamn it.* It's like, it was a shitty thing for him to do, but I don't want to make too big a deal out of it, because I still want to *like* Joseph, I still want things to go on as they've been going on, so he wakes up, a couple minutes later, and we kind of share this look, the look that says that we agree not to talk about it, that we agree to pretend that it never happened.

"And around then it kind of fizzles out. Maybe because of that and maybe not. I double down on my schoolwork, get more serious about my writing, start liking my Penn friends again, I graduate, I get the job that I want at the Philly Museum of Art, and then, poof, that's it, Joseph is gone. End of story.

"Except then, a couple years later, *bam*, my parents die, and then, *double bam*, a month later I turn into a wolf for the first time. And it fucked me up. So, yeah, I screw up a big grant, lose my job, and my boyfriend dumps me. Basically I'm losing my mind. So, whatever: I just start spending days sitting on the couch, wrapped in a blanket, drinking herbal tea and fucking *meditating* or something until I come to terms with the way my life is now and figure out what the fuck to do next. And Joseph finds me. On Facebook. He sends me this long, kinda heartfelt message about having missed me, all that shit. He doesn't mention the thing where he put his hands on my tits. And at this point I'm desperate for a friendly face from the past, and maybe I've even convinced myself that the *incident* or whatever never really happened, or it didn't happen the way I remember it, or . . ." She shrugs.

"So I friend him, and I write him back, tell him it's good to hear from him and all that, and I kinda confess that things are fucked up for me—I tell him about my parents, and my job, and my boyfriend. I don't mention the wolf thing. And that's when shit gets uncomfortable. Turns out that the record store Joseph worked at has gone out of business, and he starts talking about moving to

Philly. And the second I hear that I'm like *Uh oh*. He promptly comes up with this idea that because we're both out of work we should be roommates, to *defray the cost of living* is how he puts it. And we end up talking on the phone a bunch, and I get caught up in this stupid dance where I keep making up reasons why I can't room with him, and he keeps kind of disassembling them, which *he can do* because they're flimsy, because I don't want to say the real reason, which is *I don't want to live with you because actually you skeeve me out, and the fact that you appear to not be getting that is skeeving me out even worse.*

"In the end, Joseph does move to Philly, living on his own, and we hang out a couple of times, public places only thank you very much, and it's—it's odd. Something's changed in him. It's like his intelligence has curdled, turned into meanness. I can kind of see it in his eyes; that he either really loves me or he really hates me, and that maybe he can't exactly tell the difference anymore. So I start making all these excuses to not hang out with him, which isn't too hard, 'cause by this point I have a new job, waiting tables at this shitty fake Irish pub, and I can always beg off by telling him I picked up an extra shift or whatever. But a shitty Irish pub is a public place, right? And so at some point Joseph figures out that he can just show up there, and sit at the end of the bar while I'm trying to work, and he'll get drunker and drunker and try to get me to come home with him at closing time.

"To top it all off, I get involved with someone, one of the dish-washers. It's nothing serious. She's twenty-one years old. It's just service-industry after-hours fucking around, the two of us going out on the loading dock for cigarettes at one in the morning and making out and groping one another, trying to see how much we can work each other up. It is what it is. It's nice.

"So one night I'm out there, making out with Vicki, and who's out there by the Dumpsters and the fucking waste oil bins but Joseph. He's drunk, and his stupid hair is pushed up at like a ninety-degree angle from his head, like he's been leaning up against a wall for a while. But also he's pissed. It's like the valve in his head that holds all his shit back has finally burst. He's cursing at me, cursing at Vicki, *Fuck you you cunts*, all that. And he starts trying to climb up onto the loading dock, which he can't really do, 'cause he's stupid drunk, but it's still scary. I mean, he's a skinny dork, but he's bigger than me, and he's stronger than me, and in that second I really *understand* that he could kill me."

Billy remembers her, last night, asking him whether he was bigger than Denver, stronger than Denver. But he doesn't interrupt.

"And I realize," she continues, "that I could do something else, too. At this point I've turned into a wolf maybe six times, once a month, 'cause it's like that? But at this moment I understand that I could force the change, that I could just *will myself* into that form. I'd never done that before, but I could suddenly feel it in me. The wolf. I could feel it wanting to get out. It wanted to get out and take Joseph Meisner apart."

"But you don't do that," Billy says, quietly. "You don't just kill people."

"No," Elisa says. "I don't just kill people. But in this *particular moment* I wanted to kill *this guy*. Just for a second. But that was enough. 'Cause that's the thing about being a sex-demon wolf thing. You do what you want. And so I tore through my clothes and leapt down on him and crushed his throat in my jaws while Vicki stood there and screamed. I killed this guy, left his body mutilated in an alley, and just as a side effect I basically put the torch to my entire life in Philly. But you know what? It felt good. I *liked* it. Am I *proud* of it, sitting here now, talking to you? No. Was it the worst thing I ever did? Yes. But I wanted to do it, and then I did it. So you want to know what it's like? That's what it's like."

She climbs back into the front seat and they drive on for some more minutes, all of them silent.

Finally the van rounds the final corner of its route. Jørgen visors his eyes with his hand and peers through the windshield. "That's it, isn't it?" he asks. "I think I can see it."

"Yeah," Billy says. "That's it." The cloak no longer works on him, for some reason. He sees the tower, as menacing as it's ever looked, maybe more so. It seems to be palpably crackling with import, as though it is siphoning relevance and meaning from the surrounding city, which has begun to seem fake somehow, a generic urban setting from a film set in New York but shot in Toronto. The gallery with the Styrofoam art-shapes is now displaying prints of Instagrammed photos of food.

Jørgen yanks the steering wheel to the right and pulls two tires up onto the sidewalk. He cuts the engine and gets out of the van, and right then everything seems to go dim for a second, to waver slightly, and Billy feels a variant of nausea stir in his guts. He stifles a burp. It tastes like roast beef.

"This is what it feels like, isn't it?" Billy says. "When it happens?"

"Absolutely," says Elisa, wriggling out of Jørgen's leather coat.

Jørgen opens the van's side door. "Clothes," he says to Billy, pulling his shirt over his head and throwing it into the back. "Off."

"Okay," Billy says. He kicks off his shoes and begins to work the zipper on the jumpsuit, while he still has hands.

He cracks and extends.

This time, the change isn't as bad: breaking the bounds of his body seems easier now that he's already done it once; it's as though he has permanently limbered himself somehow. He does not vomit.

He hops out of the van and lands on all fours.

The others have changed, too. The three of them stand there for a moment, hell-wolves, bristling on the sidewalk in the Chelsea dusk, wind-borne trash whirling around them. Two pedestrians at the far end of the street pause in their stride, turn and go the other way.

It is time.

Billy leads the charge. Loping again, straight toward the red door. Somewhere in the back of his mind the part of him that is Billy wonders how, exactly, they're going to open the door: it would be his typical luck for them to get this far, this close to saving the world, only to be undone because none of them could work a doorknob.

But the wolf knows what to do. The wolf stares at the door, focuses on its surface, and something demonic rises in it. Something with *powers*.

His vision goes tunnely at the edges.

He intensifies his glare and channels hellish force out of the holes in his skull. It is as though his vision is a blade. It is as though his vision is a cold steel push knife being punched into the door again and again. The thought that a door could stop him seems ludicrous. It's just wood. It's just base matter, crude, destructible. The door trembles and warps and creaks and splinters. The red paint pulverizes; flakes of it now coat his shaggy muzzle. The brass knob smokes slightly, deforms, pops free. It takes all of ten seconds for the door's hinges to give way.

The second door is made of metal but it yields even easier. And then Billy's in the Starbucks. His jaws are open. It is fair to say he is *slavering*. Billy watches alarm crack through the blank look of the entranced employees. They scatter, their aprons billowing, the spell broken, apparently. But Billy doesn't care about them. He's here for Ollard.

And Ollard arrives, emerging from the back corridor, swollen with fury, eyes wild, teeth gnashing, shrouded in wreaths of crackling black energy. Billy turns the hate-stare on Ollard at the same time that Ollard directs a sheet of deadly-looking violet light toward Billy. The counter, caught between them, detonates. Broken glass and scones spray everywhere. Even though he has all four feet on the ground, the force of the blast still skids Billy away, into the floor plan, tables and chairs catching him painfully in his ribs.

He prepares to leap but Ollard is too fast; he strides from the wreckage first, his left hand held in the gang-sign configuration that freezes Billy, gets him aloft in the air. It's the same trick Ollard used the first time he met Billy. But it takes more effort now; Billy flexes against the spell with all the wolf-might at his disposal and can feel Ollard struggle to maintain.

And then the dark wolf that is Elisa comes out of the vestibule, leaps at Ollard from the side.

Ollard gets his right hand up, freezes her also. Billy rears his body again and nearly gets free, the force around him beginning to flicker and fail. He watches Ollard's face contort with the effort of holding them both, scans it for a sign of when the grip will finally give. Veins bulge in Ollard's forehead; both his nostrils have begun to leak blood. Yet his facial expression is a grin, the grin of a man who still has the advantage.

And then the white wolf that is Jørgen enters the room and

leaps at Ollard, jaws snapping, and it is then that Ollard's grin goes away. He drops his left hand, throws it up again, freezes Jørgen in place.

But Ollard only has two hands.

And so Billy is free.

In a second he's on Ollard, knocking him down to the floor. Ollard's head bounces off the broken concrete and his throat slides into Billy's jaws like it was the final piece of a puzzle, designed to slot there.

And all Billy needs to do is exert a particular amount of force. Which he does.

Ollard gets no final words. Instead his throat gives one horrible throb and then bursts in Billy's mouth, gushing fluids. Billy's teeth sunder the entire network of crucial vessels and tubes in there. He crushes vertebrae. He takes a human neck and reduces it to rupture and spillage.

He's larger. He's stronger. He's more powerful.

He doesn't give a good goddamn about anything else.

He drinks like a quart of Ollard's blood. He drinks it until Ollard's heart stops pumping it.

That's it, then, he thinks. *It's over.*

And then he thinks, *Oh my God, you killed a man.*

If he's having these thoughts, if they're at the forefront of his brain, then he must be changing back, and sure enough he is. His tail retracts and his skull shortens; his thumbs come back; he loses his fur. And then he's there, naked, hunched over Ollard's mutilated corpse, a quart of hot human blood swimming in his stomach. He moans, rises to his feet, turns away.

In the wreckage, Elisa is beginning to change back as well. Billy doesn't like watching her twist, doesn't like the disturbing way her form surges, so he looks back at Ollard, at the sobering sight of Ollard's wounds. Billy wonders what new conception of himself he'll need to come up with in order to manage the knowledge that those wounds were a thing that he himself caused.

You saved the world, he tells himself. *You should feel happy. Ollard was a bad dude. He wanted to die anyway. You did him a favor.*

And maybe you'll even get your book published.

None of these thoughts seem to make it okay to have made the mess that he's looking at. He begins to run through them a second time, but before he completes the litany Elisa shouts "Billy, look out!"

And Billy turns, and sees Anton Cirrus, standing there with a small duffel bag in one hand, and a gun in the other.

"Hands up, fucker," says Anton. Billy complies. He wishes he had his orange jumpsuit: it can't stop a bullet, but being naked in front of the barrel of a gun doesn't exactly make him feel *less* vulnerable.

"Everybody just hold still for a second," Anton says.

These are clear instructions, and even though Anton's voice is choked with rage and maybe even something like sorrow, he nevertheless says them loudly enough for all to hear, and if everyone in the room was human everyone in the room might even be willing to obey. But Jørgen is still a massive hell-wolf, and massive hell-wolves don't particularly care for human instructions or for the nuances of hostage situations. He gathers himself up and prepares to spring.

Anton, for his part, is smart enough to perceive that shooting Billy won't protect him, so he turns the gun onto Jørgen.

He fires twice.

The first shot misses. The other shot hits Jørgen in the joint of his right shoulder, causes him to lose his footing for a second, although he still looks like he might leap.

Anton fires two more times.

Both hit Jørgen in around the same area, which is enough to cause his front legs to crumple. His eyes flash angrily: it looks like he's trying to muster the hate-stare, but Anton has taken advantage of the moment, has sprinted through the vestibule and is already out into the streets of Chelsea.

Jørgen's wolf body leaks blood, shudders, begins to undergo the weird flesh-morph that changes it back into a human body.

Elisa finds a dish towel in the rubble and tries to maintain pressure on the wound while Jørgen's body shifts shape. She looks up at Billy. "Call an ambulance," she says.

Billy looks around, finds the phone mounted to the wall. He lifts it and is a little surprised to find that it has a dial tone. He dials 911 and gives the dispatcher the address of the tower, hopes the EMTs will be able to find the door now that Ollard is dead and the cloak has, presumably, fallen.

"How is he?" he asks, once he hangs up.

"Hard to say," Elisa says.

"Okay," Billy says. He feels worried for Jørgen, but the sensation is distant somehow, abstract; it is as though some mechanism in his psyche has lost a pin during the long battering of the day's events. He tries slowly to assemble an argument for doing something—anything—and it's then he remembers that his obligations to Lucifer are not yet concluded.

"The Neko," he says, wearily. "I know where it is. I'm going to go get it."

Elisa gives one short, curt nod.

Billy remembers the route: the long avocado corridor, the

brick stairwell, the room with the file boxes. But when he gets to the room where the Neko should be, and opens the door, he sees that it is gone. The sawhorses are there, the chalk marks on the floor, but the Neko itself? MIA, or AWOL, or something.

He makes himself undergo the effort of thinking. He stands there, naked and bloody, and thinks.

He remembers Anton Cirrus's duffel bag.

He stands in the dark, chalky room, breathing hard, and thinks about where Anton Cirrus might have gone. He considers where he, himself, ended up choosing to go when he was in the portal, with the opportunity to go anywhere. He went to work. Because that's where you go when it feels like your whole life has been up-ended. At least there you know what's expected of you. And work, for Anton Cirrus, is Bladed Hyacinth.

Billy doesn't know where the Bladed Hyacinth office is, but he has a pretty good idea of how to find out.

He retraces his steps back to the Starbucks. Elisa is there, still applying pressure to Jørgen's wound. Jørgen raises his heavy, hairy head and gives Billy a pained grin.

"Hey, buddy," Billy says.

"Did we win?" Jørgen says.

"Not yet. But I'm gonna take care of it. Okay?"

"Okay," Jørgen says.

"You hang in there. In a couple of days we'll be back home, drinking beers and getting high."

He suspects that this will not, in fact, be the case. They belong to the Devil now, and Billy's pretty sure that means they're going to spend the rest of their lives leashed up in Hell, to be brought out into the world every now and again when someone needs terrorizing. When someone's throat needs rending. Nevertheless, he carries on, hoping Jørgen will be able to take some solace from the promise of this false future.

"One day we're going to look back on all this and it's just going to be a funny story," Billy says. "You feel me?"

Jørgen winces, nods. "I feel you." His eyes close again; his head drops slowly back to the floor.

Elisa looks up at Billy. "No luck with the thingamajig?" she says. "The cat?"

"Not really, no," Billy says. "But I have a guess for where it is. I think I can get it."

"Sounds like a plan," Elisa says.

"You okay here?"

"Uh, I guess. I mean, this situation is going to be a bitch to explain to the EMTs and I'm pretty sure the presence of a shot-up dude and a motherfucking *corpse* means that I'm going to have to be talking to cops for the rest of the night. Now, I can pass myself off as somebody who doesn't know shit about shit but you know what would really help me out?"

"What?"

"Clothes."

"Ah," Billy says. "Right."

He makes a passable kilt out of a discarded Starbucks apron and he goes out to the van, changes back into the orange jumpsuit, brings everybody else's clothes inside. They can't get Jørgen into his clothes without moving him, and although neither of them really knows the first thing about first aid they seem to recall that you aren't supposed to move people who have suffered grievous injuries, so instead they fold his pants into a kind of pillow and stick them under his head, in the hopes of giving him at least a little relief.

Billy starts to wonder why the fuck the EMTs aren't here yet, and then he realizes that he's still half covered in incriminating forensics, so it'd probably be good for him to be gone before they arrive. If he can figure out where to go.

"I have to use the phone," he says.

His memory hasn't improved. Out of all the phone numbers he's ever known, he can still only remember one. Fortunately it's the one that he needs.

He calls the Ghoul.

"I heard tell that you had emerged," says the Ghoul, when he hears Billy's voice.

Billy processes this. "You talked to Anil?"

"Correct. He didn't sound well, you know. And he made it sound like you were in—something of a bad situation."

"It's all right," Billy says. "I'm just doing my job."

Silence on the other end of the line. Billy gives it a second, but he can't really wait. Forward motion. Forward motion is good.

"I need your help," he says.

"Tell me. What can I do?"

"I need the address of the Bladed Hyacinth office."

A pause. Billy can hear an unspoken *why* hovering over the conversation. But the Ghoul has never been able to resist a direct request to look something up on the Internet.

"One moment please," he finally says. Billy can hear the Ghoul's bony fingers clacking across a keyboard. "I'm pulling that up now."

He gives the address to Billy. It's also in Chelsea, close enough that someone could flee there on foot.

Bingo, Billy thinks.

He looks around for something he can use to write the address down but can't find anything. Well. He's sure he'll remember. This one time he won't get distracted and forgetful and fuck it up. *That's all I ask*, he thinks. *Just this one time.*

"Well," Billy says. "Thanks. And it's good to hear your voice. But I should go."

"Billy," says the Ghoul. "One last thing."

"What's that."

"You should call Denver. She's been really worried about you since the reading last night. I think it would mean a lot to her if you gave her a call."

"I don't—I don't think that's going to happen," Billy says. He imagines seeing Denver one final time, saying goodbye. Tries to imagine what function that would serve. For him, for her, for anyone. Comes up with nothing. Total blank. He'd rather she remember him as what he was than as what he is now. He'd rather she remember him as some goofy fuck-up who liked her movies, who found beauty in the movement of water, than as a killing machine.

He tries to come up with some way to explain this to the Ghoul, who has fallen into a pensive silence, but after a few seconds of trying out wordings in his head he just gives up and puts the phone back in its mount. It's time to go.

He shakes a set of keys out of Jørgen's pants. "I'm taking the van," he says. Jørgen seems to have slipped out of consciousness and he doesn't say anything.

"You'll tell him?" Billy asks Elisa.

"I'll tell him," Elisa responds.

"Okay, then," Billy says. "I guess it's time to hunt a motherfucker down."

CHAPTER FOURTEEN

RIDGEWAY VS. CIRRUS

GESTURES OF OPTIMISM • FANCY CHAIRS • FIST-FORMATION
OPTIONS • REALLY GOOD FOOTAGE • BACKSEAT KISSES • THE
THING WITH FEATHERS • UNO • THE WHOLE POINT OF BEING
GOOD • APOLOGIES AND PRAYERS

Billy remembers the address.

He's not the best at urban driving, and he gets turned around in traffic and heads the wrong way for a few minutes, eventually needing to correct with an astonishingly brazen U-turn. But finally he gets to the right block. He double-parks and punches on the hazard lights, the universal sign for *I'll be back in a minute*. Wresting a satanic world-destroying doodad from the clutches of a gun-wielding maniac does not seem like an errand that will conclude as tidily as, say, delivering a pizza, but he thinks it's important to make the occasional gesture in the direction of optimism.

The building that houses Bladed Hyacinth is a three-story thing, squat and ugly. From the label on the intercom, Billy gleans that the offices are on the second floor, up a flight of stairs that he can perceive dimly through the smoked glass of the street entrance. He tries the door; it's locked.

He glares at it, wondering if he can blow it to pieces. But

nothing. He remembers Elisa saying that she could will herself into the wolf form; she just needed to really want to kill someone. And so Billy thinks of all the reasons why he wants to kill Anton Cirrus. He thinks of Anton Cirrus firing bullets into Jørgen, leaving him to bleed to death on the floor of a Starbucks. He thinks of Anton Cirrus's stupid write-up. The storehouse of tired forms and stale devices. Billy grimaces.

Come on, Lucifer, he thinks. *Make me a goddamn monster.*

Nothing. He stands there with his fists clenched for a long second. He releases them.

He contemplates just using the intercom and seeing if someone will buzz him in.

And then he thinks: *Fuck this.* He returns to the van and pops open the back.

He rummages until he finds a tire iron.

The glass in the door is treated with some kind of safety film, so the first blow just spiderwebs it, albeit with a satisfying crunch. Nobody's around to see this except a few Honduran guys pushing a wheeled cart stacked with a half-dozen Igloo coolers. They give Billy a look for all of about half a second before they write him off as part of the scenery: just another insane white dude. It's a classification that Billy can live with.

He takes four more swings and the sheet of pulverized glass begins to crumple, detaching from the doorframe along one side. Enough that Billy can get a shoulder into the gap and push his way through.

He climbs the stairs, the tire iron dangling at his side, and as he climbs he imagines taking that piece of reassuringly weighty metal and swinging it at Cirrus's skull, imagines the shudder it would make when it connects.

But you don't do that, he thinks. *You don't just kill people.*

Shut up, he tells himself. *You can kill these people.*

And that ends the debate for the moment, because he's on the second floor landing and he's kicking the door open, and right behind it is Anton Cirrus with a gun, pointed directly at Billy's face.

"You're trespassing," Anton says.

"Call the fucking cops," Billy says.

"I could," Anton says, looking Billy up and down. "You'd go to jail. You killed a man. You're covered in blood."

"Like you're so clean," Billy says. "You shot my fucking room-mate. I have a witness. You want to call the cops? Go ahead. I would love to see what happens." Given the lack of subtlety of his entrance, he's a little surprised that the cops aren't here already.

"Drop the tire iron," Anton says.

When someone has a gun in your face, you feel compelled to do what they say. And so he does it.

"Get inside," Anton says.

And Billy enters the Bladed Hyacinth offices, basically a single room, dark at this hour, lit only by the light of Macintosh Thunderbolt displays running Cupertino-bred screen savers. The room contains six fancy Aeron chairs, each one stationed at a desk with a MacBook and a surprising amount of jumbled paper. On one desk, Billy notes, is also Anton's duffel bag.

"Face the wall," Anton says. "Hands up." The wall that faces the door is all bookshelves, loaded with literary magazines and proof copies of novels, and Billy dutifully reaches out and gets a grip on the edge of a shelf at eye level.

"So, what, you're just going to shoot me now?"

"Maybe," Anton says, pressing the barrel of the gun behind Billy's ear.

"Anton," Billy says. "That's not going to help you. You can kill me. You can kill my friends. But you can't kill Lucifer. You can't kill him, you can't hide from him, and you can't stop him. You already lost. All you should be thinking about is how to minimize your losses."

"And how do you recommend I do that?"

"Give me the Neko," Billy says. "Give me the Neko and I walk out of here. You never see me again. You shot my friend, but you know what? Give me the Neko and I'll just look past that. We'll call it even. I won't tell the cops. You get to keep your shitty little literary empire; you get to keep your book contract; you get to basically go on being *yourself*, which seems to be something you enjoy. All you have to do is hand over the Neko."

"Do you know what the Neko *is*?" Anton says.

"Some piece of bullshit," Billy says. "Why do you want it, anyway? You can't get the sixth seal off it and even if you could—"

"Billy, it's a *perpetual motion machine*. Get your *mind* around that for a second. What that would *mean* for the people who discover it. How much people would *pay* for it."

"Look," Billy says. "I don't give a shit about the thing. I just want it to go away. Deep down, you want the same thing. I mean, honestly, do you really have some fantasy where *you're* the guy who breaks the laws of physics once and for all?"

"Deep down inside?" Anton says. "You know what I believe deep down inside? I believe I'm intended for great things."

"Yeah, you know what? I believed that, too. But you know what? All our ambition? It made us do goddamn stupid shit. We each picked a side. We picked sides because we came across people who we thought could help us, who could provide us with some advantage. And now, we both committed felonies tonight and are both pretty much ready to commit another one, which should be an indication to both of us that we were pretty goddamn stupid to have picked the side that we picked. Look, Anton, we're in the same damn boat. Just two fucking *writers* who are trying to figure it out and maybe made some bad choices along the way. We shouldn't be fighting. We should be friends."

"But Billy," Anton says. "I can't be your friend."

"Why not?"

"Because you're a terrible writer."

Billy sighs. He may or may not be a terrible writer, but he still doesn't seem to have kick-ass rhetorical skills. Time for a different strategy. "Okay," he says. "You want to fight? Let's fight."

"It's hardly fair," Anton says. "You can turn into a wolf."

"A hell-wolf," Billy clarifies. "You have a gun to my head, though, which I think kinda evens the odds. But let's do this differently. Let's do this old-school. Old-school literary fistfight. Hemingway vs. Stevens."

Anton pauses. "Mailer vs. Vidal," he says finally. He lowers the gun. Billy tentatively turns around, looks into Anton's face.

"Ridgeway vs. Cirrus," Billy says. "That's what I'm talking about. You make me cry uncle and I leave here empty-handed. I'll tell Lucifer that I couldn't beat you, and you, you get a head start. But if I win—"

"You won't win," Anton says. He sticks the gun down into the waistband at the back of his pants and shoves Billy in the chest.

Billy takes the impact hard, stumbles back against the bookshelves. Anton's hands come up, get a grip on Billy's head. He presses his thumbs into Billy's face, as though he were violently shaping a wet lump of clay. Billy snaps his teeth, hoping that flashing his canines might send a message: keep your fingers out of my orifices. But to no real avail: Anton carries on with his attempt to use his heavy hands to smear Billy's features down to nothingness.

Billy shoots his arm up between Anton's, gets a grip on Anton's ear. He pulls, and Anton grimaces. He tightens his grip and lets himself drop down to his knees, banging one savagely on an outlet strip. Anton, not wanting to lose his ear, goes down right along with him, and the two of them thrash on the floor for a minute, each trying to get a better grip on the other.

Billy rolls over onto his back, and then realizes this was a mistake: it allows Anton to press him down, planting one hand on his sternum, the other directly on his belly—Billy groans as Anton squashes his liver, or stomach, or whatever soft organs are down there, unprotected by bones. Anton uses Billy to push himself back into an upright position, and, once risen, he begins to kick Billy with his square-toed Fluevogs. Through the pain, Billy wonders whether it hurts worse to be kicked with square-toed shoes than with the normal kind. This thought is disrupted when Anton kicks Billy in the chin, splitting it open, sending a shower of stars through his skull. One more blow like that and he'll be unconscious.

Billy rolls onto his stomach, crawls under the nearest desk, drags himself through the maze of Bladed Hyacinth's cable management system. Anton tries to lunge down, grab his ankles, drag him back out, but Billy's fear has given him the advantage of speed. He comes out the far side and keeps crawling, heads under a second desk. He gets tangled in a dangling curtain of wires but he needs to keep putting distance between Anton and himself, so he continues to advance, tugging one of the big monitors off the desk. It crashes down onto the small of his back, and he gives up a yip of pain.

But. He has the space that he needs now. Just a few feet, but that buys him the time to get back to a standing position, to strike his best imitation of a fighting stance.

Anton Cirrus lumbers toward him, slowly, clumsily, all six chairs in the place somehow in his way.

Billy makes a fist. He tries to remember whether he's supposed to put his thumb on the inside or on the outside. Which way keeps you from breaking your thumb? You put it on the inside, right, so it's protected by the other fingers? Or is it the other fingers that crush it and pulverize it if you do it that way?

In the end, he isn't even sure which one he opts for. The second Anton's head bobs into punching range Billy just pops out at it as hard as he can, fueling the jab with as much animal ferocity as he can muster, with all his frustration and anger—at Anton, at Lucifer, at himself, at the extent of all he's lost, at just the whole grand stupidity of his life now. He thinks he's aiming for Anton's chin but he miscalculates a little bit and gets him instead right in the throat.

Anton gurgles. His eyes bulge. He performs the arrested fish-gulp you perform when you try to take a breath and fail. He does it again and then he crumples down, grips the edge of a desk with both hands to keep himself from collapsing completely.

Billy steps back, bumps into the wall of bookshelves, and gets the bright idea that the grand finale here is to grab one of the bookshelves and topple it, burying Anton underneath. It would just look so cool. He turns, gets a pretty good grip on two shelves, and pulls, but it turns out the thing is maybe bolted to the wall or something? Or maybe the shelves in here were just built into the wall directly? He stands on his tiptoes to try to get a better look and when he comes back down, having learned nothing, Anton Cirrus jams the barrel of the gun into the back of Billy's jawline.

Billy puts his hands up without being asked.

"Uh," he says, breathing hard. "You're not supposed to use the gun, remember? That was the whole point of this exercise."

"Fuck you," says Anton, his voice coming out all pinched and strangulated-sounding. "Walk."

"Where are we going?" Billy asks, as Anton directs him out the door.

"What," Anton says. "You think I'm just going to shoot you here in my office? Spray your brains into my bookshelves? No. I'm going to take you out and shoot you on the goddamn street and watch you die in the gutter."

"Oh," Billy says.

But at that moment he spots someone pushing into the stairwell through the broken glass of the street entrance. A cop? He'd really like to see a cop right about now.

But it's not a cop. It's Denver, with her video camera in its shoulder-mount, its red LED blinking blithely at him.

"Hey, fuckstick," Denver shouts up at Anton, from the bottom of the stairwell. "Drop the gun."

Anton Cirrus looks down at Denver. "Who the hell are you?" he croaks.

"Let me tell you," Denver says. "I'm the one who's getting really good high-definition footage of you committing assault with a deadly weapon."

The pause that this gives Anton is palpable. He takes the gun away from Billy's head and hesitates. And that's the moment. Billy turns, and grabs Anton's shoulders, and throws him down the stairs.

The gun discharges harmlessly into the ceiling and Billy thinks, just for a moment, of Chekhov. Anton goes down the stairs, all the way down, more or less on his face, banging his elbows and knees against the walls. Denver films his entire descent until he's lying in a heap at her feet. The gun skitters to a halt next to her, and she pops a folding screwdriver off her belt, deftly lifts it by its trigger guard, and makes it vanish into some holsterlike compartment on her belt.

Billy gathers up the tire iron and the duffel bag, and hurries down the stairs to meet her. Cirrus is conscious, but dazed, and for one final time Billy contemplates smashing his skull open, reducing his human intelligence into insensate muck. But no. Instead he steps over Cirrus, and he and Denver hurry out onto the street.

"The Ghoul called me," she says. "He told me you were coming here. I thought I'd see if—if you were in trouble."

"I thought you were still pissed at me," Billy says.

"I am," Denver says. "But that doesn't mean that I don't show up. That's what I keep saying."

Billy pauses, and he lets this sink in, and he says, "Thank you."

Then he looks both ways for Lucifer, but there's no sign of him; the two hours aren't quite up yet. There are no NYPD personnel in sight, either, even though the sidewalk is covered with clear signs of forced entry. The only official on the scene is a Traffic Enforcement Agent, busy printing a ticket for the Trusty Econoline Van.

"Fuck," Billy says. "Can't she see that the hazards are on? That means *back in a minute*!" But Denver puts her hand on his shoulder, steers him away from the van, directing him instead toward a yellow cab, idling at the curb. Billy stops when he sees it.

"I told them that I'd get you, and take you to see them," Denver says.

"Who?" Billy says.

"The Ghoul. Anil. They just want to see you, Billy." She speaks cautiously, as though he may be insane.

Billy winces. He'd already pretty much assumed that after this afternoon he'd never see any of them again, and while he is still far from *coming to terms with that* there was at least a way in which he thought it would be *easier*, emotionally. He's never really liked long goodbyes and the idea of sitting with them, knowing that it's the final time, seems grueling.

He contemplates running. But then he remembers last night, at Barometer, just sitting there and laughing and enjoying everyone's company. He remembers feeling, even if it was only for fifteen minutes, like everything in his life was going to be okay. He'd like to have that experience one final time. A last toast together before Lucifer sucks him down to Hell. Sad, but it would give him a thing to hold on to, an image he could take with him down to the void. And he sees no prohibition against it; it doesn't appear to violate his vow, as long as he comes when Lucifer calls. So he lets Denver steer him into the cab, and off they go, into the night.

They put the gun and the tire iron in the duffel bag, along with the Neko, which floats serenely in the bubble of its shining final seal, and then Billy tries to fill Denver in on everything that's happened, but she has pieces of the story from Anil and the Ghoul, and she ends up shushing him so she can tend to his wound. He's grateful for that, because it allows him to not have to figure out what to do when he gets to the part of the story where he and Elisa fuck one another.

He leans his head back and lets Denver press a tissue against his chin, watches the streetlights recede through the cab's rear windshield. It'll be sad, to say goodbye to all this. This world, with all its weirdness. He will, in the end, miss it.

After the blood seems to have been stanched, he wonders if he can get away with leaning in for a kiss. He can.

They kiss for a while, and it's good.

And then Billy looks out the window. They're still in Manhattan. If they were going to Anil's place, or the Ghoul's place, or any of their normal haunts they should have crossed over to Brooklyn long ago. And they're going completely the wrong way to get back to Denver's place, where they wouldn't go anyway, 'cause Denver has eleven fucking roommates. It occurs to Billy to ask what he should have asked before he got in the cab.

"Where are we going?"

"We're going to see your dad," she says.

"That guy's not my dad," he says, beginning to get agitated. "I don't want to see him. I thought we were going to see Anil—"

"Anil gave me an address. He said we should meet him there, that there were people there who could help you—"

"You're taking me to the Right-Hand Path headquarters," Billy says, incensed at what suddenly appears to him as her betrayal. "I can't *go* there. That's like the *one place* I can't go."

"I don't understand," she says. "Everybody says that these people can *protect* you."

"They can't protect me," Billy says. "And I'm not allowed to let them try." They cross through an intersection. Billy figures out where they are on the grid; they aren't far, now, from the Right-Hand Path headquarters. "Hey," Billy says. He reaches up and raps on the scratched plane of Plexiglas separating him from the cabbie. "Hey, pull over. I have to get out."

"Billy," Denver says. "Just *wait*."

"You don't understand," Billy says. He can feel the prohibitions put in place by his vow begin to rise in him, a sort of physical discomfort, a vague, burning itch prickling over him, as though he's been sprayed with a fine mist of allergens.

They roll up to HQ. There are signs that Lucifer has been here. Billy remembers Lucifer saying that when he came for Elisa and Jørgen, he came in his full splendor. Billy didn't think too much about what that meant at the time but he thinks about it now. The building looks like a bomb went off inside it. Scorch marks, some of them fifteen feet high, mar the granite facing. Clean-cut looking men and women with violet hard hats—Right-Hand Path employees, Billy guesses—politely herd pedestrians along a strip of CAUTION tape that cordons off the site. He wonders whether the pedestrians will remember having seen the damage, or if some replacement memory gets installed in their minds before they go.

The cab pulls over. While Denver fumbles with her credit card Billy grabs the duffel bag, pops the door and hurries out. He's going to run. Or at least that's the plan. He looks both ways, trying to decide which way to bolt, but then right there at his side is Barry, the big guy with the serpent facial tattoo who plays Gorbok the Mad.

"Don't worry, Billy," Barry says, in his sweet, high voice. He places a firm hand on Billy's shoulder. "We got ya."

Billy tries to twist free but Barry's hand stays heavily on his shoulder; it sends some kind of line of force down through his body, rooting his feet to the pavement.

"Come on now," Barry says. "Let's get you upstairs. We've regrouped into the secure room, on three."

"Fuck you," Billy says. In response, Barry steps behind him, and twists his arm back between his shoulder blades.

"Don't hurt him," Denver cries, as Barry marches Billy forward. They enter the burnt lobby through a seam in a translucent tarp, stretched across the spot where there used to be a revolving door. Standing in the lobby is Laurent, wearing one of the violet hard hats.

"Billy!" Laurent says. "Good to see you, very good to see you. We've suffered some, ah, unfortunate setbacks today, you can see, the old place looked a little better this morning." He smiles. "But it's good to have you back in our court."

"I'm not in your court," Billy says, as they usher him through the lobby.

"Oh, no, I suppose not, not if we're speaking about, you know, where your loyalties lie." They push Billy through a door and begin guiding him up a flight of stairs, with Denver bringing up the rear. "We have your friend Anil in the secure room; we got his report of the situation, a layman's report, but very good nonetheless, very rich in nuances, the *fine details*, I can understand why the man became a writer. In any case! He seemed to indicate that you might be on the wrong side of some kind of Dark Oath scenario. Which would match, you know, with what happened with Elisa, and the other one, the big gentleman?"

"Jørgen," Barry offers, as they cross the second floor landing.

"Yes! Jørgen! Shame about the two of them; we may be able to get them later, very tricky right now, though, very tricky. So— where was I? Oh, yes, in our court. You say you're not. And to this we say: Of course! Of course you're not. Dark Oath, you know, it works that way. You probably see us as the enemy right now, it's terribly ironic, actually. But in a physical sense? We have you here in the building. Literally in our court. And that's very, very, very good."

"You can't stop Lucifer," Billy says. "He came and he took Jørgen and Elisa away from you. He'll take me, too."

"Well," Laurent says. "We'll see about that."

"Yes," Billy says. "We will."

They emerge into a hallway on the third floor and hustle him toward a pair of black double doors at the far end. As they approach, Billy's dad, Keith, still in his commando garb, throws the doors open. Billy glares at him as though he's an enemy.

"Is he—" Keith says.

"It's as we thought," Laurent says. "Dark Oath."

"Shit," Keith says. He looks like he might rip a phone book in half.

"Don't hurt him," Denver says, hurrying to catch up. "It looks like you're hurting him."

They enter the secure room. Fluorescent lighting, nacreous tile. Various personnel toil busily at racks of arcane-looking equipment. The room resembles a hospital operating suite jammed full of card tables, half-finished cups of coffee, empty take-out containers, and at least one ashtray. Billy sees Anil sitting in a plastic chair, safely out of the way of most of the bustle, in front of a glossy black bank of dormant technology.

"Seal the room," Laurent says to Barry. Barry lets go of Billy's arm finally and begins to do something to the door, something that involves a brilliant light flowing out of his fingertips. It hurts to look at, like an acetylene torch. Billy moves his arm gingerly, rotates it tenderly in its socket.

"We can undo the Oath," Laurent says to Keith. "It'll just— it'll just take some time."

"How long?" Keith says.

"Two days?" Laurent says.

"Two *days?*" Keith says.

"It's unfortunate, I agree. But we don't have the right components and we don't have the right staff. I could get you this

Yoruban guy, a specialist, but he's in Nigeria, and even if we *could* get in touch with him—"

"You can't keep this room secure for two days," Keith says, pressing his fingertips against his temples like a character in a commercial for a headache remedy. "Not against the Adversary."

"He has a name, you know," Billy says.

"Billy," Laurent snaps. "Why don't you make yourself comfortable. Go sit over there by the God detector. With your friend." He waves in Anil's direction.

Billy takes one more look at the double doors. They are barely visible behind a gleaming magical glyph. So, okay, fuck it, he probably can't run. He dismally considers whether he's going to need to turn into a wolf again and kill everyone in the room just to keep his word. But he feels no special compulsion to do anything other than wait for Lucifer to show up. So he goes, and he sits down in a chair next to Anil. Denver comes and joins them.

"Hey, man," Anil says.

"Hey," Billy says. He dumps Anton Cirrus's duffel bag onto the floor.

Anil puts a hand on Billy's shoulder. "Listen, man, these guys say that they're going to help you get out of this. This Oath or whatever it is that you're under."

"But that's the thing," Billy says. "I can't really root for that. I gave my *word*."

Anil gives him an incredulous look. "Are you kidding me?" he says. "Of all the people I know, you're like the *first* person to try to weasel out of your obligations. You break promises *all the time*."

Billy turns to look at Denver, in the hopes that she'll defend his honor, but all she does is give a palms-up gesture.

"So what the fuck makes *this* promise so special?" Anil says.

"I made it to the Devil," Billy says.

"Right—which means that it fucks you *even worse* than the average stupid shit you agree to! And now you're in a room with people who love you—your *friends* and your *dad* and an entire staff of fucking *magicians* who are working overtime to help you *get out of this* and you won't even allow yourself to *root for them*? No offense, man, but it's kind of a dick move."

"You know what's a dick move?" Billy says.

"What," Anil says.

But Billy has no retort.

They sit there in silence for a minute. "All I'm saying," Anil says eventually, "is just try to let yourself feel a little hope."

Billy tries it. And a little light goes on in the wing of himself that he thought had collapsed, in the part of himself that he thought had died.

"So now what," Denver says, after a minute.

"I dunno," Billy says. "Anybody have, like, an UNO deck or something?"

The lights go out. A collective murmur of dismay goes up from everyone in the room, except Billy. The lights come up again a second later, when some backup system kicks in, although the illumination they cast seems a little more feeble and uncertain now.

"He's coming for me," Billy says. He says it quietly, but a pall has fallen over the room, so no one has any trouble hearing him.

"Hold that seal," Laurent says.

"Got it," says Barry.

The room shudders ferociously. The lights flicker. An expensive-looking oscilloscope-type widget crashes to the floor, gives one single alarming bleat as it dies. Barry's glyph wobbles, blurs at its edges. Sparks peel off and bounce to the floor.

"*Hold* that *seal*!" Laurent shouts.

"It's not that easy," Barry says.

"Goddamn it," Laurent says. He turns from person to person frantically, although he does not really appear to be addressing anyone in particular. "We're not going to lose. Not twice in one day. We're the fucking good guys. The whole *point* of our *existence* is that we're superior to evil. We're supposed to *win*. Our whole building got fucking trashed by hellfire once today, okay, yes, bad, but we should at least be able to hold *one room* that a fucking council of warlocks designed to be the most mystically secure space in all of New York City." He takes off his hard hat and flings it at the wall.

The room gives another violent shudder. Barry's silvery glyph suddenly turns a dark, smoky red. Little flames spill out of its edges. Barry begins to tremble and jitter, like someone about to have a seizure.

"Oh," Laurent says, throwing his hands up into the air. "Oh. This is just perfect. We are ever so perfectly fucked."

"Billy," says Denver. She grips his leg.

"Yeah," Billy says. He doesn't look at her; he's watching the door, watching the glyph begin to burn.

"Are we going to die?"

Billy turns to look at her now, sees the fear in her face. "I don't know," he says.

"If we're going to die," she says, "I want to say that I'm sorry. About last night."

"Sorry?" Billy says.

"Yes," Denver says. "When you said you loved me. I should have said it back."

"Oh," Billy says. "Uh, you still could say it. Now might be a good time." His hope grasps at the idea that somehow love is the key to this situation, that somehow, love will save them all.

She opens her mouth, but then the room is gripped by a third groaning spasm. This one cracks about half the tiles that line the walls and shatters three of the fluorescent lights, filling the air with a harsh, choking dust. The glyph sputters out completely.

"Fuck," Anil says, rearing out of his chair. "Fuckity fuck." He fumbles around in his pockets and gets out a convenience-store packet of incense sticks, rips it open, takes all dozen sticks into one fist. With his other hand he pulls out his lighter, gets it going, lights the end of all the sticks at once. He gets down on his knees, closes his eyes and begins to murmur hurriedly, waving the sticks in the air, making tight little loops of fragrant smoke.

"What are you doing?" Billy asks.

Anil snaps his eyes open, looks sharply at Billy. "What does it look like I'm doing, nimrod? I'm *praying*."

And behind him, one by one, all 777 LEDs on the God detector begin to light up.

CHAPTER FIFTEEN

DEUS EX MACHINA

Barry loses consciousness and slumps to the floor, and the double doors swing open, revealing Lucifer, standing there, in his bloodied shirt, grinning widely. For one horrifying moment Billy can see *through* him, can see how the version of Lucifer that looks human is really just the tip, the tiniest tip, of something larger, infinitely large, really. Billy looks into Lucifer's face and it is like looking through a window into an endless abyss, an inferno as broad as the universe. Except worse than an abyss, and worse than an inferno, because it has a mind. It is intelligent, diabolically intelligent, capable of scheming, strategizing, plotting. Capable of being an opponent, the opponent of anything, the opponent of a god. Billy looks at Lucifer and he sees the Adversary. And he finally understands what it means, to have sworn himself to that, and he wills himself to break free of his vow, in the way that you try to will yourself to wake up from a nightmare, but he can't, he can't wake up, he can't break free, and the horror of this causes him to nearly lose his mind right then and there.

But something stops him. Some presence in the room.

Something stabilizing, balancing, calming. Lucifer looks over Billy's shoulder and his grin dissolves, replaced by recognition. An unmistakably contemptuous variety of recognition.

Billy turns. Behind him stands a dark-skinned Indian man, slender, young, maybe eighteen at best. He wears a keen blue suit, with a sharp yellow silk tie, and in his hands he holds a very fine briefcase. He's incredibly handsome in sort of an androgynous way, a way that seems familiar to Billy somehow, as though he recognizes this man from a movie, or as though some facet of the man's face can be found somewhere in every movie ever made, even movies that are nothing but footage of water.

The man steps out into the center of the room. "Lucifer," he says, in a voice that is light and boyish but betrays no trace of immaturity.

Lucifer responds by forcing a polite smile, the kind of smile that reveals that a smile can be achieved by just tensing particular zones of your face. "Krishna," he says. "The Protector of Cows."

No way. No fucking way. Billy turns to look at the God detector. Its display seethes with evolving mandalic patterns.

Anil still sits in front of it, staring at Krishna in a stupor of disbelief: his jaw hangs open, the incense droops in his slackened fist. Fragrant smoke merges with the thin, acrid smell of frying circuitry.

Laurent looks from the machine to Krishna to Lucifer and back again, and finally, with nothing to say for once, he drops his ass into a chair.

Denver has her camera out and she leaves Billy's side in order to maneuver for a better angle.

Billy can't immediately see where his dad is.

"Long time no see," Lucifer says. "What brings you here?"

"I received a request for intercession," Krishna says, gesturing at Anil.

"A request for *intercession*?" Lucifer repeats, incredulously. "But—I mean—you must get, what, millions of those a day."

"True," Krishna says, pronouncing the word with great precision. "But is it not apparent that the circumstances unfolding here today are unique?"

"Well, sure, but," Lucifer says. "When you really think about it, couldn't you say that *all* circumstances are unique?"

Krishna blinks, once, very slowly.

Lucifer says, "Okay, so, you're telling me that that one's yours?" Lucifer waves a hand to indicate Anil. "That's fine. I'm not here for that one. I'm here for the other one." He turns to address Billy. "Billy Ridgeway. Have you fulfilled your objective?"

"I have," Billy says.

"Are you ready to depart with me, to return to Hell?"

"I am," Billy says.

Keith Ridgeway gives a roar and springs out of whatever nook he'd been crouching in. He lunges at Lucifer with a ceramic blade in his hand. Lucifer turns, though, and snaps his fingers, and Keith vanishes in a spume of white flame. *Dad*, Billy thinks, with a jolt.

"He's fine," Lucifer says, quickly.

"What did you do to him?" Billy says, with mounting horror.

"I sent him home," Lucifer says. "Ohio. Don't worry. I have no interest in harming your father. I'm not inherently vengeful, you know." He looks pointedly at Krishna, as if this utterance is a move in some long argument the two of them have been having. "But now. It is time."

"Wait one moment, please," Krishna says.

"What," Lucifer says. "This has nothing to do with you."

"Ah, but there you are incorrect," Krishna says. He calmly approaches a metal table cluttered with Right-Hand Path crap, and, with a single fluid arc of his arm, a graceful motion, like the most sublime gesture in a modern dance piece about office life, he sweeps it clear, sending paper cups and reams of printouts to the floor. "If this situation did not fall under the scope of my dharma I would have no ability to hold you here, as it would not be rightful. And yet we can see that here you are held. Are you not?"

"I am," says Lucifer, tetchily. "Although I fail to see why."

Krishna places the briefcase on the table and pops its clasps. The report echoes off the room's destroyed tile. Lucifer winces at the sound.

"Your actions are in violation of a long-standing agreement," Krishna says.

"Nonsense," Lucifer says.

From his case, Krishna produces a document festooned with official-looking seals and at least one strip of crimson ribbon. He proffers it toward Lucifer, who makes no gesture toward accepting it. "Need I remind you, Lucifer, of the protocols established by the Treaty of Sectarian Nonaggression?"

"You don't need to remind *me*," Lucifer says, "of the protocols of the Treaty of Sectarian Nonaggression."

"I would hope that I would not," Krishna says, "as you assented to them on October 25, 1965, and you assented to an earlier yet functionally identical version of them on October 24, 1648, in the form of—"

"The Peace of Pantheons," Lucifer says, wearily. "Believe me, I remember."

"Nevertheless," Krishna says, "perhaps it would be worth taking the time to review their principles, which explicitly prohibit

any god, demigod, angel, archangel, demon, *or devil* from deliberately harming *or threatening to harm* human adherents of any
member faith. Therefore, when you endangered Anil Mallick
with hellfire—"

"But—" Lucifer points at Anil. "He's a secular humanist!"

"He is Hindu," says Krishna.

"His *parents* are Hindu," Lucifer stresses.

"It is true that he has claimed that he is not the best example
of a practicing Hindu," Krishna says. "But even a not-very-good
example remains an example."

"So, okay, maybe he's Hindu. But a treaty violation only
means—"

"Among other things," Krishna says, "what that means is that
you forfeit the right to any gains directly acquired by means of
the acts which violated the treaty. And because William Harrison
Ridgeway was coerced into—"

"He prefers Billy," Lucifer says, although suddenly Billy isn't
certain that he does, any longer.

"Be*cause* William Harrison Ridgeway was coerced into swear-
ing his Dark Oath to you in order to remove Anil Mallick from
danger, and be*cause* Anil Mallick was endangered in violation of
the Treaty of Sectarian Nonaggression, the penalties you face in-
clude an invalidation of William Harrison Ridgeway's Oath, effective immediately."

And with those words Billy feels it go, as though washed away
by cold, clear water rushing through his mind. He inhales once,
deeply.

"You cheat," says Lucifer.

"Lucifer," Krishna says. He returns the document to its case
and claps it shut. "My intercession here is complete, or nearly

complete, and so I intend to depart. But I shall leave you with one recommendation. Whatever business you may have with these people? Conclude it."

"Yes, fine," Lucifer says. "Give my best to your sixteen thousand wives."

For the first time, an irritated look crosses Krishna's face. "You *do* understand that those wives are manifestations of Lakshmi, my consort—?"

Lucifer shrugs. "If you insist," he says.

Krishna sighs, and in the sigh is the sound of a river, an infinite river, and when the sound fades Krishna is gone, although it's difficult to pinpoint any exact instant as being the one at which he disappeared, and in a way it is like he is still there with them. The situation still feels balanced. Billy turns to check out the detector, which is dormant, and he notices that Anil has disappeared, spirited away by his god. Billy senses him returned home, bewildered, worried but safe.

"So," Lucifer says, returning his attention to Billy.

"So," Billy says. "Now what?"

"Nothing has changed," says Lucifer. "I still intend to take you and the others to Hell with me, where you shall serve the purpose for which you were bred and born. No ward protects you. I can take you at any time."

"But that's not fair," Billy says. "You don't get to *take* us just because you *can*."

"I never claimed to be fair, Billy," Lucifer says, softly.

"But that wasn't the deal," Billy says.

"Billy," Lucifer says. "We made no deal."

"We did," Billy says, pleadingly.

"We did not," Lucifer says. "You are correct that I proposed a deal, originally. You will recall the terms: you were to have given me the Neko, and I was to have seen to it that your book would be published, and our obligations to one another were to mutually conclude. But you did not agree to that deal. You made a point, repeatedly, of saying that you were not agreeing to that deal. And now I want more."

"You said you enjoyed tempting people," Billy said. "Show me. Tempt me. Give me something."

"Billy," Lucifer says. "It is time to go." He raises his hand.

Billy looks Lucifer in his stupid placid face, and feels his anger and animal ferocity surge up again. He finds himself wanting blood in his mouth.

"No," he says.

"No?" Lucifer says, sounding faintly amused.

"No."

Lucifer regards Billy carefully. "Are you telling me," he says, "that you won't serve your master?"

"You're not my master," Billy says.

"I appreciate this attitude," Lucifer says, after a beat. "It reminds me of myself at your age. Very well, then. You wish to make a deal? Let's make a deal."

And with those words it is like a circle is drawn around them, a circle that no one else in the room can enter.

"Let us discuss your book," Lucifer says.

"No," Billy says. "Screw the book. My book sucks and I don't give a shit about it." He exhales after he says that, like he's letting go of a breath he's held for years. Something that had been flailing in him, all that time, finally calms, and from that position of calm he is able to speak: "Here's the deal: I give you the Neko and you leave me alone. You leave me alone and you leave my friends alone, forever. You release Jørgen and Elisa from their own oaths or obligations or whatever. You let us all go home and you don't contact us again."

"That's really what you want," Lucifer says.

"That's what I want," Billy says.

Lucifer watches him closely. "I went to some trouble to make the three of you, you know," he says, with something bordering on affection in his voice. "To let all three of you go would represent the squandering of a great deal of effort."

"You waited thirty years to track us down," Billy says. "You can't have needed us all that badly."

"Thirty years," Lucifer says. "That's nothing to me."

"Then start over," Billy says. "Invest the time. Make another set like us. In the end you'd have exactly what you want now." He feels bad, using someone not yet born in this way, an innocent person he'll never know, but he has nothing else to bargain with.

Lucifer considers the idea impassively. It is like watching a computer chew up some enormous wad of data only without the benefit of a creeping bar to mark the progress of the process.

"This is the deal," Billy says, quietly. "Take it or leave it."

After a nearly interminable interval Lucifer breaks into a smile. "No," he says.

"No?" Billy exclaims.

"Don't act so surprised, Billy Ridgeway; you're not the only one who can say no when a proposal does not suit him."

"Okay, fine," Billy says, anger in his voice. "Make me a counteroffer, then."

"I shall," Lucifer says, his smile broadening. "And here it is. You give me the Neko. I send you and your friends home. I free Jørgen Storløkken and Elisa Mastic from their Oaths and I begin to work on building another retinue of hell-wolves. But that will take time. It will take years. What I want from you, then, is permission. I want permission to contact you again, should I require your services."

"Am I obligated to say yes? When you pop up? Do I have to do what you say?"

"You do not. At that time, should it come, we will negotiate a new deal. I only ask for the right to approach you, and I ask that you consent to hear me out."

"Will I have to watch a PowerPoint presentation?"

"Yes," Lucifer says. "But any such presentation will be under forty-five minutes in duration."

"Fifteen," Billy says.

"Thirty," Lucifer says.

"Agreed."

"I have your consent?"

"You do."

"Very well, then. Billy Ridgeway, I accept our deal."

He extends his right hand, and Billy knows that the time has come: at long last, he has to shake hands with the Devil. And he does. Lucifer's palm is cool and dry to the touch, and Billy feels a little self-conscious about his own, which is coated with a clammy sheen of panic sweat.

"The Neko, please," Lucifer says, extending his left hand, without releasing Billy's right hand from his grip. Billy passes the duffel bag containing the Neko and the cache of incriminating weapons.

"I shall honor our agreement," Lucifer says, looking Billy straight in the eye. "And if you wish to go home, then home is where you shall go."

"Yes, very good," says Laurent, rising from his chair, "but, but, wait, wait just a second—"

But Lucifer does not wait a second. He releases the handshake and there is the flashbulb crackle. Everything goes white.

For a second Billy fears he's been tricked, that he's going back to Hell, on the grounds that Hell Is His True Home or some shit. Or even that he's being flung back to Ohio, where he'll have to deal with his dad. But no. When his vision clears he's happy to see he's back in his apartment, as he left it, only with one difference: Denver is next to him.

"Oh, thank God," Billy says.

Denver, looking completely drained, drops onto the couch. She shoves open a space on the messy coffee table and drops her camera there.

"I'm sorry the place is such a mess," Billy says, exhausted.

"It's okay," she says.

Billy makes a restless circuit of the room, wonders whether Jørgen will be magically appearing in the next minute or so. In the end, he figures that Jørgen is probably still in the hospital, and Elisa is probably still talking to cops—they may be free of their servitude to the Devil, but there's still some sorting out to do. He feels an impulse to try right now to call around, figure out what hospital Jørgen might be in, see if he's all right, but after patting down his jumpsuit for the hundredth time Billy realizes that he still doesn't have a goddamn phone, and the thought of getting on the Internet right now makes him squirm. Either Jørgen is all right or he isn't, and nothing Billy does right now either way is going to change that. He puts it in a great file of things that he can worry about in the morning.

For now, he can assume that he and Denver have the place to themselves.

"Hey," he says, pausing in his pacing. "Look, I don't know if we're—if we're still a thing, or what. I kinda hope we are."

"You *kinda* hope we are?" Denver says.

"I hope we are," Billy says, groping for definitiveness. "I do. I just—you know, maybe you want to go home, I get it, but I would really love it if you would spend the night here with me tonight. I could go out and get a bottle of wine"—he can't really, it occurs to him, since he has no cash and no ID—"and we could order Chinese or something and just—hang out? Or something?"

"You still have to work on your delivery," Denver says. "But yes, I would like that."

Billy breathes an enormous sigh and collapses onto the couch next to her.

"Wait a second, though," Denver says. "Do you think it's safe?"

"Safe?" Billy says.

"Well, I'm still missing parts of the story, but if I understand correctly you occasionally turn into some kind of—sex-demon wolf thing?"

"Hell-wolf," Billy says.

"And it was some kind of mystic ward or something that kept you from changing? That your dad put on you? But that ward never got put back on,"

"Oh, right," Billy says. "My dad wanted me to go back home; he said he could sort it out there."

"Do you want to go?" Denver asks. "We could—get on a bus, or—?"

Billy frowns at this. "I don't know what I want," he says.

Except he does. He knows that he wants to sit down and have

a conversation with his dad, to speak honestly with him for maybe the first time ever. But he also knows that he's done, at least for a while, with people doing things to his brain, with oaths and wards and whatever else.

Before he has a chance to really think about that, Denver speaks again. "Let me ask it this way," she says. "Do you think you'll try to kill me in the night?"

"No," Billy says, with resolve.

Denver looks into his eyes, inspecting something in his pupils. She gets a penlight off her belt and shines it into each of them in turn. "You seem normal," Denver says.

"I'm not," Billy says.

"No," Denver says. "You're not. But I think that might be okay."

They don't order Chinese. They don't go out and get wine. They drink a half a bottle of Jørgen's port that they find in the back of a cabinet above the refrigerator and they go up to the loft.

For a while they lie in bed and watch the footage that Denver captured. Billy laughs out loud at seeing Anton Cirrus fall down the stairs, but then he remembers the reality of the situation and it sobers him.

"I think you saved my life," Billy says, "showing up when you did. He really would have shot me if you weren't there." It occurs to him that that means he's on his third life. Or maybe fourth, if he counts his dad busting him out of Hell. Or fifth, if he counts Anil calling for Krishna's intercession. *Fuck*, he thinks, *I'm in debt to* everyone *now.*

And then he realizes that that's okay. Denver is right: when people love you, they show up. Sometimes that means that they get to bail you out of trouble. It's not bad when that happens; it just means that you return the obligation when you get the chance. You be a guy who is present instead of a fuck-up.

He thinks he can do that.

Billy dreams of Ollard.

First he dreams of the tower, looming, dank, writhing like a living thing.

And in this dream Billy enters the tower and finds there not a Starbucks but a room, Billy's own writing room from long ago, on the third floor of his childhood home. Ollard is there, pecking at the precious Olivetti with stained fingers, and Billy finds one of his mother's antique blades in his hand. He comes up behind Ollard and slashes his throat. He slashes again and again. Ollard gurgles beneath the blade. Blood sprays onto the page loaded into the typewriter.

And Billy looks at the page, to see what Ollard has written, and the page is blank, there are no words upon it, even the blood is gone, it is just blankness, the pure blankness of Hell, and Billy can feel himself and Ollard falling into it, forever together.

And Billy wakes, next to Denver; it is dark and he is safe, surrounded by the comforting things of this world. But the blankness hangs in his mind like a specter. He struggles for a moment to banish it, the only way he knows how. He has an idea.

CHAPTER SIXTEEN

FULL DISCLOSURE

Hello.

You are listening to the August 17 edition of *The Stolon*, the Bladed Hyacinth weekly podcast. Fifteen minutes of Q&A about books and the people who make them. I'm your host, Ethel Shira Wise. Today our guest is author W. H. Ridgeway, here to discuss his book-length lyric essay of moral inquiry, *On Killing*. Thank you for joining us.

Thank you for having me.

So. Killing. It's a heavy topic.

It is.

But not a *new* topic.

No. It's one of the oldest topics, in fact. The history of literature is, in some ways, the history of writing about killing. *Beowulf*, *The Iliad*—these are works that are intimately attentive to the act of killing.

And religious literature, as well, is certainly concerned with the topic.

Indeed. All religious traditions define themselves, partially, by the nature of their ethical values, and all of them therefore end up having to say something about killing. Usually it's in the form of a proscription of some sort, although in practice religious traditions tend to be fascinatingly inconsistent in exactly how and when they enforce this proscription.

Inconsistent. Would you say *arbitrary*?

Not arbitrary. How would I—? [*Pause.*] Provisional.

The provisional ethics of killing is a big subject in this book. Did you approach it from a background in any particular religious tradition?

No. When I began this book—I'd just turned thirty—I was existing in a very secular place, a sort of nexus of various incoherent nonbeliefs.

Midway on your life's journey, you found yourself in a dark wood, the clear path lost?

Very funny, although the pedant in me insists on pointing out that the Dante of *The Divine Comedy* is thirty-five, not thirty.

[*Laughter.*] I stand corrected.

But—yeah—you're not wrong. I *was* in kind of a dark wood, spiritually speaking, and part of the impetus behind the book is that I'm attempting, on the page, to develop a usable moral system without the benefit of any specific religious practice to fall back on.

And yet the centerpiece of the book looks extensively at the concept of "right action" in Hinduism.

Well, I had some help with that.

Yes. If I understand correctly, you've credited the author Anil Mallick with assisting you on that chapter.

That's correct.

Mallick is known, of course, for his acclaimed collection of short stories *King in Exile*, published earlier this year. *King in Exile* features contemporized versions of stories from the Ramayana, is that correct?

And the Mahabharata, yes. It's an excellent book; I would recommend it wholeheartedly.

Your book hints at something like a conversion experience. Do you consider yourself religious now?

[*Pause.*] It's complicated.

I'm sure.

[*Pause.*]

Let's shift gears. This book is a work of nonfiction, but prior to its publication you were mostly known as a fiction writer.

I'm not sure I would say *known*.

You'd published some short stories.

And I was working on a novel. But the novel—it proved to be on a topic I didn't care about, wasn't interested in, had nothing to say about.

And then the idea for this book came along?

Yes.

You decided your true topic of interest was killing?

[*Pause.*] Yes. [*Pause.*] The moral appropriateness of killing. Or lack thereof.

On Killing is published by Naginata Editions, an imprint dedicated to quote-unquote *vicious* works of fiction and nonfiction.

Correct.

And—full disclosure—Naginata Editions is helmed by Anton Cirrus, founder and former editor of Bladed Hyacinth.

Correct.

There's a rumor that the two of you didn't always get along.

[*Laughter.*] I'm not sure we get along now.

Is it true that he once published a piece on Bladed Hyacinth that panned your work? Only to take it down later?

If I understand correctly, it's the only piece he's ever withdrawn from the site.

What do you think was behind his change of heart?

I have no idea. You'd have to ask him. Maybe he'll talk about it in his memoir.

Well, we'll all look forward to that. You'll forgive me if I ask after one more rumor?

Certainly.

You've been romantically linked with the emerging filmmaker Denver Norton.

I have. [*Pause.*] That's not a question. [*Laughter.*]

There's quite a buzz around her new film, *Love Lives of the Hell-Wolves.* It's a departure from her earlier work.

That's fair to say.

It features explicit scenes of violent animal sex that have raised the eyebrows of both animal rights activists and people in the visual effects community.

Well, according to the narrative, the hell-wolves aren't animals, not in a strict sense. But I shouldn't say more—I don't want to spoil anything.

Can you discuss how those scenes were achieved?

Denver Norton is a very talented filmmaker. And she was fortunate to work with two talented nonprofessional actors: my good friend Jørgen Storløkken, and the poet Elisa Mastic, who also has a new book coming out this fall.

You appear in the film as well.

Briefly.

A nude scene.

[*Laughter.*] I'm not going to comment on that. If people want to find out they can go see the film.

And we'll have an opportunity to see it when?

It's debuting as one of the showcased shorts at Telluride next month. New York audiences will need to wait until April, when it'll be one of the Shorts in Competition at Tribeca.

Fantastic.

We all feel good about it.

You've been listening to *The Stolon*, fifteen minutes of Q&A about books and the people who make them. I'm your host, Ethel Shira Wise. Our guest today has been W. H. Ridgeway, discussing his new book, *On Killing*. Thank you for taking the time to talk to us.

Thank you for having me. It's been a pleasure.

JEREMY P. BUSHNELL is the fiction editor for Longform.org, and is also the lead developer of Inevitable, a tabletop game released by Dystopian Holdings. He teaches writing at Northeastern University in Boston, and he lives in Dedham, Massachusetts. This is his first novel.

Reading Group Guide for *The Weirdness*

1. Where do the bananas in bodegas come from? Have you ever thought about something so long that it becomes strange, the way Billy thinks "people have pets"? What started to seem strange to you?

2. What did you think about the role of religion in *The Weirdness*? When you heard the line "What about God?" repeated, were you expecting God to make an appearance? Because Lucifer was the Judeo-Christian version of the Devil, were you expecting a Judeo-Christian God to appear?

3. Why do you think Elisa asks Billy, "What is the worst thing you ever did?" Do you think she wants to share her history with him because she realizes they have a connection? Or do you think she has other motives?

4. How did your perception of Lucifer change over the course of the story? If he had given you a convincing PowerPoint presentation, do you think you would have signed on to help him?

5. What do you think Bingxin Ying meant when she told Denver that she admired her "commitment to immanentization of the ephemeral"? How do you think this phrase affects Billy in the moment she says it and when, later in the book, he tries to get closer to Denver?

6. On page 127, were you surprised to find out that Laurent hadn't read Billy's work? How did it change your perception of Laurent and his crew?

7. On page 134, do you believe Lucifer when he says Billy doesn't want to go back to his old life? Did you expect Billy to choose the Devil's side?

8. What do you imagine the warlock might do with the Neko of Infinite Equilibrium? Do you trust that Lucifer will do the right thing?

9. Billy is constantly slowed down by coffee, traffic, and other simple forms of conflict rarely represented in books. Did the story feel more realistic to you, based on these moments?

10. How did Billy change over the course of this story? Do you think Billy agreed to the right compromise—protecting Elisa and Jørgen by asking Lucifer to train new hell-wolves from the next generation?

11. Why do you think Anton Cirrus retracted his blog post about Billy's work? And why do you think Anton Cirrus opted to publish Billy's book?

12. The topic of consent recurs throughout the book. Lucifer raises it on page 24, and Billy returns to it on page 120. In what other ways does this theme occur in this book?

13. The book ends with Billy musing upon the "moral appropriateness of killing," or lack thereof. Was it "morally appropriate" for Billy to kill Timothy Ollard? Is it ever morally appropriate to kill in the world of this book, or in real life?